PASSPORT TO DANGER

PASSPORT TO DANGER

SHEILA GRANT

A SAVIO REPUBLIC BOOK
An Imprint of Post Hill Press
ISBN: 979-8-89565-100-1
ISBN (eBook): 979-8-89565-101-8

Passport to Danger
© 2025 by Sheila Grant
All Rights Reserved

Cover Design by Conroy Accord

This book is a work of fiction. People, places, events, and situations are the product of the author's imagination. Any resemblance to actual persons, living or dead, or historical events, is purely coincidental.

This book, as well as any other Savio Republic publications, may be purchased in bulk quantities at a special discounted rate. Contact orders@posthillpress.com for more information.

No part of this book may be reproduced, stored in a retrieval system, or transmitted by any means without the written permission of the author and publisher.

posthillpress.com
New York • Nashville
Published in the United States of America

1 2 3 4 5 6 7 8 9 10

CHAPTER ONE

Steve Brenner glanced up from his newspaper as the taxi jolted to a halt. The rain was heavier now, and the New York traffic was barely crawling along. He looked down at his watch—even under normal circumstances, Bill Wynter didn't like to be left waiting, and whatever he had to tell Steve was important enough that he had cabled the previous day, telling him to come home a week early from his vacation in France. Steve sighed impatiently. Trading the sunshine of southern France for the cold rain and traffic of New York City was enough to leave anyone in a dour mood. And Steve doubted that Bill had called him back to tell him good news.

He looked out the window of the cab at the people huddled under the awning of a Park Avenue apartment building. His eyes were drawn to a pretty brunette standing on the curb, her arm raised in a desperate attempt to hail a taxi. She was tall and elegant, stunningly dressed in a violet coat trimmed with mink at the collar. She reminded him of someone. But who? She was strikingly attractive—that much was clear, even at this distance. Maybe it was just wishful thinking. If he weren't late for his appointment, he'd give her a ride—she'd never get a taxi in this weather.

As the taxi slowly passed the awning, he was able to see her face more clearly. Dark auburn hair, blue eyes, classic features.

And then he felt his blood run cold. That was the face—he was almost sure of it—that had been splashed on the front page of the newspapers four years ago alongside his brother's. He remembered picking up the morning paper on that horrible day—October 27, 1967, he could still see it so clearly—reading the headline and going immediately to call his brother, hoping the reports weren't true. But they were. His brother was gone, and there was no use in dwelling on his brother's mistake.

Why would the girl risk coming back to the United States? Whatever her reason, it meant trouble—for him, for Bill Wynter, and for the country.

The taxi lurched forward as the traffic loosened. Brenner kept his eyes on the woman, still trying to hail a cab. Would she know who he was if she saw him? He didn't think so. It was a risk. But one worth taking. Bill Wynter would never forgive him if he let Nicola Neumann get away.

"Take a left at the next corner," Brenner said to the driver. "Go back around. I want to come down this same stretch again."

"You crazy?" the driver said. "All you've said since I picked you up was to hurry."

"I'll double the meter. Now step on it."

"Okay, boss," the cabbie said.

The car wheeled around the median, heading rapidly uptown, and then swung back into the stream of traffic inching down towards midtown. Steve tried to keep his eyes on the girl the whole time, praying that no taxi would pick her up before he got to her. The cab lurched forward and then stopped short as a Pontiac cut them off. The driver cursed and leaned on the horn. Steve leaned back and lit a cigarette, trying to steady his nerves. As they waited for the traffic to clear, he had a sobering thought.

PASSPORT TO DANGER

What if Wynter already knew she was in New York? Maybe he was having her tailed to see where she was going and who she tried to contact. If that was the case, then Brenner could ruin the whole operation by interfering. But then again, if she *had* slipped into the country unnoticed, it would be disastrous to let her get away.

The cab began to move again, and Brenner felt his muscles tighten. They were half a block away now; he could just barely make out the awning where he'd seen her. He scanned the street, desperate to locate the woman. But it was no use; she was gone. He cussed under his breath. What was he going to tell Wynter now?

But then, just as the cab was passing the building, he saw the woman walk smartly through the front door back to the curb, her eyes still searching the street for an empty cab.

"Stop!" Brenner said. He yanked the door open before the driver could come to a full stop and looked at the woman. Her large blue eyes appraised him, a slightly skeptical look on her face.

"You look like you need a ride," Brenner said, trying his best to smile. He watched as she scanned the street once more for an empty cab. Finding none, she nodded and slid into the seat next to him, closing the door behind her.

"Where to?" he asked her.

"The Look Building," she said. "But you can drop me on 52nd, if you're going straight down Park."

Her voice was soft and, Steve had to admit, more pleasant than he had expected. Her words were tinged with a very slight French accent, which surprised him; he had been expecting an accent, but not French. But with all her practice, he figured, she was probably adept at feigning any accent. *Who*, he wondered, *is she pretending to be this time?*

"I try to make a point to not abandon beautiful women in rainstorms," Steve said, "and I happen to be going to the Look Building myself."

"What a coincidence," the woman said. She seemed less than convinced. Steve wondered if he had made a mistake, calling her beautiful, and tried for a disarming, slightly sheepish smile.

"I'm a producer," he said. "I have to see a reporter about a documentary I'm putting together for one of the networks."

She gave him a searching look, and Steve wondered if she could see through his lie. He didn't like to lie—it didn't come naturally to him. But he didn't want to let the woman out of his sight, if he could manage it. It was one thing to know what building she was headed to, and another altogether to discover who she was going to see.

The woman turned to look out the window. It was really coming down now, the torrent so heavy that the buildings were little more than vague outlines through the rain-smudged glass, the sound of the rain obliterating all noise except the most strident horns. A savage clap of thunder burst from the skies; the young woman glanced anxiously down at the gold watch on her slender wrist.

"What's the next cross street?" she asked the driver.

"Fifty-seventh," he said. "It should clear up once we're past it."

"I hope so," the woman said. Steve wondered who she was late to meet; in her world, timing was everything. He watched as the woman caught the eyes of the driver in the rearview mirror and gave him a warm smile.

"I'm sure it must be exhausting to drive in this weather. Driving in New York is exhausting for me under any circumstances."

Steve hid his surprise. He would not have expected a woman like her to show the least bit of sympathy towards anyone. *Don't start thinking she has a nice side*, he said to himself. *Or you'll be duped like everyone else.* But now that he could study her up close, he could see why she'd been able to make fools of so many of the men she'd known: large violet-blue eyes; long dark lashes under well-shaped brows; lightly tanned complexion, practically glowing, over perfect features; rich shining auburn hair—she wore it casually, but he could tell the cut was expensive; and a body that would have caused men to stare, even if she hadn't been so beautiful. She looked younger than he would have thought; her line of work could age a person, and quickly. Most surprising of all was her warm and gentle smile—Steve had always thought one could tell a lot about a girl from her smile, but clearly he was wrong in this case.

Finally, they reached the Look Building. Steve tipped generously and then ran around the cab to get the door for the woman. She seemed wary but accepted his hand getting out of the car, and they walked into the lobby together. As they went, Steve quickly scanned the directory behind the security desk—*CBS News, 11th floor.*

"Where to?" he asked when they were in the elevator together.

"Five, please," the woman said. As the elevator began to rise, Steve tried to remember what the directory listed on the floor; *there had been a modeling agency*, he thought. What could she want there? Was her contact posing as a model? Or was she recruiting other young women? Beautiful women could be dangerous, as she herself had proved.

The doors dinged open on the fifth floor.

SHEILA GRANT

"Thank you for the ride," the woman said, turning to him with a small smile, "and good luck with that documentary of yours."

"I hope we run into one another again sometime," Steve said.

"The next rainstorm, maybe," the woman said brightly.

"It's a date," Steve said, offering a small wave as the woman walked out and the elevator doors closed behind her. He loosed a massive sigh and rested his head back against the mirrored wall of the elevator, alone for the moment. Then he punched the button for the lobby. He was anxious to get to the phone bank and tell Bill Wynter everything.

• • •

He hadn't made a pass at her, which was a pleasant surprise. Elizabeth Lamont had spent a lifetime fending off the advances of men. It hadn't used to bother her so much. But things had felt different in the year since Scott's death. The world felt a little colder now.

Indeed, Elizabeth thought that the man in the elevator seemed almost relieved once she had left him behind. Maybe gentlemen really did prefer blondes—it had been years since she was a brunette. She did not think that the man was actually a television producer—there was something quiet and studious about him that made her think he might be a stockbroker, or an academic, and, in her experience, men who worked in television were rarely studious and never quiet. It would not have been the first time that a man had lied to spend a bit more time with her. He did have the sort of tan that brought to mind West Coast sunshine. But while his clothes were clearly expensive—elegantly cut suit, demure tie—they weren't as flashy as the sort of thing worn by

PASSPORT TO DANGER

people in entertainment. Oh well—it didn't matter now what he did. She would never see him again.

She made her way down the hall towards an office marked *Richard Owens' Modeling Agency*. She hesitated outside, trying to work up her nerve to go in. For weeks—months really—she had been thinking about this conversation, imagining what she might say. It wouldn't be easy. But the time had come for her to make a break. She took a deep breath and walked in.

The office was neat and fashionable. A young woman at the front desk with dark hair and intelligent eyes was typing rapidly; she glanced up briefly when the door opened, and then went back to her typing.

"Honey, if you want an appointment with Mr. Owens, you'll have to come back later in the week," she said as she typed. "This is one of those unbelievable days, and he doesn't have a free minute."

Elizabeth laughed.

"Maggie, it's me."

The secretary looked up from her typing, astounded. She shook her head.

"I didn't even recognize you," she said. Elizabeth watched as Maggie took in her new look—new hair color, locks curling around her face instead of up, and the tan she'd gotten instead of the porcelain-white skin that Richard preferred. "Richard is going to go through the ceiling when he sees you."

"That's a good way to get a headache," Elizabeth said. But Maggie didn't laugh. Instead, the secretary seemed to be calculating just how disappointed her boss would be when he saw his top model. "Is anyone with him now?"

"He has an appointment in twenty minutes," Maggie said. She was still staring at Elizabeth's hair. "You know, blondes do have more fun. And, in your case, make more money."

Elizabeth raised her eyebrows, and then smiled.

"You could be right about that," she said as she walked into Richard's office.

His back was to the door, facing the only window in the room that looked out onto the Midtown gloom. Richard Owens was flipping rapidly through photographs; Elizabeth watched as he tossed the ones he didn't like on the floor, a steady rain of models in high fashion clothes cascading down to the carpet.

"I couldn't get a cab," Elizabeth said, taking a seat in the blue leather chair in front of his desk.

Richard was carefully studying the last picture in the stack.

"I know. The damn traffic in this city could drive a sane man crazy. And it gets worse every year. When I'm rich, I'm going to buy a helicopter and land—"

He stopped short as he turned around and saw her. After a pregnant silence, he said, "You were wearing a blonde wig this whole time."

Elizabeth was surprised.

"How do you know I didn't dye it?"

"If you tried to dye hair that blonde, it would look like brown straw, instead of silk. And you wouldn't have those gold and red highlights." He sighed. "Why did you let it grow out?"

"Because I wanted to look like myself for a change," Elizabeth said.

"You do realize how much it changes your appearance? Between the hair and the tan, I don't know if I would recognize you if I saw you on the street. Where did you even get a tan like that?"

"The roof of my apartment building," Elizabeth said. "It wasn't all that hard. You just lie there for a while."

PASSPORT TO DANGER

"In April in New York? It's a miracle you didn't get pneumonia." He studied her complexion, frowning slightly. "We're going to have a hard time covering up that tan. And you know I can't use you as one of those sun beauties modeling bathing suits. You have an image: the cool, regal, unattainable girl that every man dreams about but never gets. Do you know how hard it is to find someone like that? When a man wakes up in the morning and looks over at his wife snoring in curlers, he goes back to sleep and dreams of you—the beauty swathed in furs, neck glittering with diamonds. As impossible to get as that Cadillac he's always wanted." He looked openly annoyed now. "You look so damn healthy that you ought to be doing the Pepsi Cola commercial tomorrow. I don't know what I'm going to tell Cartier."

Elizabeth bit her lip.

"I'm not doing either of them."

He glanced at her sharply.

"You're cancelling? Why?"

"I found a substitute. Rachel Conway. She's good."

"I know she's good. But she isn't you. And you're not answering my question."

"I'm going to Greece. With Susan Graves."

"A vacation? Just like that? We have shoots booked, Elizabeth. Commitments." He shook his head again, but Elizabeth thought he looked more concerned now than angry. "What's all this about? You've never given me any trouble before. Not like the other girls. Is one of the advertisers giving you problems?"

"No. Nothing like that."

"Then what?"

Elizabeth sighed and leaned back in her chair. She had worked with Richard for three years now. She had walked into his office that first day, a young woman alone in a new and unforgiving city, put on her best smile and asked him, "Do you have a job for a starving refugee from Quebec?" He had smiled back at her, almost automatically. But he had been honest with her: told her how demanding modeling was, with long hours and hard work. Was she sure she would be interested in something like that?

She had been. Very interested. She had moved down to the city with the hope of becoming a translator for the United Nations—she spoke flawless French and English, very good Spanish and German, and enough of a few other languages to get by. But the UN wasn't hiring—she couldn't get even an interview to be a tour guide—and she was running out of money, fast. Her grandmother had died three months earlier, leaving her with enough money to come to New York. The woman had always been indifferent towards Elizabeth, shipped her off to boarding school as soon as she could. Still, she supposed that wasn't the old woman's fault—she had never signed up to look after another child. Her parents were both dead—a car crash when she was eight, her life in DC suddenly upended and everyone she'd ever known left behind. All she had wanted in the years since was to come back to the States, and this was her chance.

She had stood in Richard's office, waiting to hear what he thought of her chances. To her surprise, his next question was, "Have you had breakfast?"

She laughed and shook her head.

"Nothing since lunch yesterday."

"Good God! And you're still walking?"

She gave him her best smile.

"I'm not sure you could call it walking. Wobbling is more like it."

PASSPORT TO DANGER

"Well, come on," Richard said. "Let's have breakfast. You can tell me about yourself over some ham and eggs."

And that had been that. He had signed her to a contract later that day, sent her to the Elizabeth Arden Beauty Farm, where she lost ten pounds, had her hair fashioned into a high upswept style to emphasize her high cheekbones, and learned to cover her skin with a pale ivory foundation to give her face a fragile appearance. Fake eyelashes, eyeliner, and blue eyeshadow made her large eyes seem even more enormous in her pale, delicate face.

Richard had always said that the proof would be in those first photos. To Elizabeth's surprise, and Richard's delight, she had photographed beautifully. In three months, she had become one of the most highly paid models in New York. A year in, she had met Scott and fallen madly in love, spending every moment with him when he was back in New York and searching the papers each morning for his byline when he was reporting from Vietnam. They had talked about getting married. It was the happiest she could ever remember being in her life. And then suddenly, it had all been over. Just like that.

"What is it, Elizabeth?" Richard repeated.

She looked at him unhappily.

"I'm quitting."

"What?"

"I'm sorry. I really am. But you always told me I was free to go whenever I wanted."

"But for God's sake, why?"

Elizabeth looked down at her hands for a moment before she raised her eyes to meet Richard's gaze.

"I've been a model for three years now. That's a long time for most models. In another year or so I'll be finished anyway. You know that."

"But you're not finished. I've still got brands lining up to use you in their campaigns. There's still a lot of money to be made."

"I've made a lot already. More than I ever thought I would. But I don't feel as though I've really *done* anything with the last three years. Nothing constructive, anyway. It's like I've been living in a kind of limbo."

"Then give some of your money to charity. That's constructive." She could tell that Richard was trying hard to keep his anger in check, but it was beginning to seep through the edges. "There's no need for you to give up your career."

"But that's just it, Richard. Modeling isn't really my career. I came to New York to be a translator. And as hard as I've worked, I've never enjoyed being a model. Scott and I used to talk about me leaving all the time—doing something different, traveling the world with him. But now…"

She could hear the small fast inhalation that Richard made at the mention of her dead fiancé.

"I forget sometimes, how hard this all must be for you. You never seemed to let it affect you."

"You were wonderful, Richard, when all that happened. My world blew apart, and you helped glue it back together. I'll never forget that."

Richard looked away, trying to hide his emotion from Elizabeth.

"He was a wonderful man, and a terrific reporter."

"And he would have made a wonderful husband and father. He really cared about people. You knew him. Like those poor Vietnamese orphans he wrote that feature on. I really think he would have adopted every one of them, if he could have."

Elizabeth gazed for a moment out the window, watching the grey clouds moving like ghost riders across the sky. She could picture Scott's ruggedly handsome face—he'd had such an immense vitality, a real zest for living, and seemed fond of everyone he met. Being with him was the first time since she was eight years old that she had felt like she had a real home—Scott had been that home for her, even when he was halfway around the world. It had felt like those long, lonely years were over.

"You've been a wonderful friend since the first day I met you, Richard," Elizabeth said, "and I know how rare that is, in this business especially. I hate to run out on you. But I need some time to gather myself and decide what I really want to do with my life."

She could see across the desk that Richard knew that he had lost. He rose from his desk with a small sigh and came around, offering her a hand to help her out of her chair, and then embraced her. Elizabeth buried her face in his shoulder and tried her very best not to cry.

"You have a job here any time you want it," he said. "And, Elizabeth, call me if you ever need me. I don't care where you are. Call me and I'll come."

"Oh, Richard!" Elizabeth said, turning away and trying to choke back the sudden tears. "Thank you, for everything."

She hurried towards the door.

"Send me a postcard from Greece!" he yelled after her. She nodded and then raced past the astonished Maggie and down the hall, heading for the elevators.

It hadn't been easy, but she had done it. She was free. All she had to do now was to figure out what she wanted to do with the rest of her life.

When she reached the ground floor, she stopped at the magazine counter to try and regain her composure before going back out to the street. *Why can't I ever have a handkerchief when I need one?* She thought as she rifled through her purse.

"I think you could use this," a quiet voice beside her said. She looked up—it was the stranger from that morning, the one who had given her a ride in his taxi. He handed her a handkerchief, and she laughed and gratefully accepted it.

"You seem to arrive at the most opportune times," Elizabeth told him. She looked away, wiping her eyes, hoping her makeup wasn't ruined. "Have I smeared my mascara?"

He grinned. "You look like a very pretty raccoon."

"Oh dear!" she said, and began rubbing under her eyes with the handkerchief.

"You're only making it worse," the man said, chuckling and shaking his head. "Here, let me."

He put his hand out for the handkerchief. She had spent the last three years being poked and prodded and done up and made up by a swarm of professionals—makeup artists, hair stylists, seamstresses, designers, and photographers who wanted her to look *just so* at the camera. But it felt different, with this man. More intimate, familiar. But then she handed him the handkerchief, and he rubbed—not too hard, but not too gently—the mascara from her face.

"There," he said. "That's better."

He stepped back and appraised her once more.

"Are you all right? You seem awfully upset compared to when I left you."

"Yes, thank you. Just a tricky day is all."

"I know all about those," he said. Then he smiled at her. And for the first time in more than a year, she felt an unfamiliar flutter somewhere just beneath her chest. "Say, any chance you'd let me try and cheer you up with a little lunch?"

CHAPTER TWO

Steve Brenner wasn't sure which had surprised him more: that Bill Wynter had told him to ask Nicola Neumann to lunch, or that the woman in the lobby of the Look Building had actually said yes, and not just yes; she had appeared genuinely upset when she had come out of the elevator, her eyes teary in a way that didn't seem like a calculated performance for his sake. In fact, *nothing* the woman had done so far that day, ever since she had accepted his offer of a ride in the rain, had seemed particularly calculated. Instead, she seemed lovely, almost innocent. Was this why his brother had fallen for her charms? He had always heard Nicola described as a hard woman; he had assumed his brother was so blinded by her beauty that he had been willing to look past all the other things that ought to have served as red flags. But now, he wondered if he had been too hasty in his assessment.

The rain had quit as abruptly as if a faucet had been turned off over New York. The precipitation had cleared away the city's soot, and the air now smelled fresh and clean. As Steve walked down Park Avenue, the woman alongside him, they were absorbed in the throng of people emerging from the office buildings all around them, heading for lunch or out for a mid-day stroll. It would be easy, he thought, for her to slip away if she wanted to, blend into the crowd and disappear with no hope of him finding her again. He extended his arm out to her, and, once again to his surprise, she took it with a smile. He caught his breath. With that smile, any man would find her irresistible. He shook his head lightly. He needed to keep his wits about him.

"Since I'm taking you out to lunch," he said, "it seems like I ought to ask your name."

The woman laughed lightly.

"Where are my manners? Elizabeth Lamont."

"It's lovely to meet you, Ms. Lamont," he said. At least the KGB wasn't repetitious. They had sent her in as a French girl this time. He kept his eyes on the people coming towards them on the sidewalk. Any moment now, she was going to ask him for his name. And then he'd have a choice: lie, and risk her suspecting him even more than she already did when he "coincidentally" happened to be taking a cab up to the Look Building; or tell the truth, and reveal to her who he really was, and how he knew her. Neither seemed like a particularly appealing option, and he wondered if he would be able to avoid it until they made it down to the restaurant.

He saw an elderly woman ahead of them, brandishing her umbrella before her like a sword. He steered them towards the older woman who, as he expected, decided to continue charging ahead, oblivious to the fact that he was holding her arm. He let go, and for half a block he and the woman made their way along the crowded sidewalk, close enough to see one another but too far apart to talk. Finally, they came together again on the sidewalk just outside the Seagram Building, the woman shaking her head.

"I thought that old woman was going to run me through with her umbrella," she said.

PASSPORT TO DANGER

"This city is full of little old ladies with umbrellas," Steve said. "They scare the daylights out of me, because I think you're right—they'd prefer to impale you, if you stay still for long enough."

The woman began to laugh as they made their way into the plush restaurant of the Seagram Building. The sound was so infectious that Steve seen found himself laughing, too, in spite of himself. It was remarkable: here he was, standing with this woman who had caused so much pain and damage to his country—to his family—coming as close to enjoying himself as he could remember. *If only she really was Elizabeth Lamont*, he thought to himself sadly as he watched the maître d' come towards them.

Steve gave Bill Wynter's name and the maître d' led them through the restaurant. As they made their way to the table, Steve realized he wasn't the only one who thought the woman was beautiful—she was attracting admiring stares from nearly everyone they passed. The funny thing was, she seemed unaware of the attention, or at least uncommonly good at ignoring it. Maybe that was the KGB training coming through.

"So your name is Bill," the woman said softly to him. "I was wondering when you were going to tell me."

"Not exactly," Steve said.

The woman cocked her head to the side.

"But the maître d' said…"

"I was planning on meeting a friend here," Steve said. "I hope you don't mind."

"Oh…" the woman said. He could feel her disappointment. "Then, what is your name?"

"Steve," he said as they took their seats. "Steve Brenner."

He held his breath and studied the woman's face across the table. What would she say? Or would she say nothing at all, and turn and run? The woman frowned lightly.

"So tell me, Steve Brenner," she said. "I've been trying all day to figure out where you're from. With a tan like yours, you can't be a New Yorker—unless you've just spent a week in the Virgin Islands."

Steve was dumbfounded. The name had meant nothing to her—absolutely nothing. How was that possible? Brenner was a name that Nicola Neumann could not possibly forget, no matter how many other lives she had ruined and how many other men she had betrayed. And she wasn't acting; there hadn't been even the faintest glimmer of recognition. Was it possible that she wasn't actually Nicola Neumann?

"Is something wrong?" the woman asked. Steve shook his head and forced a smile onto his face.

"Texas," he said. "Though I spent the last week on the French Riviera."

"*Très jolie!*" the woman said. "I've always wanted to travel after the shows in Paris. But there was never any time—it was always onto Milan, or to London for a fitting, or back to New York for a commercial shoot. Well, so long to all that now. Maybe now I'll actually have a chance to see it for myself."

Before he could respond, a cheerful voice next to him cut in. Bill Wynter was standing next to their table, his arrival nearly silent.

"Steve, are you going to introduce me to your gorgeous date?"

It had been a bad week for Bill Wynter, and that was before he got the frantic phone call from Steve Brenner, claiming that he had spotted Nicola Neumann in New York City. That was the last thing Bill needed—a top KGB operative, somehow back in the country after going dark, totally undetected by him and his men. The hits just kept on coming.

PASSPORT TO DANGER

He hadn't wanted to bring Steve back to the city in the first place. It was easy, in a role like Bill's, to treat everything as an emergency, pretend that nothing else was as important. But that was a good way to burn out your assets—ruined vacations, skipped graduations, and missed birthdays added up over time, made his people less good at their jobs. But the situation with Sobokov was getting more and more dire, and no one knew the scientist as well as Steve Brenner. So he had sent the telegraph and given him instructions to come back to the States at once. He hoped that the first-class flight back from Paris was some small consolation. But he knew that Steve would have traded it readily for another week on the Riviera, if he'd had a choice in the matter.

Now, here he was, with this beautiful woman in tow, looking up at Bill with something like trepidation. He extended his hand to the woman.

"Bill Wynter," he said. "I'm so sorry to be interrupting your lunch. Steve and I had some business to discuss, but I can understand why he asked me to postpone. Steve, could you introduce us?"

"She's calling herself Elizabeth Lamont," Steve said, and Bill had to stop himself from giving Steve too withering a look. What was he hoping to accomplish, talking like that? The woman—Elizabeth—seemed to take offense as well, her formerly friendly manner suddenly turning a few degrees colder. She seemed confused, and defensive, as though she couldn't quite tell what had changed.

"There's nothing abnormal about that," Elizabeth said, "since that happens to be my name."

"I'm sure that it is," Bill said, trying to reassure her with a friendly smile. "Would you mind if I sat with you for a minute? I suspect there are some things that Steve and I might have to clear up about what you're really doing here."

The woman seemed even more uncertain now, glancing around the restaurant as though searching for an exit.

"If nothing else, I can promise you'll get an excellent lunch out of it for your troubles," Bill said.

The waiter came by and asked if anyone would like a drink.

"I think a round of drinks is an excellent idea," Bill said. He ordered himself an old fashioned; Steve ordered a Manhattan; and Elizabeth, after a moment's hesitation, asked for a daiquiri. For a few moments after the waiter left an awkward, icy silence descended over the table. Bill was about to speak when Elizabeth cleared her throat.

"Well," she said, staring daggers at Steve Brenner. "I suppose it's time for someone to tell me what the hell is going on."

Elizabeth Lamont had been a fool to think that this had all just been some friendly coincidence. What were the odds that the man was *really* going up to the Look Building too? She had been skeptical of his story of being a TV producer but had held her tongue because it was raining and she'd needed a ride. And then afterwards, when he'd been waiting for her in the lobby—how had she let herself believe that was just a happy accident, as well? She had been emotional, and he had been there, and she had allowed herself to believe, in a way that she didn't often, that the universe in its kindness was looking out for her. And now here she was, with no hope of escape.

She had seen the way that some of the other models could get, believing that all the good things that happened to them had nothing to do with the way they looked. She thought she knew better. She had been so pleased when it seemed like the man hadn't recognized her name—she'd been on her fair share of dates with men who were a terrible match for her, all because they'd wanted the rest of the world to see New York's top model on their arm. Then this kind, handsome man had come along and whisked her off to lunch, like some kind of a modern fairy tale. Sometimes, she still felt like that stupid girl back in Quebec, utterly alone and unsure of her place in the world.

The man sitting across from her now, Bill Wynter, was tall, with thick light brown hair. There were crinkles around his grey eyes that suggested a man who smiled easily, and a prominent nose that dominated the middle of his face and kept him from being handsome. He seemed friendly enough, but Elizabeth felt as though there was a fierce intelligence working behind that placid mask—the way he had immediately taken control of the situation from the minute he'd sat down at their table suggested as much.

"I can see why you made your mistake," Bill said to Steve as the waiter brought over their drinks. "She certainly does resemble Nicola Neumann."

"But I'm not," Elizabeth said. "I'm Elizabeth Lamont, and I'm feeling awfully foolish for letting myself believe that you actually wanted to have lunch with me. Why didn't you ask? I would have told you."

Across the table, Steve Brenner's cheeks were turning red. He seemed awfully embarrassed, possibly even ashamed. And yet still he had nothing to say for himself—no apology, no explanation for what he was doing.

"Don't be angry with Steve, Ms. Lamont," Bill said. "He felt like he was doing the right thing."

"And what is that, exactly?" Elizabeth said.

"Trying to find a woman who we regard as a menace to this country, and who happens to look quite a bit like you. Though, and I hope you won't mind my saying, Nicola Neumann isn't nearly as beautiful as you are."

Elizabeth ignored the compliment and instead sat very still, studying the man across from her. *It can't be true*, she thought to herself. But even as she thought it, she knew that it was.

"If you're right," she said, "then why has no one mentioned it before?"

"Nicola hasn't received that much publicity," Bill said. "I should also mention that those who would remember her best tend to forget…or aren't around anymore to remember."

Elizabeth felt a shiver run down her spine, and thought of another reason why no one might have mentioned it to her before.

"And I haven't been a brunette in three years."

Bill smiled; Steve took another sip of his cocktail and looked absolutely miserable.

"I'd only ever seen pictures," Steve said finally, still not looking at her.

"Who is she?" Elizabeth said after a moment. Steve and Bill looked at one another, as though trying to assess whether she warranted that kind of intel. "A little more information would be make for a very nice. *amuse bouche*."

Bill laughed out loud, a surprisingly high, pleasant laugh. He turned to Steve.

"Where did you find this girl?"

"On the street," Steve said, "waiting for a cab."

"Remarkable," Bill said. Then he turned back to Elizabeth. "Before I tell you anymore about Nicola, do you mind telling me a little bit about yourself?"

PASSPORT TO DANGER

Elizabeth hesitated for a moment.

"Who are you that you want to know all this?"

"I'm attached to NATO," Bill said. "Anything that has to do with Nicola is of interest to us, and our allies. I know you aren't Nicola. But you look like her, and that makes you someone I'd like to get to know better."

Elizabeth sighed and took a tiny sip of her daiquiri—it was cold and sweet. Under different circumstances, she could imagine how much she might be enjoying herself, having a lovely cocktail with a good-looking man, hearing him talk about his childhood in Texas. Instead, she had found herself in the middle of a confounding interrogation.

"What is it that you want to know?"

"Start from the beginning."

She gave him the quick version of her life story, keeping strictly to names and dates. Her father was French-Canadian; her mother was from Connecticut. Both dead after the car crash. Then back to Quebec, then down to New York for her modeling career. Now, she was here.

Bill Wynter shook his head when she was finished speaking.

"Then it's just one of those fantastic coincidences," he said. "I assume you speak French?"

"Yes, fluently," she said. "Along with German, and Spanish. I can get by in Italian. And I speak a little Russian."

Both of the men were staring at her now, and Elizabeth couldn't help but smile.

"I suppose Nicola Neumann does, too?"

"You didn't tell me you were a linguist," Steve said finally.

"You never asked," Elizabeth said. "But yes, I majored in languages because I wanted to be a translator."

"So why go into modeling, instead of doing something with your languages?" Bill Wynter said. He had taken out a pipe and was carefully loading it with tobacco. "More glamor, I suppose."

"It wasn't glamor I was interested in," Elizabeth said. "I've had about enough glamor for a lifetime. But no one was hiring for a translator, I was tall, and needed money. I was almost broke by the time I made it to New York. It seemed like the natural thing to try."

"And you were good at it, it seems," said Bill.

"I was," she said.

"I'm sorry to ask a personal question," Bill said, puffing on the pipe. "But have you ever been married, Ms. Lamont?"

Elizabeth frowned.

"No."

"Engaged, then?"

She took a deep breath; she was very much wishing this interview would end now, and she could get on with the rest of her life.

"Yes. Once. To a man named Scott Brandt."

Bill's eyes lit up first with recognition, then with sympathy.

"The journalist?"

Elizabeth nodded her head.

"I'm sorry, Ms. Lamont," Bill said. "He was a fine man, and a damn good writer. It was a shame what happened to him."

"Thank you. Is there anything else you need to know?" she said, struggling to keep the hurt and annoyance out of her voice. But what did it matter if they knew how she felt, how angry she was to be treated like this? So much of modeling involved pleasing people—the photographer, the advertisers, and Richard…. It would take time before it felt natural to let people know how she really felt, instead of hiding behind her pleasant, innocent face.

PASSPORT TO DANGER

"No, that's all for now," Bill said. "I am sorry for your loss, Ms. Lamont. I really am. I'll leave you two to your lunch. I think I see a friend a few tables over."

He rose from the table and extended a hand across to her. She shook it automatically. He turned to Steve. "Come find me after? There are still some things you and I need to discuss."

Steve made a sort of noncommittal noise, and then Bill was gone, leaving the two of them to their icy silences and hurt. Elizabeth took another sip of her daiquiri, and then stood to leave.

"Well," she said. "This has been an interesting day."

"Wait," Steve said, half-rising from the table. "Please stay."

"Why should I?"

"Because I'm sorry, for one thing," Steve said. "So very sorry. For lying to you, and for bringing you here under false pretenses. If I was in your shoes, I'd be awfully angry with me, and rightfully so."

Elizabeth hesitated. Steve seemed genuinely ashamed, and his apology struck a chord with her. Still, she wasn't sure if she wanted anything more to do with him, or with Bill Wynter, or with Nicola Neumann, whoever she really was.

"If it makes any difference, the only reason I felt I had to lie to you was because I had to be certain you weren't Nicola. If you knew the things this woman had done, then maybe you'd understand."

"So tell me."

Steve grimaced.

"It isn't mine to tell. But if you let me treat you to lunch, I'll make sure Bill comes back over to tell you whatever you want to know."

Elizabeth remained standing. There was something so pleading and innocent about the look on Steve Brenner's face, the same qualities that had attracted her to the man from the first time she'd seen him through the open door of his waiting cab. And at that very moment, a server came by carrying a giant tray of dishes, including the most delicious-smelling trout almandine she had ever seen before. She had spent the last three years consuming rabbit food: salads with no dressing, boiled lean proteins, never enough to satisfy her. If this was the start of the rest of her life, then she could do worse than begin with a good meal at a beautiful restaurant.

She sat back down, and examined the menu.

"Your friend isn't with NATO, is he?" she said. She peeked over the top of the menu and saw the surprise on Steve's face.

"What makes you say that?"

Elizabeth smiled.

"Who can say? Women's intuition?"

"Which isn't always right, you know."

"Of course not. But I have a feeling that it is now."

"Go ahead, then," Steve said. Elizabeth grinned and put down her menu.

"Bill Wynter seems like the sort of man who never tells you his real job the first time you meet him," she said. "He had to choose something to do with defense, since we were talking about a KGB spy. But I'm not sure NATO makes sense. If she's really that much of a threat, I'd say he's with the CIA. Military intelligence, maybe. Or the FBI if he works in counterintelligence. But the real reason I don't believe he's with NATO is that I don't think you'd call a NATO attaché if you really thought you found Nicola Neumann. Which begs the question—what is it that you do, Steve Brenner?"

PASSPORT TO DANGER

Steve laughed out loud—she could tell that she had surprised him.

"I'm a nuclear scientist," he said. Now, it was Elizabeth's turn to be surprised.

"Really?"

"Is that so hard to believe?" Steve said.

"I just have a hard time imagining you in a lab all day, huddled over beakers and Bunsen burners. I had taken you for a stockbroker when we first met, or maybe a banker."

"I don't spend much time in the lab anymore," Steve said. "And there isn't nearly as much money in physics as there is in those other lines of work, I'm sorry to report."

"Is this the sort of thing where you tell me you're a scientist, and then it turns out you and Bill actually work for the same folks?"

"Bill is an old friend," Steve said. "We were in the service together. I'm sure you can imagine that there are certain natural overlaps between my work and the security interests of the United States. Any other questions?"

"Just the one," Elizabeth said as the waiter approached the table. She looked up at him brightly. "What wine do you recommend with the trout?"

CHAPTER THREE

"Bill?"

Bill Wynter had been sitting across the table from Miles Reardon for a good five minutes now. He hadn't heard a damn word the reporter had said to him. His attention was still trained across the room, to where Elizabeth Lamont was now sipping a glass of white wine and cooing as the waiter deboned her trout. He turned back to Miles.

"Hmm?"

"I don't think I've ever had to repeat myself to you in all the years I've known you. Something must be on your mind."

Wynter chewed the inside of his cheek. He had known Miles Reardon since they were in the Army Intelligence Corps together in Korea. Wynter had stayed in intelligence; Reardon had gone back into journalism and was now the top American reporter in the Middle East. Wynter liked to meet up with Reardon whenever he was back in the States. With his background, and their personal connection, he could be a very useful source for timely information on the true state of play between the Arab nations and Israel. Between the failed overthrow of the king of Morocco, the attempt on the king of Jordan's life, and the briefly lived coup in Sudan, there was plenty of interest for the two men to discuss. But Wynter had more pressing issues to deal with.

"Did you ever know Scott Brandt?"

At the mention of the dead journalist's name, Reardon sat up straighter in his chair.

"Sure I did. You know how it is in the press corp. It was a real shame what happened. Makes you remember how quickly it could all go away."

"And you two would get together sometimes? Socially, I mean."

Reardon nodded.

"Whenever we were in the same city. New York especially."

Wynter pointed his chin across the room to where Elizabeth Lamont was listening intently to what Steve Brenner was saying.

"Did you ever know that girl?"

"Since when do you allow yourself time for a girl?"

"Humor me."

Reardon peered across the room.

"You may be a late starter, but you've got excellent taste. She's lovely."

"You don't recognize her?"

Reardon frowned.

"Should I?"

"She seems to think so."

"You're kidding." He looked back at the girl. "And what's your connection? Business or pleasure?"

"Business."

Wynter watched as Reardon narrowed his eyes and looked hard at Elizabeth, sifting through his mental rolodex as he tried to place the face. Suddenly his eyes lit up in recognition.

"My God, it's Elizabeth Lamont!" He turned to Wynter, dumbfounded. "I didn't recognize her until she smiled. No one else smiles like that. Sweet but sexy, you know? She's changed the color of her hair. I think I like her even better this way; more natural, less ethereal."

A small smile had spread across Miles Reardon's lips as he studied Elizabeth. But when he turned back to Wynter, his eyes appeared troubled. "Why are you interested in her, Bill?"

"Now that she doesn't look like a high fashion model, does she remind you of someone?"

Reardon considered this for a moment.

"Yes. But who?"

"Think KGB."

Reardon nodded to himself as he studied Elizabeth's face once more.

"If I looked quickly, I might say she looks a little like your friend Nicola Neumann."

"Yes. I thought so too."

"But I wouldn't get the two confused," Reardon said. "Elizabeth has a gentleness. Nicola didn't have that the day she was born. You can see it clearly on her face." He stopped himself and stared at Wynter. "You're obviously interested in her because she looks like Nicola. Why?"

Wynter shifted his lanky body into a more comfortable position. It was gratifying to have Reardon recognize the girl—it confirmed what he'd already thought. But he didn't need to tell the reporter anything more than he needed to know.

"I'll tell you about it after I hear about your trip to Egypt. I'm glad you're going back soon. We need you there."

"I was hoping you'd join me in Cairo," Reardon said. "You've been back in the States for a whole week now. I think that's a new record for you being away from your post."

Wynter gave him a direct look and spoke quietly.

PASSPORT TO DANGER

"I've been pulled out of the Middle East division. For a while at least."

Reardon was astonished.

"What do your superiors think is more important than the tinderbox in the Middle East?"

Wynter scratched the bridge of his nose.

"It's only for the next few weeks. Gerald Kimberly will be taking over for me; anything you hear you'll pass along to him."

"They're leaving Kimberly in charge? There goes the neighborhood," Reardon said with a small chuckle. "At least tell me where you're going, Bill."

Wynter pursed his lips.

"Mexico."

"You're leaving the Middle East bureau for a two-week vacation down in Acapulco?"

Wynter scoffed.

"Do I strike you as the sun and surf type?"

Reardon pretended to look the wiry old spy up and down.

"Bill, you do not. But I don't get it. Mexico is sleepy as all get-out. And you haven't covered Latin America since, what, the Cuban Missile Crisis?"

"Tell you what," Bill said, turning to watch as a waiter brought Elizabeth Lamont a dessert menu. "If you stick around, and come talk to Elizabeth with me, I'll let you in on what's going on."

"You're usually a little bit better about disguising your *quid pro quo*," Reardon said.

"Desperate times, Miles," Wynter said. "You play your cards right, there might even be a slice of pie in your future."

Reardon laughed.

"Just what exactly is it I'm helping you convince Elizabeth to do?"

Wynter stood from the table and straightened his jacket.

"Save the free world, of course."

Elizabeth had forgotten just how good food could taste.

For the last three years, food had been as much a part of her job as the makeup or the hair styling—the advertisers were very particular about the right sized girl for their campaigns, and the couture designers cut their dresses for an idealized sort of girl that Elizabeth wasn't sure had ever actually existed in the natural world. She had been rigorous and exacting in what she ate—never anything unhealthy, never too much. She had grown used to it. But now, she was beginning to realize that she had been hungry for a long time now.

She noticed Steve looking at her surprised as she polished off her trout and accepted the dessert menu from the waiter.

"You're surprised to see a woman eat?" she said. Steve smiled—he had a nice smile, she had to admit that much.

"Not at all. It's just rare to have a date show genuine pleasure in the food, rather than worry about appearances."

"You're still calling this a date, then?" Elizabeth said.

"What would you call it?"

"An apology," she said. "Or the beginning of one, at least."

She ordered herself the Crêpes Suzette and a cup of coffee; Steve got coffee as well and leaned back in his chair. Her anger with him had mostly burned itself out over the course of the lunch—she could tell that he was genuinely sorry, and he seemed ashamed to have lured her to lunch under false pretenses. He was obviously intelligent—they didn't go around handing out PhDs in physics to idiots—but unlike other men she'd been out with, he didn't seem intent on proving to her just how smart he really was. There was a quiet confidence about this man, and an air of self-containment, that she admired. That was the problem with the kind of man who typically wanted to date a top fashion model—they were much more interested in the idea of her than who she really was. Scott hadn't been like that at all. It was one of the many reasons she had loved him so fiercely.

"I don't think your friend is quite done with us," Elizabeth said. Bill Wynter was coming back towards their table, a familiar face in tow. It was Miles Reardon, one of Scott's old reporter buddies. The three of them used to go out for drinks when Scott was in New York, Miles usually accompanied by some flavor-of-the-month girlfriend—he was never in one city long enough to keep a woman for long, which seemed to suit him just fine. Still, Elizabeth had liked Miles, and rose now from the table to accept a kiss from him on the cheek.

"Are you a spy now too, Miles?" she asked brightly, noting the way Bill Wynter winced at the question.

"Bill and I are old Army buddies," Miles said. "I like to give him a bit of the local color when I'm back in town."

"The buzz around the base?"

"Something like that," Miles said with a sheepish smile.

"Are you two joining us for dessert?" Elizabeth said.

"If you don't mind," Bill said, taking the empty chair to Steve's right. "And I was actually hoping we might continue this conversation afterwards. Somewhere a bit more private."

"What kind of girl do you take me for?" Elizabeth said, summoning all the mock indignation she could muster. Miles roared with laughter as Bill's cheeks flushed ever so slightly red.

Miles got a coffee and a dish of vanilla ice cream; Bill ordered himself a brandy. They all watched as a waiter came toward their table, with a cart of crepes. Elizabeth nodded approval as he lit the orange liqueur in the pan, the flames jumping up towards the ceiling. The crepes were still sizzling as the waiter placed the plate in front of her. Elizabeth took a bite.

"Delicious!" she said. "You guys must try a little."

She passed the plate over to Steve who, after a moment's hesitation, picked up a forkful. "Isn't that just wonderful?" she said.

"You said that you were planning a vacation to Greece," Bill said.

"I did. As soon as my friend finishes filming her television show out in Los Angeles."

"Would you consider waiting a few weeks before the trip?" Bill said. "We would make it worth your while, I assure you."

Elizabeth looked over at Steve, wondering if this was part of the reason she had been brought to lunch. However, he seemed just as confused as she was, maybe even more so by the way he was staring at Bill. She turned to Miles, hoping for a little clarification, but the reporter suddenly appeared extremely interested in the ice cream melting in his bowl.

"I'd hate to put out a friend," Elizabeth said.

"I have it on good authority that the show is hitting some production snags, and Ms. Graves will almost certainly be delayed."

"But I never told you..."

"I've found its typically a good policy to assume Bill knows just about everything, Elizabeth," Miles said. "As difficult as that can be to believe sometimes."

"So first you mistake me for some kind of KGB agent," Elizabeth said, "and now you want me to drop everything for some reason that you haven't yet told me? You can imagine why I might be a little hesitant."

PASSPORT TO DANGER

"Of course," Bill said, nodding. "In fact, I'd be worried if you said yes before hearing what I had to say. I know we don't know each other well, Elizabeth. We hardly know each other at all. But I have the sense that you're a smart woman, and a good person as well. Those are rare qualities to find."

Elizabeth took another small bite of the crepe. For years now, the only compliments she had ever received from men were about how beautiful or elegant she was, or how professionally she navigated the shoots. It was hard not to feel like a commodity sometimes, or like some show animal brought out to perform her tricks. True, Bill didn't know her well. But it was nice to have someone notice something about her other than the shade of her lipstick or her model's sway as she walked down the catwalk.

"Steve," she said, turning to the scientist, "do you have any idea what Bill has in mind?"

"I wish the answer was no," he said. "But, unfortunately, I have a guess."

"And does this guess have anything to do with me looking like Nicola Neumann?"

"I think that's a pretty safe bet."

She frowned for a moment, her chin in her hand as the eyes of the three men around the table focused squarely on her.

"Just how much trouble am I getting into?"

The three men all looked at one another, none of them immediately volunteering an answer. And for the first time that day, Elizabeth Lamont wondered if she might be in real danger.

"Let's talk in my office when you're finished," Bill said. Elizabeth looked back down at what was left of her crepes; suddenly, they seemed overly sweet and rich.

"All right, then," she said. "Let's hear what you have to say."

CHAPTER FOUR

An uncomfortable silence filled the elevator as the four of them rode up to Bill Wynter's office. Steve wondered why he had invited the journalist to come along with them—usually Bill took pains to keep his different sources from spending too much time with one another, particularly when they didn't officially work for the agency. Miles Reardon seemed like a nice enough guy, and he was clearly a good reporter, but what was he doing getting mixed up in all this? Maybe, Steve thought, Bill thought that having Miles around might help to put Elizabeth at ease; they had known one another socially, and he had been friends with her fiancé before his death. But why would Bill care about putting Elizabeth at ease? Why would he invite her up to his office in the first place?

Steve spent the whole elevator ride trying desperately to think of some reason other than the fact that Elizabeth Lamont, with her new haircut, bore more than a passing resemblance to Nicola Neumann—close enough that he had spent all morning chasing her around New York City and then shepherding her to lunch. He had felt badly enough to have brought her there under false pretenses, especially once his mistake had been made clear. But it was one thing to inconvenience the woman and another altogether

PASSPORT TO DANGER

to put her in harm's way. If anything happened to Elizabeth, he wasn't sure he could forgive himself.

From the other corner of the elevator, he heard Miles Reardon begin to hum quietly to try and break the silence. But the thin sound died on his lips and turned into a cough. Everyone seemed on edge, troubled by what they did not and could not know. Steve wondered if this was how Bill felt all the time. *The man must have an iron stomach*, he thought, *or at least a very large tub of antacids somewhere.*

• • •

Elizabeth stood by the window in Bill Wynter's office, looking out at the sea of buildings. New York was a labyrinth of stone, steel, and glass, but it also had a certain beauty that no other city possessed. The crowded streets emanated an immense vitality; it engulfed everyone, whether you wanted it to or not. Elizabeth had been awed by the endless hustle and bustle when she had first come to the city; now she thrived on it. But it would be good to get away for a while. She needed some peace and quiet.

Bill Wynter's office was just about the last place she had expected to find herself today, after a morning spent fretting about how she was going to break the news of her early retirement. She could tell that Steve hadn't expected it, either, by the edgy silence in the elevator and the looks he kept shooting her way, as though she couldn't see him. She watched the cars down on Park Avenue, listening behind her as Steve and Miles talked about the latest troop withdrawal in Vietnam and Bill shuffled papers on his desk.

"You have a marvelous view," she said.

Bill looked up from his desk, a small smile on his lips. Did anyone, Elizabeth wondered, ever know what really went on behind those calm grey eyes?

"I'll have to admit it, I've had worse," he said, looking out the window himself. "The skyline always makes my heart beat a little faster."

"And these paintings," Elizabeth said, moving to the series of abstract art pieces that decorated the walls. Steve was standing in front of a painting of brightly colored squares against a royal blue background; across the room, above where Miles Reardon had taken a seat in a brown leather club chair, was a large chartreuse painting with a single, off-center black dot. "Not what I would have pictured for your office, I have to say."

Bill chuckled.

"No?"

"I would have taken you for a western man," she said. "You know, men on horses lassoing steers? Or maybe a lone man against the Wyoming mountains and a crimson sunset."

Bill chuckled and shook his head.

"I'm not much for interior design," he said. "I'd probably prefer to have paintings like that myself."

"But you didn't bring me here to show me your artwork," Elizabeth said. "Or the fabulous view."

"No," Bill said, the playfulness in his tone having been replaced by something steelier. "I didn't."

Elizabeth could feel the heightened attention of the other men in the room as Wynter stood behind his desk and appraised her with those grey eyes.

"I should start by telling you that I haven't been completely straight with you," Wynter said. "I don't really work for NATO."

"She knows that already," Steve Brenner said from the back of the room. Wynter squinted at the scientist.

"You told her?"

"No," Steve said. "She guessed."

"I'd say it's a tossup between the CIA and military intelligence," Elizabeth said. "Though I'm leaning CIA."

"And why is that, Ms. Lamont?" Wynter said.

"No real reason," Elizabeth said with a small smile of her own. "I just find it's always more fun to have a horse in the race."

"You should take this girl up to Saratoga, Steve," Wynter said before turning his attention back to Elizabeth. "You're right. I work for the CIA, and I have a problem, which means, unfortunately, that America has a problem. I've spent the last forty-eight hours trying to think of any possible solution to this problem, and so far, I've come up empty. That is, until Steve brought you into the restaurant."

"And how, exactly, am I a solution to your problem?"

Wynter scratched his nose.

"What I'm about to tell you is highly classified. Under ordinary circumstances, I couldn't possibly reveal this information to you without going through the proper security clearances. But these are no ordinary circumstances, and I have a feeling that you can be trusted. I have a few friends back at Langley confirming everything you told me and Steve over lunch, but I'm pretty sure it will all check out."

"It will," Miles Reardon said from his perch on the chair. "I'm sure of it."

"So how about it, Ms. Lamont? Can I trust you?"

Elizabeth paused for a moment before answering the man's question. On its face, it was a simple question: Elizabeth had always prided herself on her ability to keep the secrets of others. She was no gossip like so many of the other models and hair stylists, the ones who traded juicy details and rumors of torrid affairs back and forth on the sets of photoshoots like they were commodity traders in the pits of the Chicago Mercantile Exchange. If what Bill had to tell her was really so important, then she didn't expect it would be difficult to keep this information to herself.

But she could also sense the presence of another question behind his question of trust—a larger question, and a more difficult one, whose contours she could not quite yet grasp. She wasn't saying yes to that bigger question yet. But she was consenting to go down an uncertain road. She could not possibly understand where it might lead, or whether she would be able to come back.

"Yes," she said. "You can trust me."

"Good," Bill said. "Miles, you know some of this already. There is a house in Mexico. In Cuernavaca, to be specific. Inside that house is a man—a scientist, one of the finest physicists working for our country. We don't know exactly how he got there, whether he was taken against his will or went there of his own accord. What we do know is that he is being held by Soviet agents who are keeping him there until they can load him onto a boat bound for Moscow. We believe we have a week until that happens. But we can't be certain.

"Before he left—or was taken—this scientist was at work on a project that had meaningful implications for our national defense. I'm not exaggerating when I say it was something that could tip the balance of power to the US and ensure the continued prosperity of the free world for decades, if not permanently. That project—and everything he was working on for the past year—is now protected by a code that only this scientist knows. It is

PASSPORT TO DANGER

of vital importance that we learn that code from him before he leaves that house."

"Can't you decrypt it?" Elizabeth said.

Wynter frowned and shook his head.

"We tried. The boys over at the NSA put some of their top people on it. But our scientist was both smart and paranoid—justifiably so, as it now seems. The encryption is advanced, specific, and sensitive. If we attempt any brute force methods, they believe that the contents of the project will be destroyed. That is a risk we cannot take.

"We need that code, Elizabeth. I've been racking my brain for days now trying to figure out how to get it. The men guarding him are some of the best agents the Soviets have; returning this scientist to the Soviet Union would be not only a public relations coup, but also a decisive step forward in their ability to advance their own weapons system and, in doing so, counteract ours."

"Returning..." Steve Brenner said from behind her. Elizabeth turned to look at the man. His face was positively pale.

"What's that?" Bill Wynter said.

"You said, 'returning this scientist to the Soviet Union,'" Steve said.

Bill nodded.

"Yes."

"There's only one man I know of who fits that description," Steve said. Bill sighed.

"I really did want to let you have that vacation, Steve," Bill said. "But I hope you now understand what was so urgent."

"Who are you talking about?" Elizabeth asked. Steve looked at Bill, as though asking him for permission. Bill gave his assent with a very slight nod of his head.

"Anton Sobokov," Steve said. His voice was steady, but Elizabeth could see the way he was tensing his body, as though preparing for impact. "He's been in America since when, Bill? 1939?"

"Since '38," Bill said. "But who's counting?"

"One of the best minds in nuclear physics. A close friend of mine, and an American patriot. If he's with them, then they kidnapped him."

"Possible. Our sources indicate otherwise."

"That's absurd," Steve said. "He hates the Soviets!"

"You know what the Communists can do," Bill said. "It wouldn't take us long to come up with a hundred cases of citizens who have been bribed, blackmailed, or threatened into doing something abhorrent to them, people who never would have dreamed of betraying their country."

"Dr. Sobokov is well aware of the methods the Soviets employ," Steve said. He was speaking quietly, but Elizabeth could see that a certain rage was growing within him. "He saw those methods applied to his family, Bill, those who were dragged out of their bed by Yezhov or Beria in the middle of the night and never heard from again. There's no way he'd go back. Not to mention he's the most dedicated scientist I know, and if there's one thing a scientist needs, it's freedom. He told me that trying to do good science in Russia was like trying to work with a straitjacket on."

Wynter returned to his seat and methodically loaded his pipe with tobacco.

"Humor me. In your opinion, what do you think Dr. Sobokov would do if the Russians offered him a great deal of money?"

"Laugh in their faces," Brenner said.

"Do you think they could blackmail him?"

"Impossible. Anton lives as austerely as a Trappist monk. And why now? If they had anything on him, why wait thirty years? Why let him advance American weapons systems for three decades before trying to bring him back into the fold?"

Wynter took a contemplative puff on his pipe.

"Your logic is sound, Steve. I thought the same thing. But a source tells me he chose to go back."

"Can you tell me anything about this so-called source?"

Elizabeth could practically see the steam coming from Steve's nostrils now. But Wynter kept his cool.

"She's a defector. Or an attempted defector, at least."

Steve gave a dismissive snort.

"Why would you put any faith in what a defector says?"

"Because she didn't read about this plot in Pravda, Steve. For her to have known about it, she had to be involved in it."

Brenner's dark eyes narrowed.

"She?"

"Yes."

There was, for a few moments, silence in the room. Elizabeth looked between the two men; she was pretty sure she already knew the answer.

"It's Nicola Neumann, isn't it?" Elizabeth said.

Wynter nodded. Steve struck the arm of the nearby couch with his fist.

"Why the hell would you believe anything she says?"

"Because she's badly frightened. She's out of favor, and you know what that means."

"I don't give a damn if she's frightened. That woman hasn't told the truth since the day she crawled out of her mother's womb."

"I have another source. Someone high in the government. Code name Cobalt. He believed the same thing about Sobokov."

Elizabeth could see that Steve was not convinced; so could Wynter.

"This source is important, Steve," Wynter said. "He's given me too much information that has compromised the Soviet Intelligence apparatus for me to disregard what he's told me about Sobokov."

"Could it be some kind of plot?" Miles Reardon said from his chair. The other three pairs of eyes in the room turned to look at him, seemingly surprised to still see him there. "I'm just saying. Cobalt feeds you information over time, plays the long game, gains your confidence and makes you believe what he told you about Dr. Sobokov so you don't try to rescue him before they can get him back to Moscow?"

Wynter took another thoughtful puff on his pipe.

"You really should have stayed in intelligence, Miles. Your talents are wasted in journalism. I considered the same thing myself. There's just one problem: Cobalt's the one who told me that Sobokov is in Cuernavaca. If he really wanted me to believe that Sobokov is defecting, what's stopping me from taking the house any time between now and when the ship arrives in Mexico? It's no trouble to keep Sobokov from going with the Russians. It's getting that damn code from him, and ideally getting him out alive, that's the problem."

"Maybe that's it," Miles said. "If you think he's defecting, he won't give you the code anyway. It wouldn't be worth it to you."

"It's possible," Bill said. "But I don't like it, any of it. There's something we're not seeing."

Another long silence descended over the room. Elizabeth's head was spinning. Was it always like this in this line of work? All these names, all this information at once, and everyone just expected to keep up? It was clear that she was entering an entirely new kind of world, and she wasn't sure yet if she liked it. But it did have one thing going for it: After three years of posing for pictures, being painted and tousled and teased with absolutely nothing to do with her mind, it felt good to finally be thinking again.

"So what are you going to do?" she asked Wynter. He sighed.

"That's exactly the problem I've been trying to puzzle out. We can't take the house by force—too risky. If Sobokov was killed in the crossfire, there goes five years of research on our missile systems, and his minders are as clever and cautious as they are brutal. The house is functionally on lockdown until that ship arrives in Mexico—nobody in or out. But I need to get someone into that house, someone who can try to get the code from Sobokov."

"Assuming he wants to give it," Elizabeth said.

"It's a gamble, all right. But we don't have another choice. Or none, at least, that I can see."

"You said that Nicola Neumann knew about the defection," Elizabeth said.

"It *wasn't* a defection," Steve said.

"Or kidnapping. Abduction. The plan to get Sobokov back to Moscow, however it happened."

"That's right," Wynter said.

"Does that mean she was involved with the plot?"

"She was," Wynter said.

"She *said* she was," Steve said.

"And does that mean the men in the house are expecting Nicola Neumann to show up in Mexico?" Elizabeth said.

A very small, private smile—one that seemed meant just for her—briefly played across Bill Wynter's lips.

"I think it just might," he said.

CHAPTER FIVE

"You can't do that," Steve Brenner said. Bill Wynter took another thoughtful puff from his pipe as the scientist came towards his him, finger pointed like it was a bayonet and he was storming the desk by force.

"I don't know what I'm going to do yet," Bill said as calmly as he could. "But I've got to get someone into that house to talk to Sobokov."

"But this is lunacy!" Brenner said.

Bill sighed; he had known that Steve was likely to object to any plan that involved even the specter of Nicola Neumann, especially after everything that had happened between the KGB asset and his brother. But this felt like something different. Wynter had noticed the way that Steve was looking at Elizabeth across the table when he'd returned with Miles Reardon at the end of lunch. It seemed almost impossible that the two of them had only met that morning.

"Elizabeth," Bill said, "would you mind taking Miles to get a cup of coffee? I think Steve and I need to have a private conversation."

Elizabeth glanced back at Steve, less asking for permission than to see what the man thought of the idea. He was still steaming mad, pacing slightly on the deep emerald carpeting.

"I think a coffee would be just the thing after a lunch like that," Elizabeth said pleasantly, fixing Bill with a smile that, if he didn't know better, would have suggested that she thought nothing at all about this situation was amiss. Bill felt something within him lift slightly. It was one thing that the universe had thought fit to provide him with a woman who bore such a close resemblance to Nicola Neumann. But Elizabeth could really handle herself. Bill Wynter was rarely wrong when it came to evaluating talent; he just had to find a way to make Steve see that before he scared off their last best chance at getting to Sobokov.

"You'll show me the way, Miles?" Elizabeth said, rising from her seat.

"It would be my pleasure," the journalist said, extending an arm as Elizabeth led him out of the office and then closed the door behind him.

In the empty break room down the hall, Miles Reardon sat as Elizabeth served them both coffee.

"Cream and sugar?" she asked.

"No, thanks. I take it black."

"You must have a strong stomach. I think it tastes like mud without sugar."

"You spend enough time outside the country, and you begin to realize that cream and sugar are a luxury you can't always afford. You like yours with sugar, though, I see."

Elizabeth smiled broadly as she spooned another teaspoon of sugar into her cup. It was the same smile Miles had seen at so many dinners with her late fiancé and in the pages of countless magazines. She really was an elegant woman. He took a sip of coffee and then lit up a cigarette.

"At least I don't have to take it black anymore," Elizabeth said. "I think I could get used to eating and drinking stuff that actually tastes good without having to worry about all the calories."

"So you're really done with modeling, then?"

"You know how it is," Elizabeth said. "Girls like me all come with an expiration date. I was just lucky enough to get to go out on my own terms, instead of trying to cling on desperately after nobody wanted me anymore."

"I can respect that," Miles said. "Is there any of it you'll miss?"

Elizabeth chuckled and shook her head.

"I'm sure I will, eventually. The money was good. I was good at the work. But for now, I'm so glad to be out, I can't even imagine having to go back in for a shoot." She blew on the top of her cup to cool the coffee, and then took a delicate sip. "How did you get yourself mixed up in all this, Miles?"

"Korea," Miles said. "It feels like a lifetime ago now. After the disaster on the Yalu, when our intelligence believed that China would stay out of the war, it became a priority to make sure our agencies were actually helping, rather than hurting, the war effort. The CIA was brand new; no one quite knew what to make of them. McArthur didn't trust them. I hate to think of how many lives we lost because of that hubris.

"Bill and I were both in military intelligence. I thought it was going to be some kind of grand adventure; I hadn't been old enough to serve in World War II, and like all young men I was stupid enough to believe that war was mostly about glory and honor. Well, I learned quickly otherwise. Bill was something of a mentor to me back then, me and a number of other men. Always level-headed, always thinking about things from the broader strategic perspective. It was no surprise that he stayed on with Langley after Korea. I'm not sure I've ever met a man better suited for intelligence work, to be honest."

"Scott always told me he believed that if more people could see war first-hand, there would be a lot less of it," Elizabeth said. "I wasn't sure I always agreed. But I thought there was something noble about that. He really believed in his work, Miles, as I'm sure you do too."

"I know he did," Miles said. Then, "You must miss him terribly."

"I can't believe it's been a year already. Sometimes, it feels like no time at all has gone by, and other times, well, other times I think it was another lifetime ago."

"I know what you mean."

For a few moments it was quiet in the room, the two of them sipping their coffees and thinking about the man they had once both known so well.

"You know, it's funny," Elizabeth said after a time. "After Scott died, I used to lie awake at night, dreaming that there would be some way for me to even the score with the Communists. It was a silly idea—the world is too big and complicated for things to work like that, and for all I know, Moscow just as soon would have preferred if Scott was still alive. He was certainly no jingoist, but I needed to believe, in those months, that it was possible to get something like even, that I could avenge him in some way. It was foolish to think like that, I knew it even at the time, but I couldn't help myself.

"And now here it is, a chance out of the blue to get back at the Soviets. What I can't tell is whether, if Scott were here now, he'd see this all as some kind of grand adventure or tell me that I was being hopelessly naive."

She sighed and stared down into her coffee.

"Can I trust him, Miles?" Elizabeth said finally.

"Who?"

"Bill Wynter."

Miles nodded slowly and while contemplating his answer.

"In my experience, it's best to take everything that a CIA man tells you with a healthy dose of skepticism," he said. "If he's giving you information, there's a reason for it, and it usually isn't your own edification. You have to remember that they're seeing a much, much bigger chess board, and you're only a small piece on it. Especially a man like Bill, who's been around long enough that he can see more of the board than most."

Miles watched Elizabeth taking this in, making her own calculations.

"But Bill Wynter is an honorable man," Miles said. "He isn't in it for the glory, or to advance his own agenda. In all the years I've known him, his only goal has ever been to try to make the world a better, safer place. If we had a few more men like him running things, I think we'd all be better off for it."

"I used to play chess as a girl," Elizabeth said. "After my parents died, I was sent back up to live with my grandmother in Quebec. Those were not good years. But she had a chess set that had been my grandfather's, and she taught me how to play. I never got very good at it; that isn't how my mind works. But I remember her explaining that sometimes, the best move on the board required a sacrifice. That was always difficult for me."

"I don't think Bill would do anything to put you in a situation that you couldn't handle," Miles said.

"Like impersonating a KGB operative to get access to a Russian safehouse and try to extract information from an American nuclear scientist?" Elizabeth said with a little smile.

PASSPORT TO DANGER

Miles chuckled a little and took a nervous sip of coffee.

"Well, when you put it that way."

"You'd tell me if you thought I was making a mistake, wouldn't you?"

"We don't even know what his plans are," Miles said. "I say hear him out. Listen to what he proposes, and if it seems like too much, you walk—fly off to Greece, take that vacation you deserve, and never worry about it again."

"Is it really possible to forget about a thing like that?" Elizabeth said. "It feels like the more you learn about the true state of the world, the more difficult it is to leave things like that behind."

"You might be right," Miles said. She was smart, this woman. He had forgotten just how sharp she was. He looked down at his coffee cup. "I wouldn't mind a slug of brandy in here."

"So that's how you do it," Elizabeth said.

"Do what?"

"Forget about everything you know," she said.

Miles laughed. "It helps," he said. "But, no. You never really forget."

"I didn't think so," Elizabeth said.

It was warm in the little break room, but even so, Miles felt a quick chill go through him.

"I can't believe you," Steve Brenner said as soon as Miles and Elizabeth left the office. "Actually considering a thing like this."

"It's my job to consider things like this," Wynter said to him, "and consider things much, much worse. Like, for instance, the Russians setting back our weapons program by a decade, and stealing our best nuclear scientist."

"I realize you have a problem, Bill. A very serious one."

"Do you?" Wynter said. "Because your little performance suggests to me you might not fully grasp the magnitude of what we're facing here."

"I know about Dr. Sobokov's work," Steve said.

"Then why don't you tell me why it would be such a problem if they actually got him back to Moscow," Wynter said. Steve was silently fuming—who was Bill Wynter to lecture him like this, as though he was a misbehaving schoolboy who had been called into the principal's office? But Wynter clearly wasn't joking around anymore. "That wasn't a rhetorical request, Steve."

Steve took a deep breath and tried to calm himself—yelling at Bill wasn't going to do any good, or help to prevent Elizabeth from getting caught in the middle of this mess. If he wanted to keep her safe, he was going to have to appeal to Bill's rational mind. It was the only way he had ever seen the old master spy make a decision.

"Dr. Sobokov was part of the original team who developed MIRV for our ICBMs," Steve said. "The Russians have far more intercontinental ballistic missiles than we do. They've got the SS-9 missile, more powerful and formidable than any of our missiles. They can mount a twenty-five-megaton warhead on it that could knock out our entire Minuteman system, and we don't have a similar weapon to send back at them. Not to mention they have a much larger missile defense system than we do."

Bill Wynter nodded; Steve figured he was on the right track.

"But they haven't been able to perfect their multiple warhead re-entry vehicles, have they?"

"No," Bill said. "Which means that one of our Poseidon missiles is worth more than any of their more powerful weapons. Each one of the MIRVs on a Poseidon missile can detach itself and strike a separate target hundreds of miles away. We can equip each of our ICBMs with three to ten multiple warheads. We can maintain the upper hand. For now."

"Unless the Russians were able to find a scientist willing to work out the kinks in their system for them," Steve said. He had known that losing Sobokov would be a blow, but he hadn't conceptualized just how dangerous it might be.

"And that's not all," Wynter said. "The last five years of Dr. Sobokov's work will be lost if we aren't able to get him back, or at least get the code from him that will allow us to unlock his work. Think about it—you move the Soviets forward by a decade, and you set us back by almost the same amount. The next thing you know, they have us over a barrel."

"I can appreciate the implications," Steve said. "It's a hell of a fix we've got ourselves into. But that doesn't mean you can send Elizabeth Lamont on a suicide mission!"

"I would never ask her to do anything unless I thought there was a real chance of success," Bill said. "I'd hoped you knew me well enough to understand that I don't see my people as expendable assets to be deployed at will. Especially not a girl like that who, until this morning, had probably never given espionage a second thought."

"You can't ask her to go into that house!"

Bill sighed.

"Do you think I'd even be considering something like this if I felt I had any other option?"

"She's not tough," Steve said. "She's smart, and she's perceptive. But Nicola Neumann is tough as tempered steel. Anyone who tries to impersonate her will have to be that tough too, or they'll see right through her."

"You only met the woman this morning," Wynter said. "She managed to fool you for several hours. What makes you think you know her so well? She might continue to surprise you.

"All I'm asking of her now is to listen with an open mind. We tell her more about Nicola Neumann and the situation down in Cuernavaca. We flesh out a possible plan and the role she will be expected to play in it. If at any point she feels she can't be involved, then she walks, no questions asked."

Wynter sighed.

"I know she didn't sign up for any of this, and it's a hell of a lot to throw at her all at once. I haven't even gotten her security clearances yet; for all I know, she had some dalliance with a Quebecois separatist group that would make it impossible for me to use her in the first place."

I hope so, Steve found himself thinking. *At least that way, she would be safe.* Though he suspected, in his heart, that things wouldn't be nearly that easy.

"I need your help on this, Steve," Wynter said. "No one knows Dr. Sobokov better than you. And Elizabeth Lamont, despite the dubious nature of your meeting, appears to trust you and value you opinion. I want her to feel as comfortable as possible. If she does end up agreeing to work with us, it needs to feel like it's her decision, not something we're forcing her into."

"I think you're making a big mistake here," Steve said.

"I'm taking a risk," Wynter said. "There's a difference."

"Nothing I say is going to change your mind, is it?" Steve said.

"Not unless you have another way into that house," Wynter said. "Now, why don't you go see if Elizabeth and Miles have finished their coffee break?"

PASSPORT TO DANGER

Elizabeth Lamont was back in Bill Wynter's impressive office, with its majestic views, plush carpeting, and surprisingly modern art. But all of that faded away now as she stood before the CIA man, looking at him as he prepared to speak. Her conversation with Miles hadn't done much to allay her concerns—if anything, he had confirmed what she thought. She liked Bill Wynter; under other circumstances, she would have happily sat next to him at a dinner party, listening to his stories of traveling the world trying to advance the interests of the United States. But this was a different matter altogether. She noticed, almost absently, that her hands were shaking.

It's ridiculous to be so upset, she thought to herself, trying to slow the rapid beating of her own heart. *All I have to do is tell him he's crazy and walk out. Nothing's stopping me.*

But she didn't. Instead, she stayed where she was as Bill Wynter cleared his throat and began to speak.

"Elizabeth," he said. "I'd like to have you briefed. For the next few days, my people would explain the situation to you in greater detail—how we got into this mess, and how we think we might be able to get out of it. After you've heard what we think, it will be entirely your decision whether you accept or refuse my request. If you don't think you can do what we're asking you to do, or simply don't want to, I'll send you back to New York. You'll be free to do whatever you like, as though none of this ever happened."

Elizabeth stared at him with wide eyes. *This wasn't a briefing?* She thought to herself. It had sure felt like one. She was in an entirely new world, one she had scarcely known existed before today. She'd been thinking about Scott more today than she had for some time—she found the hurt was different than it had been in the immediate aftermath, less of a sharp-toothed thing, more bittersweet. *If he was here,* she thought, *and he knew he was the only one who could get into that house, he would have gone to Cuernavaca.* But Scott had been fearless, and she wasn't. That was one of the reasons she had loved him so fiercely.

"Where would I be briefed?" she asked.

"If you agree," Wynter said, "you, me, and Steve will fly down to Washington tonight, and from there onto somewhere safe."

"Steve is going?" she said. At almost the same moment, she heard a sound of surprise coming from where Steve was standing in the corner of the room.

"Yes," Wynter said. "I need him. I'll arrange with his superior to give Dr. Brenner a leave of absence until we get Dr. Sobokov back."

Elizabeth took a deep breath.

"I can't promise you anything," she said. "But I'll go down to Washington with you, and hear what you have to say."

Wynter looked immensely relieved and grinned broadly at her.

"That's wonderful. Will half an hour give you enough time to get ready?"

Elizabeth laughed lightly.

"You don't know much about women, do you?"

Wynter laughed too, his head cocked to the side.

"Fine. An hour, then. There's a car downstairs waiting to take you to your apartment." His grey eyes softened. "Thank you, Elizabeth. I know I'm asking a lot of you. Today has probably gone very differently from how you imagined when you woke up this morning."

"I'll walk you down," Miles Reardon said. Elizabeth nodded, and then took one last look at Steve Brenner before she walked out of the office. Bill Wynter was right—today had gone nothing

PASSPORT TO DANGER

at all like she had imagined it would. The end of her modeling career was the last thing on her mind now. Instead, her thoughts were down in Mexico, trying to imagine just what it was that was happening in that little house that was so important to the fate of the free world.

Once Elizabeth and Miles were gone, Steve Brenner shook his head grimly.

"I just can't believe there isn't another way."

"If there is, we'll find it," Wynter said, glancing down at his watch. He began to pack up his briefcase.

"Elizabeth isn't a trained—"

"She is the only one who can prevent a bloodbath, and give us any chance of getting Dr. Sobokov out alive."

"So you think they're just going to let her waltz in and out as she pleases?"

Wynter snapped the clasps on his briefcase shut.

"I think that's precisely what they'll do. Now, unless you have any more specific objections, we have a plane to catch."

"I still don't see what you need me for," Steve said, following Wynter out of the office.

"It's that sunny, can-do attitude of yours," Wynter said as he called for the elevator. "I'm just not sure how long I can go without it."

CHAPTER SIX

It was a lovely evening, clear and cool, with stars sprinkled over the black sky burning bright and steadfast, so long in the heavens that Elizabeth felt as though she could almost reach out and touch them.

She was standing on the back patio of the two-story colonial home, looking down at a pasture flooded with silvery moonlight. The pasture was bordered by a belt of pines, almost black against the meadow's ghostly hue. Cicadas were singing cheerfully, as though they were glad darkness had fallen, and somewhere in the forest a nightingale fluted a song. It smelled so different here than it did in the city: the sharp, resinous smell of the pines; the sweet fragrance of honeysuckle coming from the garden below; the clean smell of newly cut hay.

It was a beautiful place, Elizabeth thought as she stared out into the night. She could imagine that, under different circumstances, she might feel fully at peace here. If she was back in New York, she'd be surrounded by millions of glowing lights beneath a smoggy sky and the honking horns of impatient cabbies, the air sickly with soot. It was amazing that one could move, in a matter of minutes, from the hectic city to this quiet Virginia countryside. But not nearly as amazing as how quickly she had been swept away from the frivolous world of glamor into the silent world of intelligence officers, where the decisions affected not next year's collections but the future of the country, and, seemingly, that of the world.

Bill Wynter had made it clear to her that she wasn't committing to anything by coming down here with him. But now that she was here, it felt like she was in much deeper than she had been before. What would he do if she decided that she couldn't impersonate Nicola Neumann, after all? She was almost certain that she wasn't as capable as Wynter seemed to think she was—no. Elizabeth shook her head at that foolishness. He probably didn't actually think she was capable, either—he was just desperate. Miles had said that Wynter wouldn't use an amateur unless there was no one else; too much could go wrong when an amateur was involved. Intelligence agents required years of training before they were sent on a mission. She had three days.

A bat soaring out of a tree startled her out of her thoughts. She heard a door open behind her and prepared herself for another pep talk from Wynter. The men had been quiet on the flight down to DC—the little prop engine plane had been so loud that they probably wouldn't have been able to talk much, anyway. Then in the car on the way out to Virginia, Steve and Wynter had talked of nothing but Sobokov. She was tired of all that talk. But when she turned around, she saw it was Steve Brenner coming onto the patio. In spite of herself, she felt her heart lift.

She had known this man for less than twenty-four hours—her introduction to him had come by way of him tricking her into lunch under false pretenses—and yet every time he looked at her, her pulse quickened. What was wrong with her? But she couldn't help the way she felt. Part of the appeal was his appearance—he was quite handsome with his black hair, dark brown eyes, high cheekbones, strong jaw, and deep tan. It surprised her that a scientist dressed as well as he did, with his excellently tailored clothes accentuating a muscular build that suggested a college athlete who had kept himself in shape after leaving school. She tried to imagine him as he must have been back then, coming out of a lecture hall with his head full of equations before heading down to the docks to calm his mind on the water.

But it was as much his personality as his looks that drew her to him. He was masculine without working at it; confident without being arrogant; amusing without trying to be funny; easy and relaxed, but she could tell that beneath his outward presence, he was alert and astute. She heard the way he had challenged Wynter; he had strong convictions, but his opinions could be changed if he heard a sensible argument. Maybe that was why Wynter had insisted that he come along with them to Virginia—because the man had known, on some level, that she would follow wherever Steve went. It had been a year since she had even thought about another man, and now here he was, at the least convenient time possible. But then, wasn't that how it always went?

"I was hoping I'd find you out here," Steve said, coming over to where she stood. He was carrying two little tumblers with brown liquor in them. He handed one over to her.

"I'm not usually much for whiskey," she said. "But after the day I've had..."

"Believe me, if there was anything stronger, I'd pour both of us a double," he said. "But bourbon will have to do for now."

Elizabeth took a sip of the drink and felt the warmth spread through her against the chill of the night air.

"You seemed surprised when Bill asked you to come down with us," she said after a time.

"I was," Steve said. "I still am, in fact."

"Is it because of Dr. Sobokov? It sounded like you followed his work closely."

"Dr. Sobokov was—*is*—a great mentor of mine," Steve said. "And a top-notch nuclear scientist."

"But that's not why you think he invited you down here," Elizabeth said. Steve gave her a weak smile.

"The CIA knows more about our nuclear weapons program than I ever will," he said. "I don't doubt that my personal connection with Dr. Sobokov is a useful perspective for Bill to have, but no, I don't think that's why."

"It's because of her, isn't it?" Elizabeth said. "Nicola Neumann."

Steve sighed.

"Elizabeth," he said, lighting a cigarette, "there's a lot you're going to hear about Nicola Neumann over the next few days, things you need to hear, so you can make up your mind on whether or not you want to go through with this plan of Bill's. But before you do, there are some things I want to tell you. I know it's late, but will you hear me out?"

"Of course," she said. Steve took a long swig of whiskey.

"I'm going to start by telling you a story about a girl named Nicola," he said. "Nicola grew up in East Berlin, suffering terrible hardships under the Communists. Her mother died in childbirth; she had no other relatives. She was a ward of the state. Once she was in her teens, they put her in a brothel. A terrible thing, but all too common in that place and time. A few years later, when she was released, she became a waitress in a brauhaus. She started going to night school, teaching herself typing and shorthand. Eventually, she became a secretary for one of the Colonels in East German Intelligence—no easy thing for a girl like her, but she was smart, quick, and pretty. Seven years later, she escaped into West Berlin. She asked to speak with someone in British Intelligence, and got connected with a man who sent her to London. The British questioned her thoroughly, but her story checked out—there had been an Anna N. Neumann, born to Heinz Neumann, a soldier killed during the war. Mother dead from childbirth, just like the woman told them. No other known relatives.

"Nicola gave the British some valuable information about the East German intelligence apparatus and tipped them off about some double agents, because she hadn't just been twiddling her thumbs during her time as a secretary. She had been plotting her revenge, vowing to strike back against the Communists when she got her chance. The British, as it turned out, already had their doubts about these agents, which only added to her credibility. Six months after her escape from East Berlin, the British gave Nicola a visa, at her request, and sent her to the United States. Land of the free, home of the brave, all that.

"And that," Steve said, "is where she met my brother."

He paused there. Elizabeth could see his jaw tighten. She watched him for a moment, quiet and sympathetic—she could tell how hard this was for him. But all the same, she felt like this was something that she needed to hear, and from him, before the rest of the intelligence apparatus engulfed her in the morning.

"Carl was a Senator from Texas and a member of the Committee on Foreign Relations," Steve said. "At the time he met Nicola, his wife was back in Texas; her mother had had a stroke. A month after he was introduced to Nicola at a party, she leased an apartment in his building in Washington and began to arrange 'accidental' meetings with him. Unfortunately, my brother was too naive to realize that these meetings were no accident."

PASSPORT TO DANGER

Steve ground out his cigarette with an abrupt movement.

"Most men would have realized what kind of woman Nicola was. But I guess that despite all his apparent sophistication, Carl was just a green country boy, especially when it came to women."

Steve was having a hard time keeping the bitterness from his voice. Elizabeth felt sorry for him. It must be difficult for him to tell her all this, and in doing so, relive it all over again.

"After they'd seen each other a few times, Carl began to get interested in her. She pretended to like the same things he did—horse racing, baseball. And, even more importantly, she appeared to *hate* the Communists. Carl had advocated for a hard policy against the Soviets ever since he had become a Senator." Steve's face hardened. "They began an affair. Carl thought he was in love with her. He even tried to get a divorce—but his wife refused, because of their four children." Steve lit another cigarette—he was smoking too much, Elizabeth thought, but she wasn't about to tell him that, given everything he had been through. "Someone leaked the affair to the Press, which would have been bad enough. But it also came out that Nicola was a Russian agent."

"That must have been awful," Elizabeth said quietly. She thought for a few moments about what Steve had said. "I suppose the Soviets were the ones who started the rumor about her being an enemy agent."

Steve nodded.

"That's right. So Carl found himself embroiled in both a sex scandal and a security crisis."

"And he was singled out because of his policy against the Communists?"

"Yes."

"So what happened?" Elizabeth bit her lip as soon as she had asked the question; there was no way for this story to end, other than disaster.

"After the initial story broke, the Press let it die down. Carl had always been popular with the newsmen, and they realized the Communists' purpose in using Nicola was to discredit a US Senator, and embarrass the government. Giving the affair a lot of publicity would be playing right into the Communists' hands."

"Well, that's good then, right?" Elizabeth said.

Steve took a long drag on his cigarette.

"My brother was in a hunting accident, down in Texas, shortly after the news of his affair came out."

Elizabeth stared at Steve's profile; the man was looking out, unseeing, into the dark country night. Was "hunting accident" another way of saying a suicide? Noticing the pain in Steve's black eyes, she decided that it must be. *How horrible*, she thought, glancing away.

"I'm so sorry, Steve."

He nodded, though she wasn't sure if he had heard her—his mind seemed far away now.

"When it became known that Nicola was a spy, American Intelligence started to look into her past. Her real story. She was German by birth—that much had been true—the illegitimate daughter of a top Nazi General. She'd kept her mother's last name, Mueller. But when the General discovered that his mistress was a quarter Jewish, he decided that it would be prudent to get rid of her. Nicola wasn't home when the SS came to get her mother—otherwise she would have been sent to Dachau, too. But a neighbor intercepted Nicola on her way home and made arrangements for her to leave the country with a band of refugees. They escaped by an underground route through Czechoslovakia to Kiev. For several years, she lived with one of the families she had escaped with. Then, in her mid-teens, she became the mistress of the head of the Secret Police. He recognized something in her—it wasn't just that she was pretty, she was also smart, and ruthless. So he sent her to spy school in Leningrad. She was a natural, and not just with languages—mannerisms, customs, the difference between how someone from the North of England would drink a beer compared to a born and bred Londoner. Nicola was good enough to convince anyone that she was a native of whatever country she was sent to. The NATO countries, it was decided, would be her targets.

"When the Communists decided that she was ready, they put her in beautiful clothes, gave her an American passport, and sent her to France. She became involved with André Villiers, the newly elected head of one of the largest French labor unions. The union had been cooperating with the Communists, but Villiers had never got on with the Soviets—he didn't like them, or trust him. He intended to change the union's policy. But after the story of his affair with an East German agent became public, he was ruined. Even for the French, this was too much.

"Nicola disappeared for a year. Then she turned up in England, on a Spanish passport this time. Her target was one of the most influential men in Parliament. Again, the leak and the scandal. It wasn't quite the Profumo affair, but it was just as disastrous.

"She escaped before the British could capture her, went to ground, and got across the channel at Dover. She made her way back to Germany through Belgium, where she supposedly retired. But two years later, she made her so-called escape from East Germany."

SHEILA GRANT

Steve flicked away the cigarette, the butt glowing in the night as it tumbled down to the paving stones of the patio. Elizabeth waited to make sure that he had nothing more to add to his story.

"I can't understand why the British didn't recognize her," she said finally. "She'd been in England two years earlier, involved in a high-level affair, and this after all the noise she made in France. What am I missing?"

"The woman is a chameleon," Steve said. "Not just with her looks—though I'm sure a woman like you knows what someone can do with makeup and a new wardrobe, and the KGB are wizards. She was a thin blonde with blue eyes in France, a dark brunette fifteen pounds heavier in England, very Spanish-looking, and every bit an Eastern Bloc refugee when she finally left East Germany. But it was more than that. According to people who knew her, it was like talking to a completely different woman, like the other versions of Nicola had never existed. She just completely disappeared into whatever story her minders had come up with for her, and then discarded those personas as soon as they no longer suited her."

"And she escaped again, after everything with your brother?"

"No," Steve said. "We got her this time. But she was traded for one of our spies. A good deal, people tell me, and I haven't heard anything more about her."

"That must have been difficult for you," Elizabeth said.

"Keeping her wouldn't have brought my brother back," Steve said, "or changed anything that happened. If it meant another family got their husband and father back from the gulag, who was I to stop them? Not that anyone asked me."

"Still, I can't imagine what you must have thought this morning, when you saw me. I'm shocked you kept your cool!"

"It was the only way I could keep you from slipping away," Steve said. "Of course, who knows if it would have worked if you were the real Nicola Neumann? But for the record, I'm very glad you weren't."

"Why's that?" Elizabeth asked.

"Because otherwise, I never would have had a chance to meet you."

"Is it difficult, being around someone who apparently looks so much like her?" Elizabeth said. Steve chuckled and shook his head.

"The more I get to know you, the less you remind me of Nicola Neumann."

Elizabeth smiled for a moment, genuinely pleased to hear Steve say it. But then her face fell.

"What is it?" Steve asked.

"If I remind you less and less of Nicola the more you get to know me," she said quietly, "what does that mean for those men in the house down in Cuernavaca?"

Steve sighed.

"I don't know," he said. "But we should get some rest. I have a feeling tomorrow is going to be a long day."

"I'll be in in a minute," she said. She needed another moment to herself, to process everything he had told her. The more she learned about this woman, the more dangerous she sounded. How was she ever going to convince anyone that she was Nicola Neumann?

In the library of the house, amid a haze of pipe smoke, Bill Wynter sat hunched over a desk, reviewing the information that his men had gathered on Elizabeth Lamont. To his right, John Reynolds paced back and forth—this was John's farm, and a frequent getaway for Bill when he was back in the States. John was technically retired now but had kept his security clearances, at Bill's request, so that they could keep using the horse farm as a planning station. If John minded the company, he never mentioned it. In fact, Bill was pretty sure the old spy would have gotten bored if it wasn't for these meetings.

"I got in touch with our friends in Canada right after you gave me a call," said Alex Connor. The man was in his early thirties, with sandy brown hair, even features, and intelligent grey-green eyes. He spoke with a deep southern accent. He was Bill's go-to asset when it came to doing deep research, and he found the man's ability to synthesis information second to none. He'd had him drive out from Langley as soon as he got a yes from Elizabeth. Connor looked down at a legal pad in front of him. "The grandmother wasn't involved in anything political or subversive—she loved Quebec, but everyone up there does. No leftist affiliations among Elizabeth's school friends. Most of them are married with children; husbands are lawyers, doctors, engineers. I was expecting something a little more glamorous, given her background as a model."

He glanced up at Wynter.

"I'm also checking with a few of her professors. The men are being told that she's being considered for an embassy job that requires a background check. Standard stuff."

"What about Richard Owens, and her business associates?" Wynter asked.

"Owens had nothing but praise. He said she was self-reliant, very intelligent, gentle, and a little shy. An ideal model. But hardly the attributes you'd typically look for in an operative," Connor said.

PASSPORT TO DANGER

"Stick to the play-by-play," Wynter said. "Keep the color commentary to yourself."

Connor grinned; he had known Bill Wynter for nearly a decade and appreciated the man's candor.

"He's not wrong, though," John Reynolds said.

"Now I'm getting it in stereo," Wynter said, feigning a grimace. He turned back to Connor. "Keep going."

"Owens' secretary said about the same as him, as did the models our men talked with. Everyone remarked on her good looks."

He took a stack of magazines down from a pile on the filing cabinet in the corner and plopped them down on the desk.

"I had the girls back at Langley go through these and mark the pages where Elizabeth Lamont appears in each of these magazines."

"Good," Wynter said. "I'm anxious to see those pictures."

"I bet you are," John Reynolds said.

The men hovered around the desk as Bill Wynter began flipping through the magazine. It was impossible to imagine that any of them would have ever thought she resembled Nicola Neumann. These photos depicted a gorgeous creature—elegant, expensive, serene, and completely untouchable. But Wynter preferred Elizabeth as herself rather than as the model; the model was a pale copy in comparison with the vibrant girl he'd secreted down to Virginia. He gazed at the picture of her in a full-length chinchilla coat with a diamond necklace around her throat.

"She's wearing more money than I could make in a year," Wynter said. "Wouldn't it be nice if you could keep everything you model?"

"If that's the way the game was played," Reynolds said, "would you model fur coats and diamond necklaces?"

77

"Hell yes!"

Connor and Reynolds laughed. When Connor recovered, he drawled, "I'll tell you something, Bill, those bowlegs of yours would sure look good sticking out from under that chinchilla coat."

Wynter grinned.

"Well, since you boys don't think anyone is going to hire me to model, I'd better get back to earning the money the government is paying me. We've got some long days ahead of us, gentlemen."

CHAPTER SEVEN

There were a few seconds, after Elizabeth woke in an unfamiliar bed, when she was blissfully unaware of where she was and what she was doing. For those sweet moments, there was just the sound of tiny feet on the balcony outside her bedroom, the clean cool Virginia air coming in through where she'd left the window cracked the night before, and the bright sunshine that suffused the farm in morning light.

And then she remembered: She was in a CIA safehouse an hour outside of DC, waiting to see whether or not she could impersonate a KGB agent and sneak into a house in Mexico to extract state secrets from an American nuclear scientist who, for all they knew, may have willingly defected back to the USSR. All of this on what was supposed to be her first day of retirement! She was supposed to be sitting at the Pan Am Lounge, sipping a glass of champagne while she waited for Susan Graves to get in from the West Coast so they could fly to Greece together. So much for all that.

The clock on her bedside table read a little after six in the morning. Elizabeth had never been one to sleep late—she had spent the last three years waking up in the dark to be in hair and makeup for hours before the photoshoots started. She had idly thought that, now that she was leaving the modeling life behind, she might learn to sleep in. But some habits, it would seem, take a bit longer than one day to break.

She stood by the window for a moment, watching a man dressed in blue jeans and a red shirt leading three horses into the nearest pasture; another man followed with two more horses, their colts prancing behind them. How nice, she thought, to have a job so straightforward and clear; she imagined that these men were good at their work, good with the horses, and confident in their abilities. *I wonder if any of them would be interested in trading places with me*, Elizabeth thought, *though I suppose they don't look much like Nicola Neumann.* So instead she dressed quickly, put on a little makeup, and ran a comb through her hair before wandering downstairs in search of coffee.

In the kitchen, she found a man already padding around in a pair of khaki slacks and a clean oxford button-down. He looked, she thought, like the men she sometimes saw in New York on the weekends, heading into the office to do a bit of extra work—a studied kind of dressing meant to tell themselves that they were off the clock, no matter if they actually spent those hours back in the office, catching up on paperwork or getting ahead of the Monday pitch meetings. The man—Connor was his name, she remembered now, Alex Connor—looked over his shoulder at her approach and offered her a friendly smile.

"You're up early, Ms. Lamont," he said. His intelligent green eyes were sparkling slightly as he appraised her.

"Elizabeth, please," she said. "It's a habit of mine, I'm afraid. I can't remember the last time I saw the other side of eight a.m. from bed."

"Not exactly the glamorous image people have of famous fashion models," Connor said. Elizabeth laughed and shook her head.

PASSPORT TO DANGER

"I found I often surprised people. It's remarkable, isn't it, the assumptions that we make based on people's line of work?"

"I suppose so," Connor said.

"Like you, for instance," Elizabeth said, thinking back to the evening before, when Wynter had made hurried introductions to these men who were already at the farm when they had arrived. "Bill Wynter introduced you as an attaché, but something tells me that if that were true, you wouldn't be here for something like this."

Alex Connor laughed out loud. Elizabeth grinned, proud to have gotten it right—he did work for the Agency, after all.

"Bill said you were sharp," he said.

"I'm even sharper after a cup of coffee," Elizabeth said. Connor grinned and took a mug down from the cabinet.

For a time, the two of them sat at the breakfast table, drinking coffee and reading the morning paper. More trouble in the Middle East—there had been a rash of assassination attempts in the region, and everyone seemed to be waiting for the other shoe to drop between Israel and their Arab neighbors. She thought about Miles Reardon, probably on a plane back to Cairo by now. Had it really just been luck that he'd been in the restaurant yesterday when Steve brought her around? It must have been—Wynter had no way of knowing she was coming. Still, she was starting to feel, after the last twenty-four hours, as though she was vacillating between paranoia and naivety.

Footsteps down the stairs echoed a few moments later, and then Wynter appeared in the kitchen, his grey eyes crinkling as he greeted them.

"You two are up early. I hope you slept well, Elizabeth."

"Never better," she told him with a smile.

"Good. I never bother to ask Alex how he sleeps because he always snoozes like a baby. A clear conscience, I suppose."

Connor gave him a lazy grin.

"What else?"

Elizabeth marveled at Wynter's cheerfulness. He didn't seem like a man with a hundred grim problems on his mind. Was he truly able to disconnect from his work, or was he just putting on a good face for her sake?

More footsteps on the stairs, and soon Steve came into the kitchen, chatting with John Reynolds, the man who owned the farm. They were talking about the colts. Elizabeth studied Steve quietly. He seemed larger than she remembered—in his sweater and slacks, his shoulders looked broader, his arms more muscular, and his waist and hips narrower. His red sweater accented his dark coloring; he looked very handsome.

"A full kitchen before seven in the morning," John Reynolds said with a grin. "This feels like a real farmhouse now."

"Your guests aren't usually early risers?" Steve said.

"Not like this," Reynolds said. "Then again, we don't usually have quite as much to do. Breakfast?"

They ate a quick, pleasant breakfast—Reynolds's cook made eggs and toast along with salty country ham that she fried up in her skillet until it was crisp and delicious. Elizabeth, whose typical breakfast was a cup of coffee and a piece of fruit, thought that everything was delicious. She had previously thought she might be too anxious to eat but instead found herself ravenous.

After a second cup of coffee, Wynter rose from the table and led the group into a lovely library: marble fireplace, walnut bookshelves lining three walls, antique furniture, expensive Chinese porcelain, and a green and yellow handwoven Portuguese rug over darkly stained hardwood floors. Wynter went over to one of the bookcases, pulled out a leather-bound volume of the Canterbury Tales, and pressed a switch that had been hidden behind it. Slowly, the bookcase swung open, revealing a hidden door behind it. Elizabeth found it impossible to contain a gasp of surprise.

"Hidden doors?" she said.

"A little dramatic, I'll admit," John Reynolds said with a self-deprecating chuckle. "But if Bill insisted on using the old farm for a little work, I figured I might as well have some fun with it."

"Especially when the Agency was footing the bill for the renovation," Wynter said with a small smile.

"Well, naturally!" Reynolds said with a chuckle. Wynter pushed open the door, and the group began to descend down a flight of stone steps into a dim, dank basement space.

"This used to be the wine cellar," Reynolds said as they made their way down. "It still gets damp after we've had a good rain."

Wynter flicked on the lights, which came to life with a slow electric groan. Elizabeth could see that the space had been partitioned into little rooms as they passed by the closed doors. It was hot and dank in the narrow corridor, and Elizabeth was relieved when Wynter opened the door to an airconditioned office. There was a large table in the middle of the room; on it was what appeared to be a scene someone had borrowed from a model train set—a few streets from a little hillside town, the buildings charmingly rustic. Little flags of different colors were arrayed around one building in particular. Elizabeth bent forward to get a better look.

"Cuernavaca," Wynter said in answer to her unasked question. "We had it set up as soon as we learned where Sobokov was being held. This way," he said, holding out a hand to the conference table on the far side of the room.

The men and Elizabeth arranged themselves in the comfortable leather chairs around a long mahogany table. A projector had been set up on the table pointing at a screen that was spread across the opposite wall.

Gone now was the relaxed atmosphere at breakfast; it was time for work. Elizabeth could feel the air of expectancy in the room. Once they were seated, Wynter opened a manilla envelope that was sitting on the table, extracted a handful of photographs, and handed them over to Elizabeth.

"These," he said briskly, "are pictures of Nicola Neumann."

Elizabeth took them from him, a little surprised at how eager she was to see the girl she'd been mistaken for. The first photograph, dated May 1962, was a distant shot of a pretty girl, her hair blowing in the breeze, face titled up as she regarded a man walking beside her. Her features weren't clear—the picture had been taken at too great a distance—but it was obvious that nature had endowed Nicola with a superb figure.

The second photograph was a close-up of the first, a good three-quarters shot of Nicola's face. Elizabeth studied her carefully. Yes, there was a likeness between Nicola and herself—she had spent enough time looking at photographs of herself to be able to tell that much—but she hoped she didn't look that hard, or cold. It was a depressing thought. She glanced at the third photograph, aware that the men were watching her closely, studying her reactions. This one was a closeup of Nicola striding down the street; the face here was clearly older than the previous photographs. Wynter pointed to the picture.

PASSPORT TO DANGER

"This is the most recent one we have. It was taken on St. Thomas, just after she left Alex at Bluebeard's Castle."

Elizabeth looked at the photograph again.

"She's aged a lot in ten years," she said slowly. *Too much*, she thought. *What has she been through?*

Elizabeth studied the other photographs, paying careful attention to Nicola's expressions and posture. The woman was a little shorter than she was, and maybe ten pounds heavier—her old boss would have sent her off to the fat farm before he ever put her in front of a camera. But she wasn't really fat, just well endowed. Elizabeth studied the last photograph for some time, then handed the pictures back to Wynter, who signaled to Connor to switch off the light and run the projector.

"This film shows Nicola and her Control at the Russian Embassy in Paris; the French had a camera in the room," Wynter said. Nicola was listening to a man with his back to the camera, her face hard and intent, without a trace of softness, her blue eyes cold and calculating. When her lips moved to answer a question, Elizabeth tried to imagine her voice: *Cool, slightly sharp*, she thought.

"Run it ahead to the next one, Alex," Wynter said. "This time, she's at an embassy ball in Vienna."

Elizabeth stole a quick glance at Steve—after everything he'd told her the night before, this must be agonizing for him. But his expression was remote, indifferent; whatever he was thinking, he was careful to keep his thoughts hidden. She looked back at the screen and watched as Nicola danced across the ballroom, flirting vivaciously with her partners. She left the dancefloor and began to circulate among the guests—though, Elizabeth noticed, she only seemed to be talking with men. Nicola was the most seductive creature Elizabeth had ever seen, her every move and gesture intended to be provocative. And then there were her clothes, the neckline of her gown so low that it left little to the imagination.

Is Bill Wynter trying to scare me? Elizabeth wondered. *It would be hard enough to impersonate a shrinking violet, but to pretend to be someone like Nicola...*

"That's enough, Alex," Wynter said after a time. The picture stopped on the screen, and then disappeared as the lights came back up in the room. He turned and looked at Elizabeth. "What do you think? There's more, but first impressions."

"I'm amazed that none of the embassy wives tried to take her out themselves, the way she was flirting with their husbands," Elizabeth said. The men around the table chuckled at this—except, she noticed, for Steve, who seemed to wince slightly. Immediately Elizabeth wished that she hadn't said it like that, but it was too late. She looked down at the table for a moment to collect her thoughts, her gaze resting briefly on a cigarette burn in the wood.

"There might be a physical resemblance between me and her, I'll give you that much," Elizabeth said. "But I'm having a hard time with her personality. There's a...hardness about that woman. A coldness that's clear even in the photographs. Nicola is the product of a police state, and she acts like it. Even if the men in that house down in Cuernavaca haven't met Nicola personally, do you really think I'll be able to pass for some cold, autocratic Soviet spy?"

Wynter pursed his lips and sucked a little air through his teeth. Elizabeth couldn't tell if he was disappointed or not.

"You're asking the right questions," he said. "We have three days to decide whether or not you can. I'd never send you down there if I didn't believe that you could, and I think the best way for you to do that is by learning all you can about Nicola. If you understand the woman, maybe it can help you become her. Are you willing to give that a try?"

"I've already come this far," Elizabeth said, trying for a brave smile. "I might as well."

"Good," Wynter said with a curt nod.

Steve Brenner cleared his throat.

"If you don't need me," he said, "I think I'll get some fresh air."

"Go ahead," Wynter said.

"I think I'll join you, if you don't mind," John Reynolds said, walking with Brenner towards the door.

When the two men had left, Wynter sighed and leaned back in his chair. Alex Connor lit a cigarette and took a long inhale.

"The water was a little rough for him," he said.

Wynter nodded grimly.

"He's probably wondered how in the hell his brother could have been such a fool."

"So am I," Elizabeth said. The other two men turned to look at her. "She's so obvious. At least in the Vienna footage. I'd have thought a woman like that would need to use a bit more discretion."

"I agree," Wynter said. "But I've learned never to underestimate the stupidity of men in the presence of a beautiful woman. In its own way, her lack of tact in Vienna is a kind of cover—that kind of shameless flirt suggests a woman interested in doing a little social climbing, or finding a wealthy benefactor, rather than a Soviet agent intent on undermining the leaders of the free world. Her track record speaks for itself, Senator Brenner sadly included."

Elizabeth nodded, and then turned to Connor.

"Bill said that the last photo was just after she met with you in St. Thomas," Elizabeth said. Connor looked to Wynter—asking for permission, maybe, Elizabeth thought—and then back to Elizabeth after Wynter gave him a small nod.

"That's right."

"I'd like to hear about her," Elizabeth said. "What she was like the last time you saw her."

Connor turned again to Wynter.

"It's a shame we only have three days," Connor said. "Ms. Lamont is asking all the right questions. We could make a real agent of her."

"We still might yet," Wynter said. "That's a story you should hear. Unfortunately, so should Steve, and I think it's a good idea to give him a smoke break for however long he wants. Do you mind if I show you a few more films until he's back?"

"Go right ahead," Elizabeth said, settling back in her chair. If she had any hope of passing for Nicola Neumann, she needed to see everything they had to show her.

CHAPTER EIGHT

Steve Brenner stood on the back porch of the farmhouse, smoking a cigarette and glowering into the distance. Forty-eight hours earlier, he had been lounging on the French Riviera, drinking a sweaty bottle of beer and feeling the Mediterranean sun beat down on his back. Now, he was stuck in an old basement, watching an endless parade of photographs and video recordings of the woman who had ruined his brother's life. It was a particularly cruel form of psychological torture, made all the worse by his knowledge that all of this was absolutely necessary, if Bill Wynter really intended to go through with this insane plan of his.

Elizabeth, he noted, appeared to be taking this all remarkably well. Somehow, she had looked even more beautiful this morning, her face fresh and her bright eyes glowing as she concentrated on the screen, trying to determine whether or not she could pass for a hardened Communist agent. Anyone who had ever met Nicola Neumann would be able to make her in two seconds cold, wouldn't they? And yet nothing seemed capable of deterring Wynter from the notion he had in his head.

John Reynolds came out onto the patio holding a mug of coffee and tapping out a cigarette from the soft pack in his front shirt pocket. For a few minutes, the two men stood next to one another in silence, looking out at the morning rising over the farm and the men working the animals in the distant pastures. Steve wondered what kind of man John Reynolds had been when he was still working in the field. He had the quiet, thoughtful demeanor of a man comfortable with spending long times alone and still—he could have imagined him as an advance scout, staying silent and hidden as he tracked enemy positions. Then again, to have a place like this, he must have been someone important to the Agency. He wondered if Reynolds resented Bill Wynter stopping in unannounced like this, or if a part of the man still craved a little action, even in his ostensible retirement.

"Pretty morning," Steve said finally. Reynolds grinned and nodded.

"Rained for three days before you all showed up. That girl must be good luck."

"I'm not sure I'd call her lucky, given what she's gotten herself into."

"Bill seems to think otherwise."

"I've noticed," Steve said, taking a long drag on his cigarette. He was smoking too much, but that hardly felt like it mattered now, given everything else that was going on.

"How long have you two…" Reynolds started.

"I've known Bill since college," Steve said.

"Not Bill. You and Elizabeth."

Steve turned and looked at Reynolds.

"Would you believe me if I told you I met her yesterday?"

Reynolds let out a roar of a laugh and shook his head.

"Get out."

"I was in a cab. We had rain up in New York, too. She was standing under an awning, looking for a ride. I thought she looked familiar so I offered her a lift and then took her to lunch to meet Bill."

"Well, isn't that something.... I would've sworn the two of you had been together for some time now."

"What makes you say that?" Steve asked with a frown.

"Two things," John Reynolds said. "First is the way you look at her."

Steve looked down at his shoes. Had he really been that obvious about it? He wondered if Elizabeth could tell too—a woman like that had to be used to all manner of creeps staring at her all day long. He didn't want her to put him on that list.

"Yeah? What's the second?" Steve said.

"The way she looks at you."

Reynolds threw down the butt of his cigarette and crushed it under the heel of his well-worn boots. He put his hands on the small of his back and bent backwards, lightly straining as he looked up at the sky.

"You two kids have had a hell of a couple days," he said after a time.

Steve nodded.

"And something tells me it's not about to get any easier," Steve said.

"It never is with Bill," Reynolds said. "But you already know that, or you wouldn't be here. What do you say we head back in?"

Steve looked out over the landscape for another moment, trying to steel himself for another barrage of Nicola Neumann pictures and discussion. Then he pictured Elizabeth, sitting in that basement conference room with an earnest expression on her face. He wanted suddenly to be close to her. The feeling was so strong that for a moment, he didn't trust it, like it was some external thing that had arrived without his knowledge or consent. But the longer it stayed, the more he could tell that it was true.

"Alright then. Let's get this over with."

The three of them—Elizabeth, Wynter, and Conner—were still sitting around the conference table when Steve walked back into the room, a thin haze of smoke veiling the still photo of Nicola on the slide projector. It showed her in a coral dress, with a matching chiffon scarf over her hair and dark glasses. Behind her, ocean water glowed turquoise. He could feel the other eyes in the room watching him as he poured himself a cup of coffee from the carafe in the corner.

"She's dressed like a spy," Steve said as he took his seat.

"She's dressed like a tourist's idea of a spy," Wynter said. "Which is actually decent camouflage. Especially for a woman like that, who's going to be noticed one way or another."

"Where is she? The Amalfi Coast?"

"Puerto Rico," Connor said. "Where she had me meet her."

"When was this?" Steve said.

"About three weeks ago," Connor said.

"That's when Sobokov went missing," Steve said, looking to Wynter.

"Alex was just about to tell us what she told him," Elizabeth said. "We thought you might like to hear the story."

Steve nodded for Connor to continue. The southerner cleared his throat.

"I met Nicola years ago, when I was posted to Moscow as an attaché," Connor said. "I think she thought I might be an easy target. She seemed to lose interest once I rejected her overtures. I was flattered, believe me, but I turned her down all the same."

PASSPORT TO DANGER

"What remarkable self-restraint," Steve said coolly. Connor held up a hand in apology.

"Anyway, I hadn't heard anything from her since then. A few weeks back I'm on vacation down in Jamaica. Crocodile hunting, of all things—an old college buddy swore by it, set me up with his guide and everything. I'd just gotten back to my hotel in Mandeville after a day on the Black River, dreaming of cocktails and a very long nap, when I found a cable waiting for me from my sister. Which was curious, since I don't have a sister.

"The cable," Connor explained, "was from Nicola. She was in San Juan, and wanted to meet." He had no idea how she knew that he was in Jamaica, or where he was staying. He was exhausted from the hunt and annoyed that Nicola was trying to ruin his vacation. But he was also curious—if Nicola was reaching out to him, he assumed there was a good reason for it.

"And I knew Bill would have had my ass if I passed up a chance to talk with her, after everything," Connor said.

"Bill does seem to delight in ruining vacations," Steve said, taking a sip of coffee.

The cable told Connor that he was to meet Nicola at El Morro, the old Spanish Fort, the next morning for the eleven o'clock tour. He was to come alone. So he caught a flight to Kingston that same night, and first thing the next morning, he flew up to Puerto Rico—tired, annoyed, and, most of all, curious.

"I thought it might be a trap," he said. "It wouldn't be the first she set. But the more I thought about the note, the more I started to suspect that she might be in some trouble, and I was right."

Connor made it to the fort in time for the tour. As soon as the guide began herding his flock into the fort, a woman wearing a bright red dress fell back from the front of the group to join Connor near the back. She had changed her hair from auburn to light brown and was sporting a deep tan, but it was always easy to recognize Nicola—she had a way of swaying her hips when she walked that was unforgettable. No one seemed interested in them, as far as Connor could tell, and he hadn't noticed any tails on his way to the fort. They waited until they were on the ramparts. The rest of the group had gone ahead before Nicola said anything to him.

"I have a lot to say in a short time, Alex, so pleasure forgo your usual jokes until I can enjoy them."

"I'm dog tired, Nicola. You had me running all over the Caribbean to be here. Now tell me what you want."

"I realize I'm not exactly anyone's favorite person up in Washington," Nicola said. "I don't expect you to welcome me with open arms. But I'm in trouble. And if you help me out, I'll make it worth your while."

Connor stared at her, and then laughed.

"Are you trying to defect?"

"I'm asking for asylum."

"Oh, come on. Who would be stupid enough to believe you?"

She hissed an ugly name at him.

"See if you think this is a joke. Your precious Dr. Sobokov is returning to the Soviet Union. You won't read about it in Pravda, though. It's a secret."

Connor did his best to hide his astonishment.

"I don't think Uncle Sam will take too kindly to your people kidnapping Dr. Sobokov."

"My dear, don't be silly. He's coming voluntarily. Well, perhaps not entirely voluntarily, but let's just say he *feels* that he must."

"You don't have him, Nicola. You're lying."

"I made it a personal policy of mine to never lie when my life is at stake. It just happens to be my good luck that I have something you need. I'm not asking for permanent residency. I just need someplace safe to lie low until a certain man, in high places, meets his demise, which, I hope, will be soon. But it's not safe for me to risk any sort of exposure as long as he's still alive."

Connor mulled this over while watching the water crash against the rocks below. This could be an elaborate ruse to determine once and for all whether he was actually an attaché. That seemed too elaborate given the situation that Nicola had laid out, but Connor decided to proceed with caution.

"I hate to break it to you, Nicola, but I don't believe you. And even if I did, I couldn't help you. I just don't have the right connections."

Nicola stepped closer to him, her nostrils flaring in barely contained rage and frustration.

"Don't play games with me, Alex. I know *who* you are, and *what* you are. And I know you're good—you've kept yourself out of the Kremlin's files. You're as far above suspicion as any attaché. If you weren't, I wouldn't have contacted you."

"How do you know?"

"I heard about you through Tamara. You know, your old Russian contact? You probably wondered why you never saw her again. She got careless. The KGB came for her. I happened to be with her at the time—just my luck. She thought I was a British agent. She told me to tell you that she hadn't talked. She died before they reached her. Cyanide tablet."

Connor hoped he didn't appear half as nervous as he felt. It was real, then, and the stakes were much higher than he had anticipated.

"I can't understand why she'd give my name. I never met her."

Nicola sighed and looked up to the sky.

"This is getting tedious. I didn't tell anyone. I kept your name to myself, in case I should ever need you."

"And now you need me," Connor said before forcing a dry laugh. "I find it hard to imagine myself in the cloak and dagger business."

"I nearly fell over when she said your name," Nicola said. "You're the most cheerful spy I know, Alex. You wander through life, joking and laughing, as though all is wonderful and good in the world."

She pulled down her dark glasses just enough to give him a glance of her cold, appraising eyes.

"If you want to know any more about Sobokov's disappearance, meet me at El Convento restaurant at nine tomorrow evening."

She held out her hand.

"It's been lovely chatting with you, Mr. Connor," she said, smiling wide for the benefit of a passing tourist. Then she left him, catching up quickly with the tour.

"I was tempted to follow her," Connor said to Steve. "But she was an experienced agent; she'd make me long before she reached wherever it is she was going. If I'd had more time, I could have set up relays to tail her, but even then, I bet she would have given our men the slip. She's done it before. So I called my Control back at Langley and told him what Nicola had said. That's when he informed me that Anton Sobokov had disappeared two days earlier."

PASSPORT TO DANGER

So the next night, Connor was at El Convento. He waited until midnight, nursing a few rum and cokes, but Nicola never showed. When he returned to his hotel, irritated and worried, he had another message from his "sister" telling him to meet her on St. Thomas, at Bluebeard's Castle. The next morning, he was on another plane. He was enjoying lunch at his hotel when Nicola joined him. This time she was wearing a sleeveless yellow dress, which set off her tan; her hair was black, and she had traded her glasses for a pair with extremely dark lenses. She was definitely on the run, working hard to keep whoever was after her off her trail.

"I've been doing a lot of island hopping, thanks to you," he said as she sat down across from him. "And you've ruined my vacation."

"You call alligator hunting a vacation?" Nicola said.

Connor raised his eyebrow—how did she know so much of what he'd been up to?

"Well, you were right about Sobokov. So what happens next? You're calling the shots."

"I'm glad you're in a more agreeable mood, Alex. You were awfully boring the last time we met." She took off her dark glasses, and Connor noticed the dark circles under her eyes. Her hand shook as she picked up a fork to try a bite of his rum cake. "I want forty thousand dollars and a private plane at my disposal. I may need to vanish in a hurry."

"You sound like a bank robber," Connor said.

"That kind of money is nothing to you people," Nicola said. "Call your Control. If he agrees to these terms, I'll tell you where Sobokov is. He'll be in this hemisphere for three more weeks. I'll also tell you what pressure the Communists used to get him to go with them. If you move fast, you can get to him before they leave."

"Why would he change his mind?" Connor said. "If two days ago he wanted to defect?"

"I'm not playing all my trumps until I hear from your Control," Nicola said.

Connor decided not to press her further.

"I should have an answer for you by this evening."

Nicola smiled, and seemed to relax slightly.

"Lovely. But I can't risk meeting you again. I shouldn't have come tonight, but I didn't trust the phones. We'll have to use a drop."

"Alright."

"Do you have an agent in Nassau?"

Connor cocked an eyebrow.

"If you don't, you can get one," Nicola said. "Who knows? You might even get to do some more island hopping."

"So considerate," Connor said. "Where's the drop?"

Nicola gave him quick directions.

"And a backup? In case something goes wrong?"

Nicola laughed humorlessly.

"If anything goes wrong, anything at all, I won't need your answer. I'll have gambled and lost."

Connor saw her shoulders sag, and for a moment, Nicola forgot to look sexy and provocative. She looked forlorn, and afraid.

"Why don't you come to Jamaica with me to collect my gear, and we can go back to the States together? I'm a terrific chaperone. If you're a good girl, I might even take you gator hunting."

"It breaks my heart to have to turn you down, Alex, but I'm afraid I must." Her voice became serious. "If you have a message for Sobokov, I'd be happy to pass it along."

Connor nearly fell out of his chair.

"You'll what?"

"I'll give him a message."

"But you just told me you need to defect!"

"That's right, but I'm only in trouble with one man and a few of his friends. He's important, but I don't think he will be for long, and the man who masterminded the Sobokov affair, code name Midas, has ordered me to rendezvous with them. How do you think I knew about all this? I'm to tell them the exact date and time that they are to leave for Russia."

"Midas is a good capitalistic code name," Connor said, hoping he could get Nicola to offer more information about the man. "Is he like that? A rapacious, greedy capitalist?"

Nicola grinned wickedly.

"No games, Alex. Remember?"

Connor laughed and shrugged.

"Can't blame me for trying. Does Midas know anything about the man you're running from?"

"No. I've been out of contact for days, anyway. If you give me asylum, I can still make the rendezvous."

"Why would you do that?" Connor said. "And don't tell me it's because you're suddenly fond of America."

"I'm even less fond of Midas. If he botches this operation, he'll spend the rest of his life in Siberia, and he deserves a good case of frostbite more than anyone I know."

"That might be true. But, Nicola, if you're really in trouble, I think you're crazy not to come with me now."

"So do I!" Nicola said. "Who but an idiot misses a chance to go alligator hunting? But in case I don't see you, I do hope you get your wandering scientist back. I'd like nothing better than to see Midas dealt with, once and for all."

Connor watched as she stood and then, as quickly as she could, disappeared from the restaurant.

"We had a team trail her," Connor said now to Steve and the rest of the group gathered around the conference table. "She managed to ditch them neatly. Our agent in Nassau watched the drop for three days, but she never showed to pick up the message."

"Did something happen to her?" Elizabeth said. Connor nodded.

"It's possible. We haven't heard anything, one way or another."

"But if they caught her…" Elizabeth said. Connor shot a quick look over at Wynter.

"There's no way the men in that house in Cuernavaca would know," Wynter said. "They're still waiting for Nicola to show up and tell them when they're leaving."

"How do you know that?" Steve said. Wynter allowed himself a very small smile.

"Because we got lucky."

CHAPTER NINE

Wynter went to pour himself a cup of coffee, feeling the other eyes in the room on him. It was remarkable in this line of work how much depended on happenstance and dumb luck: who happened to be in the right—or wrong—place by freak chance. The fortunes of entire nations, the fate of the free world—so much of it was random. The key, he found, was to not let oneself be overwhelmed by how little one could control, but to use that to one's advantage: to remember that nothing is ever impossible, to not let oneself get overconfident when things seemed good or to despair when things seemed hopeless.

"When Nicola mentioned that Sobokov had been taken, I spoke with an agent I've had in place for the last year in the Soviet Union," Wynter said. "He's given me very valuable information in that time. I try to be judicious about when and how I contact him. But this was important enough to risk everything for. Lucky for us, he was able to track Sobokov to the house in Cuernavaca, and find the identity of the four men keeping him there. They're waiting for a Russian ship, the Leningrad, which is on its way to Cuba. Once it arrives, they'll fly to Cuba and board it."

"Why the layover in Mexico?" John Reynolds asked. "Seems like they'd be safer waiting for the ship in Cuba."

"I had the same question," Wynter said. "Any guesses?"

For a few moments it was quiet around the table. Finally, Elizabeth raised her hand as though she was back in grade school.

"I'm guessing it's not because someone in that house hates the rumba?" she said.

Wynter grinned.

"You're actually not far off. The man in charge of the operation is Nikolai Mavich. He's a legendary Soviet spymaster. More importantly, he can't stand the Cubans—and the feeling is mutual. He tried to talk some Cuban agents in the General Directorate of Intelligence into working for the KGB. This didn't go over too well with the head of the DGI."

"I can imagine," Reynolds said drily.

"Mavich has also been outspoken in his opinions of Cuba. He claims it's a drain on Russia's already sick economy."

"He's not wrong," Reynolds said. "But it's bad politics."

"Especially for a man as cautious as Mavich is in every other aspect of his job," Wynter said.

"I assume Mavich feels the climate in Mexico is a little healthier than it would be in Cuba," Alex Connor chimed in.

"Exactly," Wynter said.

"If your Russian contact was able to find out so much, he must know why they claim that Sobokov is defecting," Steve Brenner said.

Wynter grimaced and shook his head.

"He's as baffled as we are, which is surprising, because my contact—code name Cobalt—is up in the hierarchy of one of the Soviet intelligence agencies. GRU, KGB, I'm not sure which. But he has access to important files, sees influential people, and attends top secret meetings."

"Sounds like KGB to me," Connor said. "It's the baby of the clique that's currently in power. They trust it more than military intelligence; they feel like they can control it. Of course, how often does that end well?"

"Either way, if he doesn't know anything about Sobokov's disappearance, how did he find out where Sobokov is?" Brenner asked.

"By brilliant deduction," Wynter said. "If Nicola was telling the truth, then we had two pieces of information: Sobokov would be somewhere in this hemisphere for three more weeks. Cobalt decided that waiting that long meant waiting for a ship, probably sailing out of a Communist-controlled country. The next Russian ship with passenger accommodations docking in Cuba was the Leningrad—sure enough, it was docking in Havana in three weeks' time. If Mavich needed somewhere to lie low before that, the most likely place was Mexico—they still have diplomatic relations with Cuba, which means they can charter a plane. Then, Cobalt got a list of spy masters who have worked in Latin America. There were two exceptionally good men. One was in the hospital in Moscow. The other in a house in Cuernavaca."

"Your Cobalt is a sharp fellow," Reynolds said, chuckling a little.

"I don't understand why they didn't stick him on an Aeroflot jet and take him straight to Moscow," Brenner said. "It's all so circuitous. Seems to me they are going to a lot of trouble."

"They are," Wynter said. "But they must have felt that the risk of being recognized at Kennedy was too great. Apparently, they intend to slip him into Russia, unnoticed."

Connor took the cigarette he was about to light out of his mouth.

"You mean there isn't going to be the usual fanfare over a sheep returning to the fold?"

Wynter shook his head.

"They think he's more valuable to them as a weapons expert than a political celebrity," Wynter said.

"Which makes sense if he's being taken against his will," Brenner said.

"It's possible, but Nicola was adamant that he was defecting," Wynter said. "In any case, the Soviets want that information about our weapons systems, *desperately*. That could be disastrous for our missile defenses. Fortunately for us, we know that things are not going smoothly in the house in Cuernavaca."

"Now, how do you know that?" Reynolds asked. Wynter stuck his unlit pipe into his mouth.

"Mavich is sending a radio message to Moscow every day from somewhere in the city. Another house, an office maybe, we don't know for sure. We have an electric measuring device mounted on a mobile receiver—we drive it around in a florist truck. It can track down the location of an ordinary radio signal by indicating whether the signal is getting weaker or stronger as the truck weaves around the city."

"But you can't locate the radio," Connor said. "So this is no ordinary transmission."

"Not in the least," Wynter said, shaking his head. "Mavich's radio operator is using a high-speed transmission, prerecording his message on tape, and then playing the tape at breakneck speed. His receiving station in Moscow records the transmission and replays it back at a tempo that's intelligible. He's only on the air for twenty or thirty seconds at a time, and we're having a hell of a time pinpointing the location of the transmitter."

"I can see why Mavich is a successful spymaster," Reynolds said. "Do you think they're sending a message every day because they're having problems with Sobokov?"

"It's a distinct possibility, and I'd like to know what those problems are."

Connor sat up a bit straighter in his seat.

"Isn't it risky, using an illegal radio like that every day?"

Wynter nodded emphatically.

"For someone as cautious as Mavich, it's like jumping off the Eiffel Tower. If we had enough time, we could find the transmitter."

"You've got a tail on him?" Reynolds asked.

"Oh, I put a tail on him alright. Our men are monitoring the house, but the security is as tight as Fort Knox. The only man he lets into the gates is the grocery man, and he has to leave his packages in the driveway. He accidentally got too close to the house once, and one of Mavich's men came out pointing a shotgun at him. They won't let anyone in that house—not even a plumber or an electrician—unless he's one of their own men.

"The only time we can follow him is when he goes to make his radio transmissions. But he switches cars several times every trip, and he's smart enough to pick up on our presence if I tail him any closer. He might try to move Sobokov. If he did, I'd have to have my men pick them up. Mavich would, of course, resist, and Sobokov could get killed in the fight. That's not a risk I want to take unless I absolutely need to."

"So what are you going to do if you find the radio?" Brenner asked as he lit up yet another cigarette. Wynter tried to remember if he had ever seen the scientist smoke like this before.

"If we could locate the radio, we could make it look like the Mexicans had picked up an illegal transmitter on the air. Mavich must be worried about that anyway, and I don't think he'd feel the need to move. He'd assume the Mexicans couldn't break the code on the tapes, and he wouldn't have told a hireling like the radio operator where he's hiding. But I don't know how much time it'll take to find that damn transmitter, and time is one thing we're running out of."

"What are you hoping to find?" Elizabeth said. The rest of the room fell silent as the men seated around the table all turned to look at her.

"What do you mean, Elizabeth?" Wynter asked in the patient voice of a schoolteacher who's just heard the most ludicrous proposed answer to a simple math problem.

"With the transmitter. I've been trying to think of how it changes anything, but I can't. Whether you find it or not, they still have a nuclear scientist in that house with advanced knowledge of our missile systems, not to mention the passcode to his own top-secret work. If he isn't able to transmit, Moscow won't know what's happening. But that won't actually stop anything from happening, will it?"

There was another long silence around the table as the men considered this comment. Then Connor began to chuckle to himself.

"Damn," he said. "She might not be wrong."

"It isn't that direct, Elizabeth," Wynter starting to say, feeling himself flush slightly as the beautiful woman gazed across the table at him. "We do what we can on the margins in a case like that, try to find any avenue to give us a slight advantage, or access to information we didn't have previously. You never know what might end up being valuable, so you pursue every angle, even if it doesn't seem immediately obvious."

"Oh," Elizabeth said, looking down into her lap. "I guess I could understand that. I'll keep my questions to myself from now on."

"On the contrary," Wynter said from across the table with a warm smile. "It's good sometimes, having the perspective of someone who hasn't lived through a few dozen of these situations before. Sometimes we get so wrapped up in playing the game that we lose sight of the bigger picture. In any event, if you're going to be involved, it's important that what we're doing makes sense to you. I've made that mistake before—not making sure I let people in on why what they're doing is important. Sometimes that's necessary, in this line of work. But if you're going to agree to this, it has to make sense to you."

Elizabeth looked up from the table and fixed him with a brave smile. "Thank you, Bill," she said.

God help us, Wynter thought to himself. *How is this girl scout ever going to convince anyone she was Nicola Neumann?*

"I think it's high time for a bit of lunch," Wynter said. "Fried chicken, anyone?"

"You dog, you!" Connor said, patting his stomach in anticipation. "You know my weakness."

"I can't remember the last time I had fried chicken," Elizabeth said with slightly wide eyes.

"I'm sure we could have the cook fix you something else if you'd prefer," Reynolds said. Elizabeth shook her head.

"Oh, no," she said. "Fried chicken sounds *absolutely* amazing."

CHAPTER TEN

The rest of the day passed in a blur for Elizabeth Lamont. After an afternoon spent watching old footage of Nicola Neumann, and having Bill Wynter quiz her on the layout of the house in Cuernavaca using the scale model he'd had drawn up, she had suddenly found herself face to face with a tall man, with receding red hair and glasses. At first, she had thought the man was part of the hired staff; he had brought in a plate of sandwiches for dinner, along with a small cooler full of beer and cold drinks. But to Elizabeth's surprise, he had joined them, and her surprise had changed to amazement when he suddenly addressed her in German before switching abruptly to Spanish, and then over to French. He even tried to work in a little Russian, which Elizabeth barely spoke at all. It had been years since Elizabeth had an excuse to practice languages, and she had little experience switching so fluently between them like this. In another circumstance, maybe this would have been a fun challenge for herself. But now, like this, with all the other men around the room sipping their beers and staring at her, it was hard not to feel like she was under the microscope.

After about half an hour, the man—Chris Johnson was his name, and who just a moment ago had been asking her about her favorite season in German—turned to the rest of the table and smiled.

"Your language skills are remarkable," the man said. "Especially considering what you mentioned about not having had a chance to keep them up, except for during the occasional work trips to Europe."

"They couldn't have cared less what I spoke there," Elizabeth said, "as long as I held the smile long enough for the photographer to get the shot."

"Your Russian, however...leaves something to be desired."

Elizabeth shot a worried glance over at Wynter, who managed to keep his face cool.

"I'm afraid it's not exactly flawless," she said. She tried to imagine what was going on inside his head—had this evaluation at all changed his perspective on whether or not she was capable enough to be sent into that lion's den down in Cuernavaca? She watched with renewed surprise as Wynter's mouth relaxed into a grin.

"Your Russian is the least of my worries."

Elizabeth frowned in bewilderment.

"Why? Nicola must speak excellent Russian after living in the Soviet Union for all these years."

Wynter shook his head.

"She never perfected it. Too many dialects for her taste. Her associates and friends were also mostly KGB agents who spoke the language of whatever Western country they'd been sent to. A spot of luck for us, no question." He paused, thinking for a moment. "If I had to bet, I'd guess that Mavich and his men will probably speak in Spanish. One of his men uses it more comfortably than any other language."

Elizabeth heaved a sigh of relief—after French, Spanish was the language she felt most at home with, and the one she had the most opportunities to use in New York.

Chris Johnson pushed his chair back. "Well, you may have a few problems with your Russian, but you certainly don't have to worry about your other languages." He rose from the table and walked over to the door, then paused and looked back at Elizabeth. "I hate to tell you, but you missed your calling. You're a born linguist."

Elizabeth gave him her best smile.

"I wish you'd been able to tell that to the United Nations. They wouldn't even give me an interview for an interpreter role."

"Well then, they were fools, all of them," Johnson said with a small smile. He turned to Wynter. "I'll stick around in case you need anything else?"

"Thanks, Chris. I owe you one."

"Don't mention it. This was a pleasure, truly."

And then the man was gone. Elizabeth let out a long sigh.

"I haven't felt that much pressure since I was back at school," she said. "I never did like tests. I performed well enough, but beforehand, I'd make myself just sick with worry, even when I knew the material cold!"

Wynter leaned back in his chair and lit his pipe, squinting through the smoke at Elizabeth.

"You did well with Chris. He isn't shy in sharing his opinions when someone's languages aren't up to snuff. I can't tell you how many prospective field agents we've had test with him, and it turns out their 'fluent' Arabic or Serbian was actually anything but. If he vouches for you, it means you're good."

PASSPORT TO DANGER

Elizabeth smiled warmly and accepted the compliment. It was good to remember that she had capabilities beyond those important to the world where she'd just spent the last three years; she hadn't had much of a chance to do anything other than look pretty and act professional during the shoots and promotional campaigns. She wondered again how different her life might have turned out if she had managed to land a translating job when she'd first come to New York—the pay wouldn't have been nearly as good as what she had made working for Richard Owens, but she would have had a career that she could keep at for as long as she wanted. She tried to imagine herself picking up new languages as a hobby, talking with the other interpreters over lunches where they changed languages fluidly, delighting in their knowledge and mastery. That world seemed impossible now. But then again, so did the one that she currently found herself embroiled in.

"I know I don't have to tell you this," Wynter said, puffing away. "But that house down in Cuernavaca is going to be a little more of a pressure cooker than a standard French test."

Elizabeth nodded.

"Yes. I know."

"Good," Wynter said. He reached for the stack of file folders in front of him and began rummaging through. But before he could reach whatever it was he was looking for, Alex Connor burst through the door, looking slightly out of breath.

"You're going to want to hear this," he said, looking pointedly at Wynter who tapped out his pipe and rose from the table, pushing one of the files across the table in Elizabeth's direction.

"A little light afternoon reading. A walk might do you some good—we've been working you hard, and it's a beautiful afternoon."

Elizabeth was about to ask if she could come with them—if they had news from Cuernavaca, she wanted to know what it was. But something about the urgency with which Alex Connor had come into the room convinced her otherwise.

"I think a walk sounds lovely," she said. "I'll catch up with you boys later."

Connor said nothing as he led Bill Wynter along the narrow corridor in the basement to the room where they kept the radio equipment. John Reynolds was already standing when they arrived, and soon, the room was cramped with the three of them.

"What happened, John?" Wynter said.

"Our men found Mavich's radio today."

"And yet I don't get the sense that this is good news," Wynter said. Reynolds grimaced and shook his head.

"The radio operator managed to destroy the tapes. We don't know any more about what's going on in that house than we did before."

Wynter cursed briefly and shook his head. He turned to look at Connor.

"You know what this means, don't you?"

"That we're up shit creek without a paddle?"

"It means Elizabeth was right. She said that finding the radio wouldn't change anything, other than putting Mavich on guard. Do you notice that her instincts are almost always right, even when they go against what we think?"

"In fact, I did notice that," Connor said. "She's smart, Bill."

"Chris Johnson just gave her the nod for Spanish, French, and German, too."

"Then we got lucky. Do you know what the odds are of finding a girl like that?"

"We have Steve Brenner to thank for that. Now, John, tell me what happened."

Reynolds straightened his back.

"Our men discovered the radio with our truck. They notified the Mexicans—we couldn't send our own agents into the building, because Mavich couldn't know that we were connected with the seizure of the radio. But the Mexicans don't know the Russians like we do, and they were a little slow making their entry. As they were trying to break in the door, the operator put the tapes into a machine that shredded them into confetti."

Wynter ran his hand across his forehead, massaging his temples with his fingers.

"But we got the machine, at least?"

"We did," Reynolds said. "But our agents couldn't figure out how the damn thing worked. It's on its way to Langley as we speak. The Soviets have obviously developed a new device to destroy top secret material. I guess they decided after our fiasco with the Pueblo that they didn't intend to get caught with any data they couldn't destroy quickly."

Wynter shook his head at the mention of the USS Pueblo. The ship had ostensibly been an environmental research vessel—though the Navy had retrofitted it to be a covert intelligence ship. The North Koreans had captured it a few years earlier, taking the crew captive and seizing valuable intelligence. The whole affair had been a reminder of just how a dangerous game they were all playing—and how easily one misstep could put American intelligence, and lives, at risk.

"There was one message that the radio operator didn't manage to destroy; he either forgot it or he didn't have time to get them all. Our analysts have managed to decode it: It says that Mavich is to expect Nicola Neumann with information on the Leningrad's arrival, and that she will call him from Las Mañanitas restaurant, as he requested. She will wait there until someone comes to get her."

"That's a stroke of luck, at least," Connor said.

"You left out one possibility, John," Wynter said. The old spy frowned at him.

"How's that, Bill?"

"You said he either forgot about the message, or didn't have time to destroy it. But there's a third possibility: that they wanted us to find the message, and they're leading us into a trap."

There was silence in the little room as the three men considered this grim possibility.

"That said," Wynter said after a time, "we proceed with the plan as intended. They didn't know the Mexicans were coming and are currently unaware of Nicola's disappearance. I doubt they'd think to set a trap like that."

"There's one more piece of bad news, Bill," Reynolds said.

"You are just a ray of sunshine this afternoon."

"We've lost all contact with Cobalt."

This news hit Wynter like a punch to the gut. Cobalt was one of the highest-ranking sources he had in the Soviet intelligence apparatus—the man had given him invaluable information and, so far, he had never been wrong. Wynter had also sensed in the man a kind of kindred spirit—the right blend of caution and appetite for risk that made for an excellent agent and asset.

"Any guesses as to what's happened?" Connor said.

"I don't like to even think about it," Wynter said. "What was the last thing he sent through?"

"Late last night he gave the name of the man in charge of the operation—a Grigory Valenkov, code name Midas. He said more information would be coming soon, but we haven't been able to raise him all day."

"Do we have anything on Valenkov?" Wynter said.

"Nothing so far," Connor said. "We're working on it."

Wynter's thoughts went back to Cobalt.

"If we knew who Cobalt was, I could tell our agents in the Kremlin to look into any possible disappearances. But the only thing I know about him is his code name—some help that is in a situation like this."

"Don't jump to any conclusions, Bill," Reynolds said. "You and I have both seen our fair share of assets go dark for good reasons."

And most of them never came back, Wynter thought. But it would be no help to say something like that aloud; the other two men in the room both knew full well. Wynter wondered if he had put the man in harm's way by asking too many questions—the stakes were so high with Sobokov's disappearance that he hadn't been as discreet as he usually was. He looked up at the low ceiling of the room and hoped that, if Cobalt had been caught, his death would be a quick one. That at least would be some kind of mercy.

"You're right, though, Connor. That message about Nicola was a break for us. It could have just as easily told Mavich that Nicola had disappeared and that they were sending another courier."

"That would have smashed our plans, all right. But here's what I can't figure out: Why *wouldn't* Valenkov tell Mavich to expect another courier? If we can't find Nicola, with the source of resources we're pouring into the Caribbean, I know they can't."

Wynter thought about this for a moment.

"Mavich is cautious. Super cautious. That makes him a good spymaster, but it also means that he's a little brittle. My guess is that Valenkov—Midas—is afraid to switch couriers at this point. He thinks Mavich would call off the operation if anything as big as that was altered, which means Mavich has done his homework on Nicola Neumann; he knows who he's expecting. The Communists can't send him any information about another courier. Mavich wouldn't want anything like that sent through the mail. The Russians all assume that anything that's in the mail will be read by the state, because that's how it is in the Soviet Union, and he can't believe it wouldn't be like that in the West. The only way for him to gain access to new material is through a courier he trusts. But if the new material is *about* a new courier, then they're caught in a paradox."

"So what do you do, if you're Midas?" Connor asked. Wynter appreciated the question—Connor always cut to the heart of the matter, saw what was important and went after it.

"The only thing he can do: Try and find Nicola Neumann, and you can bet he's having a fit right about now, seeing his whole operation go up in smoke because she's disappeared." Wynter smiled. "I never thought someone else's problems could give me this much pleasure. I just wish Midas had a hundred others more serious than this one."

But Alex Connor was still frowning.

"What's wrong, Alex?" Wynter asked.

"I was just thinking how disastrous it would have been if we hadn't intercepted that message and sent Elizabeth into that house anyway."

"God, what a fiasco," Reynolds said, shaking his head.

PASSPORT TO DANGER

"It also means we have to get them down to Mexico as soon as we can," Wynter said. "Who knows how long Mavich will be willing to wait for Nicola? Or how long Midas will search for her before he calls the whole thing off."

Another grim silence came over the group when Alex Connor suddenly raised his head.

"What do you mean, send *them* down to Mexico?"

The long shadows of the afternoon fell across the field as Steve Brenner searched for Elizabeth. Wynter had told him that he sent her on a walk, and Brenner couldn't tell whether his offer to go retrieve her was welcome or not. He scarcely noticed the beautiful surroundings as he passed through the farm grounds.

At the edge of a pasture he heard the sound of running water. He headed in that direction for a few moments before he came upon a stream. Sitting on the opposite side of the water, several yards downstream, was Elizabeth. He stood quietly, watching her as she read the file on her lap. There was a small frown on her beautiful face, her dark silky hair slightly disarrayed by the breeze, little wisps of it gently curling around her face. *God, she's lovely*, he thought to himself. Maybe when this was all over, the two of them might have a chance back in New York, this whole affair a distant memory, something to laugh about when friends asked how they had first met. He'd bone up on the theater, opera, art, all sorts of cultured things so that he could talk with her about what she enjoyed. He'd try not to bore her with talk about work, though between the minutia of his physics research and the work he couldn't talk about because it was classified, there wouldn't be much there to discuss anyway. He would be a man worthy of her, if she would have him—and if she somehow made it out of this maelstrom he'd unwittingly thrust her into.

He took a step towards her and a twig snapped beneath his foot. Elizabeth looked up quickly, startled at first, but her expression blossomed into a smile when she saw that it was him.

"Isn't it lovely here?" she said.

All the more so because you're here, Steve thought to himself. But instead he just murmured in agreement. He stepped across the stream and came to sit lightly in the grass next to her.

"How are things back at the house?" she asked.

"All right. It's just, the deeper we get into this, the more I'm wishing Bill Wynter had never met you. He'd be thinking up another plan to get Sobokov out of that house in one piece, and you'd be back in New York, safe and sound." He glanced down at the sparkling blue water of the stream. The tops of the pines were mirrored in the clear, cool water; the woods were full of the sound of chirping birds, chattering squirrels, and the noises of small animals moving through the bushes and trees. The air was replete with the smell of honeysuckle, mint, pine, and wild roses. It was so peaceful that a man could almost forget his troubles. *But not quite*, Steve thought, stealing a quick glance at the girl sitting beside him. She was watching him, quiet and intent.

"You're worried about Dr. Sobokov, aren't you?" she said.

"Bill still seems to think that he defected," Steve said. "But I just can't see it. Dr. Sobokov always said that he could never go back to the Soviet Union; that, after a man had lived with the freedom that we have in the United States, he'd rather die than return to a country where he had no freedom."

"You think a lot of him."

"All of us who worked with Dr. Sobokov admired him. He was kind, dedicated, and compassionate. He was never too busy to help a younger colleague and always eager to give credit to someone else. I'm not sure how many labs you've seen, but those are rare qualities indeed. I've never known a more unselfish person."

Brenner shook a cigarette out of his pack and offered it to Elizabeth. When she shook her head, he lit one for himself.

"Will you be in Cuernavaca?" Elizabeth said.

"I don't know. I'd like to be. But that's Bill's call, in the end."

Above them, an eagle soared. He was heading their way then suddenly dove towards something he'd spotted, disappearing behind the tops of the trees.

"How are you feeling about all of this?" Steve said, nodding down at the folder in her lap. "I don't have to tell you where I stand. But in the end, it's your choice."

Elizabeth was quiet for a moment, and in that long second, Steve allowed himself to believe that maybe she had finally seen the folly in Bill Wynter's plan. This gentle woman next to him was no killer; Mavich would see through her ruse too quickly. Maybe she had finally come to her senses.

"I have to go," she said, fixing him now with a direct, resolute look. "There's no one else who can get into that house, and if I don't get in, Sobokov is as good as gone, along with the last five years of his research. If you told me that didn't matter, I'd believe you, but you know how much that means."

Steve took a long drag on his cigarette and said nothing. It was true: Dr. Sobokov's research was invaluable to the defense of the country. Losing it would be a massive blow, to say nothing about his personal feelings for the man who had been the main mentor and supporter of his career.

"I know I'm not a perfect choice," Elizabeth said. "But for the moment, I'm the only one we have."

Their eyes met then, and for several seconds, they studied one another. Then Steve pulled Elizabeth to him, kissing her long and hard. They came apart, Steve holding Elizabeth slightly away from him, searching for some sign on her face that she felt the same way he did. This time, she was the one to come forward and kiss him again, hard, their bodies so close that they seemed to melt together.

Steve came away. He traced the line of her cheek gently with his forefinger.

"If anything happened to you, Elizabeth, I don't know what I'd do. I need you to promise me you'll be *very* careful. I don't know how this all happened, but somehow, in the last two days, you've become the most important thing in my life."

"Oh, Steve," she said, her voice catching. He kissed her once more.

After a time, they started back towards the house. From here, they couldn't even see the chimney, only the winding stream and the ranks of pines marching towards the distant Virginia hills. As they crossed the field, the sun slanted towards the west, streaking the sky with crimson, mauve, and pink. A golden moon already hung in the pastel heaven.

CHAPTER ELEVEN

Bill Wynter handed a glass of brandy to Elizabeth Lamont. She was standing beside him at the bar cart in the library; the other men had arrayed themselves on the easy chairs and couches in the room, sipping from their own drinks. The air was thick with cigarette smoke—Brenner was smoking like a damn chimney, though Bill could guess why the man's desire for nicotine was higher than usual, given what a stressful few days they had all had. Wynter made a mental note to himself to have a carton of Steve's favorite brand waiting at the border; things were going to get harder before they got easier.

Elizabeth thanked him for the drink and returned to her chair by the fire. She watched as the vibrant flames lapped against the logs, seeming to swallow them up. It had been a warm day, even at twilight when Steve had found her by the creek. But with nightfall, it had turned abruptly chilly. She was grateful for the warmth from the fire, and the brandy. She had changed before dinner into a wool dress with long sleeves, its violet color setting off her clear skin, dark hair, and violet-blue eyes. She noticed that all the men in the room were looking at her—probably waiting to hear officially the decision she had made on whether or not to go down to Cuernavaca. All of them...except for Bill Wynter, who had his steely grey eyes trained on Steve across the room.

SHEILA GRANT

Steve couldn't stop looking at Elizabeth. He kept thinking of the two of them together, on the banks of that little stream, feeling the delicate softness of her lips against his. He had never fallen so hard for a woman before, never in his life. She was the most lovely creature he had ever laid his eyes on, with an active and lively mind to match her beauty, exactly the sort of woman he had always hoped to meet. But why did it have to happen now, under such dangerous and inconvenient circumstances?

The only thing that distracted him from the figure Elizabeth cut in her wool dress was the stare of Bill Wynter from across the room. Steve stubbed out his cigarette and resisted the urge to immediately light another—he had wheezed his way up the stairs that evening to get changed before dinner. He frowned as he looked at the old spy master, trying to imagine what was happening behind those grey eyes. Wynter would have guessed by now that Elizabeth would be saying yes to his proposition, no matter how insane; he wouldn't have brought them all together like this if he didn't feel confident in his read on the girl. But there was something else at play here, the contours of which Steve couldn't yet grasp. Finally, he took a long drink of the bourbon that John Reynolds had poured him out of his "secret stash," cleared his throat, and cocked his head in Wynter's direction.

"Penny for your thoughts, Bill?"

Bill Wynter had played it all out in his mind. That was what he did: considered the variables, imagined the counterfactuals, thought through everything that could go wrong and all the things he could not know. It was, necessarily, imprecise work—bets made by a man who knew just how high the stakes were. Most of the time, he tried to limit the risk. But sometimes, when the status quo was unacceptable, the only way to give yourself a chance was to increase the risk, and massively.

Alex Connor and John Reynolds had already told him they didn't think Elizabeth was up for the task. Steve Brenner had looked nearly ready to sock him in the nose when he first mentioned he was thinking of sending her down to Cuernavaca. He respected all these men's opinions—there was nothing mean or petty about them, none of the political games that dogged some of Langley's other operations, men jockeying with one another for a better posting or a share of the credit that would only be known by a special inner circle. They all wanted the same thing.

If Wynter did nothing, then the Soviets would put Sobokov on that freighter ship and send him back to Moscow. Five years of advanced weapons developments would be lost—and the Soviets would have the best man in the world for developing precisely the sort of MIRV systems that, for now, were keeping the balance of the Cold War slightly in the favor of the free world.

Which meant he had to try *something*. No matter how slim the chances that that *something* would actually work. Wynter took a sip of his brandy and forced a smile at Steve Brenner.

"I was just thinking how nice it would be to go for a long drive through beautiful Mexico right about now," he said.

"A drive?" Brenner said, stealing a nervous glance at Elizabeth.

"Nothing quite as romantic as the rural highways of Northern Mexico," Wynter said.

"Romantic?" came the incredulous sound of Alex Connor's voice from across the room.

Wynter turned to look at Elizabeth. None of the other men in the room had guessed what he was up to—that was unusual, but not impossible, considering just how unorthodox the plan he had hatched. The timid, uncertain smile that had been on her face all evening was gone, replaced now by a look closer to genuine wonder. If Wynter didn't know better, he'd say that she was excited.

"Bill," she said, addressing him with the same tone that a lady might use when you've surprised her with a particularly stunning tennis bracelet for her birthday. "Are you sending Steve and me down to Cuernavaca together?"

Now, it will Bill Wynter's turn to smile. There was something about this woman. True, it would be damned hard work for her to pass herself off credibly as a hard-as-nails East German agent for too long—that was the risk, and what all the other men saw when they counseled against it. But she had the looks, and there was something else, too—a magnetism that drew people to her, that made them turn around when they walked past her on a block in Manhattan and wished they had the nerve to run back and ask who she was. It might not be the Nicola Neumann that the Soviet agents down in Mexico were expecting, exactly. But there was no doubt that they would be intrigued by her. It was easy to imagine that, in a different life, she might have made a very powerful intelligence asset. They just had to convince a house full of dangerous men (and one wayward nuclear scientist) that this was real life.

Before Bill could answer, the little room exploded in pandemonium.

Steve Brenner couldn't believe what he was hearing. Sending him down with Elizabeth? Driving through rural Mexico, when time was of the essence? Steve wasn't even a field agent, damn it—he was a nuclear scientist who got called in to do a little consulting work, and sometimes had off-the-record conversations with other scientists at conferences around the world. He'd never done a thing like this before in his life.

PASSPORT TO DANGER

Fortunately for him, he didn't have to bother making his objections known between the volume and vociferousness currently coming from both Alex Connor and John Reynolds.

"Have you lost your damn mind, Bill?" said John Reynolds, his voice recovering the long-lost twang of his youth as it did when he was too upset to check it. "Using the girl is bad enough, now you want to send Dr. Lovebird down there with her?"

"Who knows how much time we really have," Alex Connor said. He held up his watch as though he had programmed the dial to track the movements of the cargo ship currently bound for Cuba. "And you want to send them on some back-road honeymoon? For what?"

"Sometimes you get dealt a crap hand and you just have to play it, Bill," Reynolds said. "Not try to bluff your way to the pot with your whole stack! Take the loss, move on the house, and let the cards fall where they may."

"Do you know what you'd say to me if I suggested some kind of crap like this?" Connor said. "*Cowboy stuff.* And you hate cowboy stuff. You know why?"

"Because cowboys get hurt," Steve Brenner said. The others in the room turned to look at him. "You know, as the only confirmed Texan in this room, it's probably my jurisdiction to decide what qualifies as cowboy stuff, Alex."

Connor waved a dismissive hand at him and sat back down, but made no move to interrupt. Steve nodded over at Elizabeth.

"And it occurs to me that we've never formally asked Elizabeth whether she's on board with any of this plan, which seems like a good first step to me."

"How about it, Elizabeth?" Bill Wynter said, taking a long drink of his brandy as he waited for her answer.

Elizabeth nodded for a moment, as though collecting herself, before she gave her answer.

"I know you're only asking me because you're out of options," she said. Then she turned to look across the room at where John Reynolds and Alex Connor were sitting. "And I know you all don't think very highly of the chances of this plan working. I know that's nothing against me—if I was sitting where you are now, I'm sure I'd feel the same way.

"But I also know how important it is to try and get Dr. Sobokov back. Or, if we can't do that, then at least get that password before the Soviets take him. There are relatively few moments that come in a person's life where they have a chance to make a real difference—not just for themselves, but for the world. I was in love with a man who believed in seizing those moments when they came around. He ended up dying because of it. But I believe he changed the world more in his brief life than most other men ever dream of doing—and I believe that was a life well led, no matter how much I miss him now.

"So if you really feel, Bill, like there's a chance I can make this work, then I'm willing to do all I can to help; and if you want to send Steve down with me, well, I can't think of much better company."

The room was quiet for a few moments after that, the men all thinking about what she had said. All of the men in that room had served their country, in one capacity or another; they knew what it meant to risk yourself for something greater, whether it was the men you were leading or the patch sewed onto the shoulder of your uniform. How many of them, in Elizabeth's place, would have walked away from what Bill Wynter was asking them to do? Each knew that they would have said yes, no matter the objections and the counsel against it, and if that were the case, then who were they to say no?

"Well," John Reynolds said after a time, "can we at least talk through this darn foolishness of sending Steve down there with her?"

Bill Wynter smiled and reached behind him for the atlas that he'd brought up with him to the meeting, anticipating a moment just like this. He quickly cleared off the coffee table in the library and spread the map out wide.

"Alex, you asked about flying her down. Care to guess why I think that's a bad idea?"

"You think they'd make her in Mexico City?" Connor said.

"Worse," Wynter said. "I think she looks just enough like Nicola for them to flag her when she flies in. But Mavich would know that an agent like Neumann would never even consider flying in through a commercial airport, which means he'd know she was an imposter even before she showed up. Best case, they pick up house and move before we can get to them."

He left the worst case unstated, but they all knew how much danger Elizabeth would be in if Mavich suspected from the jump that she wasn't who she claimed to be.

"Who's to say he won't check the US border to see if she crossed there?" Reynolds said.

"I think he will," Wynter said. "The four main crossings where we could go through are here, at Eagle Pass, which takes her through Piedras Negras to Saltillo, down to San Luis Potosí on the fast road until the slower Highway 86 to Valles. Or she could cross at Laredo, McAllen, or Brownsville, go down to Ciudad Victoria until Valles."

"Why not cross at one of the smaller towns, then?" Brenner said, lighting a cigarette as he studied the map carefully. "Somewhere between Laredo and McAllen?"

"It's a tricky balance," Wynter said. "True, there's less of a chance that Mavich has eyes at the smaller border crossings. But if he does, you can bet Elizabeth gets noticed going through. The border patrols in the big cities are busier, more predictable—you don't attract as much attention that way."

"But if you think Mavich has eyes on those four points, what is Elizabeth going to do?" Reynolds said.

Bill looked back over at Elizabeth.

"How do you feel about being Elizabeth Lamont, international model, for just a little while longer?"

Elizabeth smiled and straightened up in her chair.

"Everyone's always going out of their way to tell me that blondes really do have more fun."

"My thoughts exactly," Bill said. "And, Steve? How do you feel about celebrating your recent nuptials with a Mexican honeymoon?"

"My recent *what?*" Steve said. The others in the room noticed the way his cheeks went deep crimson at Bill Wynter's suggestion. But when they turned back to look at Elizabeth, she was beaming from ear to ear.

"Like I always imagined," she said.

"Good," Bill said. "Then let's get started. We have a lot of work to do before we send you lovebirds on the first trip of the rest of your happy lives."

CHAPTER TWELVE

From his desk at the Customs Building, Juan Cortazar could see the cars driving across the bridge that spanned the Rio Grande, crossing from the United States into Mexico. When he had joined the Army a decade earlier, Juan had expected excitement—gunfights with bandits, rescuing kidnapped damsels, and all the other adventures he had grown up seeing in Westerns. But for the most part, he had sat here at this desk, reading visas and dealing with gringos speaking cheerful, atrocious Spanish at him. Still, there were worse jobs, he knew, and the Army had gotten him off the farm where the rest of his siblings still woke at dawn to feed the chickens and tend to the cornfields. He'd take a boring shift with a newspaper and a thermos of coffee over breaking his back in the hot sun any day.

The pay wasn't much, but there were other ways to add a little to what he took home at the end of the month. It was a little like a game: at the start of each week, he met a man for breakfast who gave him a brief list of names to be on the lookout for, and a phone number to call if he saw anything interesting. At the end of the month, he received a nice little envelope of cash, plus a bonus if he managed to report anything of note. Juan was smart enough to know that asking too many questions about his benefactors—

like who, exactly, they were, and why they were so interested in those names—was unlikely to do him any good.

But this week had been different. The man who met him for a cup of coffee and a sweet roll on Monday had none of his usual jokes or easy smile, and there hadn't been the typical list of names like there had been the week before. Instead, there had been a single photograph of a woman—beautiful, yes, but also cold and severe, Juan could see that much even from the small, grainy snapshot that the man passed to him beneath the table. His instructions were clear: If he saw anyone who looked like that woman, he was to call the number immediately.

It was enough to make him sit up a little straighter in his little Customs office and pay a bit more attention to the sea of faces that passed through on their way down to Mexico. But so far this week, there had been nothing out of the usual: The standard parade of workers and day laborers heading back home from a hard day's work; teenagers road tripping for cheap beer and sunshine; gawking American tourists in garish shirts and pants with elasticized waistbands barely looking up from their guidebooks as he stamped their visas.

Now, here came another—a newer model Chrysler with dark brown paint, its windows rolled down as it made its way across the bridge. Americans, no doubt about it, in a car like that; and sure enough, as the car parked in front of the Customs Building, out came an American man in a blue sports shirt and a pair of tan slacks, dark sunglasses on his eyes, and bright white teeth when he reached up to stretch as though he'd already been driving for hours. He came around to the other side of the car and opened the door, and Juan watched as first one milky white leg, and then another, emerged from the Chrysler.

PASSPORT TO DANGER

She was, simply put, the most beautiful woman he had ever seen in his life. Blonde hair piled high on her head, a knock-out figure—nothing like those skinny American women who seemed to be so popular these days—and a warm, generous smile that he could see as she thanked the man for opening the door for her. When she stepped into the building and removed her sunglasses, he could see her violet-blue eyes. It wasn't often that someone like this came through his post, and he could feel the eyes of all the other Customs officers on her as well.

The man and the woman came up to his desk, and the woman gave him another bright smile and handed their visas across the desk. He glanced down at the documents, and then back up at the woman.

"Where are you going?" he asked in English. The woman's smile intensified.

"*Vamonos a Acapulco*," the woman said. Her Spanish was much better than most of what Juan heard from Americans passing through the border—a bit of an accent, perhaps, but more the way someone from another Spanish-speaking country might sound on a visit to Mexico. He shifted to Spanish and complimented her on how well she spoke.

"*Gracias! Me encantan los idiomas*," she said with another winning smile.

Juan asked what the purpose of her trip was. At this, she turned to the man traveling with her with a look of pure love, and then looked back at Juan.

"*Como se dice 'honeymoon' en Espanol? No creo que pueda ser 'luna de miel.*'"

Juan allowed himself a small chuckle, though really what he was thinking inside his head was: *You lucky bastard*. He told her that was exactly what they called a honeymoon, and the woman smiled even broader to hear that she had gotten it right. Juan tried to think of other questions to plausibly ask the woman, just to keep her here a little while longer, to continue to bask in the light that seemed to emanate from her and spread all throughout the low-ceilinged building. Finding nothing, he took his stamp, applied the ink, and approved both of their visas, watching as they took their luggage to be checked by his fellow officers.

It was only later, once the American honeymooners had left the office and were speeding off down the road in their car, that Juan bothered to think about the photograph that the man had given to him earlier that week. He took the photo out from his desk and studied it for a long moment. True, there was more than a passing resemblance between the two women—the hair color was wrong, but she could have been wearing a wig, or dyed her hair. But the longer he stared at the photo of Nicola Neumann, the more certain he became that they couldn't possibly be the same woman. The woman who had passed through his office was an angel of the light; the woman in the photograph had a darkness about her that made it difficult to look at her for too long before feeling a chill work its way down his spine. No, it wouldn't be worth calling this one in, even if there was a higher-than-usual bounty. Let the woman go enjoy her life and her honeymoon. He just hoped the man knew how lucky he was, and would treat her well, the way she so clearly deserved.

Miles down the highway, Elizabeth gazed out the window as two burros grazed along the side of the road. The adrenaline of the border crossing was starting to seep out of her, and it was only as it left that she realized just how nervous she had been. But it had all gone so well, far easier than she had imagined. They had slipped into the country undetected, just the way that Bill Wynter had designed it. And now, they were driving through some of the most desolate terrain she had even seen before. Miles and miles of scrub, cactus, and isolated maguey. The only soft color in this dry rocky world was the bright yellow of the dainty flowers blooming on the cacti.

"Your Spanish is even better than I thought," Steve said from the driver's seat, fingertips casually on the wheel and sunglasses focused on the road in front of them. "What did you and the Federale talk about?"

"I told him it was my honeymoon, and how excited I was to get you down to Acapulco," Elizabeth said, feeling the breeze through the open windows of the car. She sighed. "It was nice, to pretend for a little while, as if Dr. Sobokov was already back home, safe and sound. Or, better yet, had never been taken, and we really *were* on our way down to a beach somewhere, to stick our toes in the sand and sip drinks with those frilly little umbrellas."

"It's all I can think about," Steve said. Then he shook his head. "We have to keep our focus. Neither of us have done this before, and we can't get lured into complacency just because you managed to sweet talk your way past a sleepy border guard."

Elizabeth sighed again.

"You're right, of course. But we've got two days of driving ahead of us. What do you propose we do?"

"Let's go over the men in that house."

"Again?"

"Trust me. You'll need to have them down, cold. The way Nicola would have."

Elizabeth stole one more glance out the side of the car at the foreboding landscape, then closed her eyes briefly.

"All right. Where do you want me to start?"

"At the top," Steve said. "Tell me everything you know about Mavich."

"Nikolai Mavich," Elizabeth said, keeping her eyes closed as she tried to visualize the file that Wynter had given her to study for the flight down to Texas. "Russian. A top man in the KGB. Has organized spy networks across the globe."

"Where, specifically?"

"England, France, West Germany, Spain, Eastern Africa…"

"And?"

Elizabeth bit her lip, trying to remember the last locations. Then she grinned and turned to Steve.

"Japan. And Latin America, naturally."

"His wife's name?"

"Trick question. Mavich never married. He drinks moderately, doesn't smoke, is a snappy dresser, and apparently an excellent tennis player."

"Armed?"

"Nearly always. Wears a revolver in a shoulder holster. Is considered, and here I quote directly from the dossier, 'ruthless and very dangerous.'"

Elizabeth stretched her hands nonchalantly over her head and then turned to smile at Steve.

"How did I do?"

"Flawlessly. You must have been a real terror back at school."

"Memorization has always come easily for me. I think it's what makes me so good with languages. You should hear me with song lyrics."

"Enough bragging," Steve said with a wide smile. "Tell me about Mendoza."

As they drove the rutted highway down to Monterrey, Elizabeth proceeded to reel off the names and key details of the other men stationed in the house in Cuernavaca with Dr. Sobokov. There was Carlos Mendoza, the Director of Latin America, the son of a French mother and a Venezuelan father who had spent ten years in Russia before returning to oversee Communist activities in the area. He had been the liaison between Castro and the Kremlin during troublesome periods. He was also—and Steve couldn't help but notice that Elizabeth recounted these details with a bit more zest—known as something of a ladies' man, an expensive dresser who liked to race sports cars and was known to gamble—and lose—big sums of money.

"You think if I ask him to flip a coin for Sobokov, he'd be game for it?" Elizabeth asked.

Steve shook his head. What he didn't say: If they could get their odds of recovering Dr. Sobokov up to the fifty-fifty chance of a coin flip, that would represent a significant improvement in the likelihood of all of this going well.

"What do you give him if you lose?"

"A kiss, I suppose, and a chance to go double or nothing."

"Not on our honeymoon!" Steve said, trying to keep his voice light even as he could feel his hands gripping more tightly to the wheel.

"Oh, all right," Elizabeth said, putting an arm outside the window to feel the hot rushing wind. "Is the assassin next?"

"Betrin," Steve said with a nod of his head. "Tell me about him."

"We don't know much, which makes remembering it easier," Elizabeth said. Yuri Betrin was, in all likelihood, not the man's real name; there was no birth record for him, and his age and place of origin were both unknown. But for the last nineteen years the man had gone as Yuri Betrin. He was thought to be in his mid-forties: medium height, medium build, dark brown hair, and a face so average looking that he wouldn't be noticed in a crowd. But of all the men in the house, he was the one trained killer; he'd been a ranking member of the assassination squad in his twenties, then was the NKVD superintendent of three different Siberian labor camps. A dangerous man, no doubt about it.

"I still don't know why he'd be involved with Dr. Sobokov," Elizabeth said, shaking her head. Steve frowned.

"How do you mean?"

"I understand they'd want protection," Elizabeth said. "But his skill set is...a little too specific for anything I can imagine them needing. Do you know what he's doing there?"

Steve shook his head.

"No, I don't. But you're right—it's bad news for us that the Russians thought it would be useful to have him as part of this operation."

"Maybe he'd just always wanted to see Mexico," Elizabeth said.

"Let's hope so," Steve said as they passed another few burros chewing pensively on the scrub grass by the side of the road. For a few minutes, they drove in silence—the ruse of the honeymoon temporarily forgotten in favor of thinking through the mission that lay ahead of them at the end of this drive.

"You haven't mentioned Caslov," Elizabeth said after a time.

"The less time spent thinking about that man, the better," Steve said.

"Still," Elizabeth said. "It's important. Even if just to remind me to avoid him like the plague."

PASSPORT TO DANGER

"All right," Steve said. "Tell me all about Boris Caslov."

Of all the men in that house, Caslov was the one who worried Elizabeth the most. He was a GRU lieutenant colonel who had been a successful spymaster across Europe: Paris, Bonn, Vienna. He was fluent in five languages, a big powerful man with attractive features and a white scar on his left cheek. But it was his personal life that was the most troubling. He apparently considered himself God's gift to women and had an explosive temper—a terrible combination. There were several known cases of rape in his background and more that were merely suspected. He had been in several fights over women and left at least one man dead as a result. The GRU had overlooked his behavior because of his value to them. It felt a bit unnecessary, Elizabeth thought, to include the summary in his dossier that the man was "considered highly dangerous and unpredictable"—what other conclusion could she have come to, having read through those details?

Their recollection was interrupted by the Army checkpoint appearing on the horizon. Both of them were quiet as they eased the car to a stop before the Mexican official, the soldiers behind him holding their guns with studied indifference. Steve put on a big fake American smile and handed the official their car permit as Elizabeth pretended to study a map in the passenger seat, glancing up briefly to add a smile of her own. The man went away to study the permit.

"If we need to, do you think we can outrun them?" Elizabeth said breezily. Steve looked over, shocked.

"Are you crazy?"

"Just curious," Elizabeth said. "Don't worry about it. He's coming back now to say, 'Welcome to Mexico.'"

Just as she had predicted, the man returned in a moment and passed the permit back through the window. With a friendly grin, he waved them through. As they headed down the highway again, Steve could feel his heart rate returning to its normal steady beat.

"Do you really not get nervous at things like that?" he said to Elizabeth.

"Of course I do," Elizabeth said. "But the last three years have trained me to smile and be pleasant no matter what's happening around me. It comes in handy, it turns out, even outside of photoshoots."

"If only Nicola was known to be charming and smiling," Steve said.

"That would make things easier, yes," Elizabeth said as they sped down the road.

An hour and a half later, they reached Monterrey, a bustling industrial city sprawling on the plains of Northern Mexico beneath the enormous Cerra de la Silla mountain. Elizabeth had enjoyed the drive more than she expected to—she'd loved Sabinas Hidalgo, a veritable oasis in the desert with palm trees and flowers abounding; the little Mexican villages they'd driven through; and a unique cactus forest with cacti as big as oak trees. But she found she was glad as Steve pulled into the hotel: hardly plush, but clearly clean and respectable. Bill Wynter—or whoever at the agency did the travel arrangements—had done nicely. Steve went to the front office to get their key, and then let them into the room.

"I think a cold shower and a long cool drink is in order after that drive," Elizabeth said, stepping out of the car and stretching.

"You go ahead," Steve said. "I should give Bill a call and let him know how we're doing."

"Give him my best!" Elizabeth said as she padded off to the bathroom. Soon, Steve could hear the water running, and it took real effort to drag himself from the room and over to the public phone in the lobby.

"We made it to Monterrey in one piece," Steve said.

"Were the roads crowded?" Wynter asked.

"With burros," Steve said. "The way those damn things roam all over the road, you'd think they owned it. I nearly ran over one. Scared the hell out of me."

Bill Wynter laughed on the other end of the line.

"No one seemed interested in Elizabeth, then?"

"Our agent in Customs seemed just about ready to propose to her," Steve said. "Bad news for him that she's taken."

"Hiding in plain sight," Wynter said.

"Anything happening in Cuernavaca?" Steve said.

"Nothing yet. Mavich hasn't even left the house since we picked up the radio."

"Easier to keep an eye on him that way, I guess," Steve said. "Now, if you'll excuse me, I have a honeymoon to attend to."

"Make sure to get some sleep," Wynter said. "The roads tomorrow will make today look like a cakewalk."

"I can't wait," Steve said drolly before hanging up the phone and heading back to the room. Elizabeth was out of the shower, her hair up in a towel as she sat in front of the small mirror in the room, applying a bit of makeup. Steve came up behind her and gave her a small kiss on her neck, drawing a smile from her mirrored image of her face.

"Can you believe we're here?" Elizabeth said.

Steve chuckled and shook his head.

"You mean on a road trip through Northern Mexico with my new, fake wife? I think I would have had some questions, if you told me all this a few days ago."

"I'm glad you're here with me," Elizabeth said with a big smile.

"So am I."

"Good," Elizabeth said. "Now go get cleaned up. I'm famished, and I think we've earned a proper dinner after that ride."

Steve thought about telling her Bill Wynter's warning about the roads tomorrow, but decided to keep that detail to himself for now. Elizabeth had plenty of more important concerns on her mind, and unlike her performance at that house, there was nothing that she could do about the potholes. As he ran the water in the bathroom, he could have sworn he heard her humming to herself out in the bedroom.

Later that evening, after a simple but satisfying meal at the hotel's homey restaurant, Elizabeth was getting ready for bed as Steve took a pillow and the spare blanket and made himself a little nest on the floor next to the bed. Elizabeth came out of the bathroom wearing a pretty nightgown and fixed him with a mock frown.

"Well," she said, "this isn't at all how I pictured the first night of my honeymoon!"

Steve chuckled as he fluffed the pillow.

"We should get some sleep," he said. "We have a long day of driving ahead of us."

"And what exactly am I supposed to say if someone was to see my new husband sleeping on the floor?"

"Tell them I said something stupid that made you mad," Steve said. "Trust me, they'll believe you."

"And you really don't mind sleeping down there?"

PASSPORT TO DANGER

"I was an Eagle Scout back in Texas," he said. "At least this floor is level. I can't tell you how many tree roots I've managed to sleep on in my life."

"You really are a gentleman, Steve Brenner," Elizabeth said, stepping into bed and leaning back onto her pillow with a sigh.

"Don't you forget it," Steve said with a little smile.

Elizabeth turned off the lamp on her tableside, and the only light came from a lone streetlamp outside the hotel that filtered through the room's curtains. The two of them lay there, one in the bed and one on the floor, both thinking of what was still ahead of them.

"It's not too late to change your mind, you know," Steve said after a time. "No one would think any less of you. We could have you back to New York by the end of the day tomorrow."

"I think we both know it's a little too late for that," Elizabeth said. "And who knows? Maybe by the time we've made it down to Cuernavaca, Bill will have whipped up a whole new plan that doesn't require my particular skills at all. We'll all get to laugh about the fact that we ever had this plan in the first place."

"Wouldn't that be something," Steve said. He didn't think, between the stiff floor against his back and everything that was on his mind, that he'd be able to get much sleep at all that night. But his exhausted body had other thoughts, and before long, he was out.

CHAPTER THIRTEEN

Bill Wynter had no new ideas.

He had been in Cuernavaca for nearly a day now. The Agency had rented a house next door to where Mavich and the Soviets were holding Dr. Sobokov. A little too close, Wynter thought, for comfort. If Mavich knew how close they were to him, and how dearly they wanted Dr. Sobokov back, he might pack up in the middle of the night and make a run for it. If that happened, Wynter would have a terrible decision to make—intercept, and risk the lives of not only his men but also Dr. Sobokov, or let them go. Both seemed like bad options to him.

The house where he was staying was festooned with photos of the Yucatan jungle and intricate, detailed diagrams of the Mayan ruins. That was their official cover: archaeologists doing research for a book, retreating from the jungle where they'd been doing field work in order to actually write the book. True, there were no ruins particularly close to Cuernavaca, but it wasn't uncommon for artists and writers to rent houses in Cuernavaca. If anyone pushed them, Wynter could explain how a few weeks among the insects, snakes, and other creepy crawly things beneath the jungle canopy could make anyone yearn for modern conveniences. So far, no one had asked, and he was very much hoping that things stayed that way.

PASSPORT TO DANGER

"Any movement?" said Alex Connor, coming into the kitchen where Wynter had arrayed a map of the house next door. Wynter shook his head at Connor's appearance—the man had gone all in on their cover story, and was wearing a ridiculous field vest and an oversized sunhat.

"You know, not every mission has to be Halloween," he said, turning back to the map. When he glanced back up after a moment, Connor looked hurt. "Ah, hell, don't you get mopey on me."

"You're the one who decided we should be archaeologists even though we're a hundred miles from the nearest ruin of interest," Connor said.

"Fair enough," Wynter said. "No movement at all. They're still waiting on Nicola."

"That's good news, right?" Connor said. Wynter gave him a curt nod.

"We still don't know exactly what Elizabeth is going to be walking into when she gets here tomorrow," he said. "But I haven't seen anything that makes me think we need to change course."

Connor was quiet for a moment, chewing on the inside of his lip the way he did when he was thinking something but unsure of whether or not to say it. When Wynter had first met Connor, he'd thought this was an unacceptable quirk for someone in his line of work: Why let somebody know what you were thinking when you could otherwise conceal your true feelings? But in the years that they had worked together, Wynter had come to realize that this was Connor's way of being tactful; he was telling you that something was wrong, and it was up to you to ask him what it was. Usually, asking was a good idea; Connor was a perceptive analyst, and often saw things that others didn't. In this case, however, Wynter was pretty sure he knew what the man was going to say.

"Be honest with me," Wynter said. "What odds do you give this plan of working?"

Connor looked momentarily surprised by the question, but then took a seat and put his chin in his fingers, thinking hard.

"Worse than a coin flip," Connor said. "Maybe much worse, because I can think of lots of different ways that this blows up in our faces, and I'm having a hard time thinking of ways that it actually works."

"If we get lucky," Wynter said. "And if Elizabeth does what I think she can."

"You're putting a lot of trust in a woman who was, at this time last week, a high fashion model who'd never heard of Dr. Sobokov."

"I'm in the talent identification business," Wynter said. "No matter where that talent comes from."

"I guess I was just hoping you'd come up with another idea by the time we got down here," Connor said. Wynter allowed himself a single, long sigh.

"So did I," he said. The two men went back to poring over the map of the house next door, walking themselves through what might happen, and trying hard not to think only of everything that could go wrong.

Steve Brenner awoke with a sore back and the smell of coffee suffusing through the little hotel room. Sunlight was streaming through the open window where the curtains had been drawn back, and Elizabeth was sitting in a chair across the room, sipping a cup of coffee and reading a newspaper. When she heard him stir, she fixed him with a smile and brought him a cup of coffee.

PASSPORT TO DANGER

"What time is it?" Steve said, sitting up and wiping the sleep from his eyes.

"Still early," Elizabeth said. "I figured I'd let you sleep a little. You looked like you needed it. Milk, no sugar, right?"

Steve gratefully accepted the cup of coffee as Elizabeth perched herself on the edge of the bed and looked thoughtfully down at him.

"Any interesting dreams?" she asked. Steve chuckled and shook his head. He was grateful that the answer was no—all the last week, his nights had been haunted by the specter of his dead brother, and a shadowy figure just on the edges of his perception that he was pretty sure was Nicola Neumann, coming to taunt him once more. But Elizabeth didn't need to hear any of that, and so he sipped his coffee.

"We should get going soon," he said, rubbing his neck.

"Bags are packed," Elizabeth said. "I'm ready when you are, dear."

Steve chuckled at the thought of returning to their guise as a young couple on their honeymoon. At this moment, he felt anything but carefree. He finished his coffee and shuffled over to the bathroom.

They managed to get out of Monterrey without getting lost, Elizabeth with her nose in the road atlas and Steve driving slowly along the narrow, rutted roads. They drove through a pleasant valley circled by verdant hills, with the Sierra Madres soaring in the background. Strung along the road were small homes with thatched roofs; potted flowers were scattered in front of many of the homes, their bright colors riotous against the drab adobe.

The shoulder of the road was crowded with villagers, and Steve slowed down, worried one of them might inadvertently wander onto the highway. Elizabeth looked on with interest as they passed; several women carried pails of water on their heads; others, with babies secured to their backs by rebozos, drove burros laden with produce to the market in the next village. An old man, dressed in worn but clean clothes, was perched on a rickety cart with wooden wheels, drawn by ancient white oxen. Women with piles of colorful laundry in their arms were taking their clothes to a stream to be washed.

They all waved to Elizabeth as the big car passed, but the brown-eyed children playing in the dust in front of their homes waved the hardest, yelled out *Buenos días!* the loudest. Elizabeth waved back, warmed by their friendliness. Steve, she noticed, kept his eyes firmly fixed on the road ahead of them and did not respond to their warm entreaties.

The valley floor widened, with the Sierra Madres receding until only their jagged peaks were still visible. Off to her left, a small lake reflected grassy slopes and the deep blue of the sky. To her right, orange trees with golden globes like tiny moons masked the softly curving hills. The breeze blowing in the car window smelled like oranges and spring flowers.

"It's beautiful here," Elizabeth said.

Steve made some soft noise of distracted assent but said nothing further. He seemed even more tense than yesterday, coiled like he was waiting for something to go wrong. Elizabeth wondered if it was the night spent on the hardwood floor of the hotel room that had caused this apparent discomfort, or if he, too, was thinking about what still lay ahead of them. She decided to leave him to his silence; they still had a long drive ahead of them.

They passed through Ciudad Victoria, with field after field of agave, then through Mante, with miles of golden green sugar cane rippling like satin in the light breeze. They were up in the mountains now; the ascending road appeared as a ribbon, then as a thread, and finally disappeared as the mountains piled up, one upon the other. The rich green valley far below gradually turned to purple and blue in the haze of the distance. The air smelled fresh and cool. The steep mountainsides were carpeted with crops, farmers dotting the landscape as the tiny figures moved slowly along their fields.

The road was descending now, twisting and turning like a corkscrew. In a very short time, she would metamorphosize into Nicola Neumann. She wondered if that would make this all feel more real; the long hours in the car had brought on a sense of unreality, that this strange series of events was more like some waking dream than anything else.

They were on their way to Valles, where they were scheduled to spend the night, when Steve Brenner took an unexpected exit. Elizabeth frowned down at the atlas, and then back up at Steve.

"Do you know some kind of Mexican short cut that isn't showing up on my map?" she said.

Steve shook his head.

"Do you trust me?"

Elizabeth sighed.

"Is this some kind of plan to convince me not to go through with this?" she said. "Because if it is, you're wasting your time."

"I know that," Steve said with a small smile. "I'm through trying to change your mind. But there's something I want you to see first."

Elizabeth settled back into her seat, curious and a little apprehensive. In their brief time together, Steve had never struck her as the impulsive type—what else, she wondered, would she discover about this man?

For a time, they drove along the rutted mountain roads. But then, almost so suddenly as to make her wonder how it was possible, they found themselves in a beautiful little village. It was a tropical place yet surrounded by mountains, cloaked with luxuriant forests full of multi-hued flowers and tropical birds that flashed through the trees.

Steve brought the car to a stop in the middle of the small town square and killed the engine. He looked over at Elizabeth with a little smile on his face.

"What is this place?" she asked.

"Tamazunchale," he said.

"What a paradise," she said.

"Come on," Steve said. "We have time for a walk."

"But Wynter…"

"We'll be quick," Steve said. "And for all he knows, we just got caught behind a particularly stubborn burro on the road. Trust me. The phone call can wait."

Steve got out of the car, and after a moment's hesitation, Elizabeth joined him. Side by side, they walked through the little village. It was early evening, and the street was crowded with men and women walking briskly or riding bicycles, heading home after a long day of work. White-washed houses were covered with crimson bougainvillea, and every yard had a fruit tree or two—oranges, lemons, and other citruses that Elizabeth couldn't identify. The sweet scent of rose, jasmine, and magnolia filled the air.

"It's gorgeous," Elizabeth said after they'd been walking for a time.

"I thought you'd like it," Steve said.

"It would be nice to stay here for a while," she said. "Rent a little house. Spend all morning reading in bed with a pot of strong coffee. Go for long walks. Not worry about getting back in time for anything, because there would be nothing to get back for. Doesn't that sound nice?"

"I'd go crazy, after a while," Steve said with a little smile. "The truth is that I'm much better at working than I am at relaxing. Even when Wynter yanked me out of the French Riviera, I pretended to be annoyed. But there was a part of me that was excited, too, because it meant that something important was happening, and that I got to be part of it. I don't really know how to turn off that part of myself."

"Maybe when all of this is done, we can come back here," Elizabeth said, "and I can teach you a thing or two about relaxing."

"Last I heard, you'd been working yourself to the bone on those photo shoots for the past three years," Steve said. "I'm not sure you're exactly an expert on doing nothing."

"But I'm a very quick study," Elizabeth said, "especially when I'm passionate about the subject matter."

Steve gave a little laugh at that and reached out to take Elizabeth's hand. Her hand felt small in his, but surprisingly strong, with a firm grip that made him wonder how much of her bravado was a show that she was putting on before tomorrow. But was the show for him, or for her? He couldn't quite tell.

"Thank you for bringing me here," Elizabeth said. She looked quickly around the street and, seeing no one, came in for a quick kiss. Steve smiled, and then shook his head.

"Come on," he said. "Let's get you to Valles before Wynter has a stroke."

• • •

Once they'd reached their hotel, Steve called Wynter to let him know that they had made it. The plan was for them to spend the night, and then drive on to Mexico City the next morning. There, Elizabeth would transform into Nicola Neumann and get a different car to drive herself to Cuernavaca.

"You still don't think I should drive her?" Steve said. "I don't like the idea of her alone on these roads."

"She'll be safer if she isn't seen driving into the city with anyone else," Wynter said.

"Only if she makes it there in one piece," Steve said. "These roads are hell."

"Steve," Wynter said. Steve Brenner sighed.

"Right. Get her to Mexico City. Get her to the car. Let her do the rest."

"She can do this, you know," Wynter said.

"You really believe that, Bill?"

"I wouldn't be doing this if I didn't."

Brenner let his head lean back until he was resting against the wall of the phone booth.

"Yeah, alright. I'll call tomorrow."

At dinner, Steve and Elizabeth shared a bottle of wine. Her bright, talkative mood from earlier in the trip had dimished; she seemed distracted, looking around the restaurant as though expecting to see someone watching them.

"It's starting to feel more real," she said after a time.

"I know what you mean."

"Where will you be, once I leave you?"

PASSPORT TO DANGER

"I'm going to follow you down to Cuernavaca," Steve said. "Far enough away so no one would suspect we were traveling together. Bill's got a house close to where Mavich has things set up. I'll be right next door the whole time."

"Mavich doesn't strike me as a man who enjoys nosy neighbors."

"Bill's got a whole cover story cooked up. Something about Mayan ruins? Apparently Connor's driving him nuts, playacting as an archaeologist."

This was enough to get a laugh from Elizabeth, who shook her head and took another sip of the wine.

"I can just imagine that," she said. "I bet Connor did some acting back in school. They're an odd couple, aren't they, Bill and Alex?"

"That they are," Steve said. "But it seems to work for them. Bill's at his best when he's got someone to point out the things he might be missing. Most men I know aren't willing to put up with that. It bruises their egos, and the agency is full of delicate egos."

"We got lucky, then, to have him running the show."

"I wouldn't trust anyone else."

"Well, then."

Steve paused for a moment, and then raised his wine glass.

"I just want you to know, whatever happens over the next few days, I will always be grateful for this time together," he said, "and I'll be waiting for you on the other side, ready to go wherever you want."

"I'll think on that," Elizabeth said with a small smile. "I'm beginning to suspect I might have to tell my friend Susan that she'll have to go onto Greece without me."

"Yeah?" Steve said. Elizabeth nodded.

"I think I have another travel companion I'd rather spend my time with," she said. They clinked their glasses and tried their best to enjoy the rest of their meal, ignoring everything that was looming before them.

In the morning, they woke early and began the drive to Mexico City in the half-light of dawn. They were quiet for the long miles, the only sound the bumping of the car against the road and the breeze whistling through the open window. Elizabeth watched the odometer closely as they passed the mile marker outside the city; Bill Wynter had given the specific directions about picking up her car. After two and a half miles, she directed Steve down a narrow alleyway until they came to a garage, its metal door still rolled down. Elizabeth slipped the blonde wig off her head, shook out her natural dark hair, and fixed Steve with another smile. *She is such a beautiful woman*, Steve thought. He wondered if he would ever see her again.

"Well, this is me," she said lightly. "Thanks for the ride."

"Be careful, Elizabeth," he said.

"I will."

She came across the center console and kissed him.

"I love you," she said.

"I love you, too," he said.

And then she was out of the car, rapping three times on the metal door. For a moment, no answer came. But soon, with a creaking, groaning sound, the metal door began to open. Elizabeth slipped inside. Steve waited in the car until he heard the sound of an engine starting, and then a rust-colored Datsun sedan pulled out in front of him. Steve raised a hand in a wave, and from the other car Elizabeth gave a cheery toot of the sedan's horn. He watched the car recede in a growing cloud of dust. Elizabeth turned the corner, and then she was gone.

It was a little under two hours to Cuernavaca. As Elizabeth drove, she tried to shed all vestiges she could of her former life. She wasn't sure that this was going to work, or if they would make her the moment she sat down at the restaurant where they had arranged to meet. But if she had any chance, it had to be Nicola Neumann who sat down, not Elizabeth Lamont. So gone were her parents, dead now for nearly twenty years; gone, too, her grandmother. Gone was boarding school in Quebec, her time at college, and the three years she had spent modeling. Gone were the friends and colleagues she had made along the way. Gone, most painfully, was Steve Brenner, the man she was beginning to suspect may just be the love of her life. All that remained was the East German agent with cold eyes and a colder heart, and everything she had seen and read about in that file. Elizabeth felt a shiver run down her spine as she drove along the road. She'd find out soon, one way or another, if she was fooling anyone.

CHAPTER FOURTEEN

Elizabeth Lamont could feel a bead of sweat falling slowly down the back of her leg as she sat at a table on the terrace of Las Mañanitas restaurant. The warm day alone couldn't account for how she was feeling; she tried to flag down a passing waiter to ask for something cool to drink, and then remembered Bill Wynter's warning about drinking the local water, even from a fancy place like Las Mañanitas. So instead, she looked out onto the beautiful, smooth lawn, the dazzling flowers whose sweet scent perfumed the air, and the peacocks preening as they moved across the soft grass. Elizabeth would have been relaxed and happy if she had been waiting here for Steve Brenner, and if this had been her actual honeymoon. But Steve was now with Bill and the other CIA men, and here she was, waiting for one of Mavich's men to pick her up.

She had called the house as soon as she'd arrived in Cuernavaca. She told the person who answered the phone that she was Nicola Neumann, and that she would wait at Las Mañanitas for half an hour, no longer. She'd hung up before the man had a chance to speak, afraid that if she talked much longer he'd be able to detect her nervousness. Elizabeth glanced at her watch; the call had been twenty minutes ago. If no one showed up by the time she had set, was she really meant to leave? She thought back to Alex

PASSPORT TO DANGER

Connor's story of chasing the *real* Nicola Neumann all around the Caribbean, the cautious way she had tried to stay a step ahead of both the CIA and whoever else was chasing her. Yes, she decided; if no one showed, she would leave the restaurant and try again somewhere else. She'd have to work herself into a real lather to dress down whoever it was who had missed her pickup; she wondered, for perhaps the hundredth time that day, whether she was really up for all this.

Who, she wondered, *would Mavich send?* None of the men in the dossiers that she and Steve had reviewed on the drive seemed like particularly savory characters. She was simply hoping that it wouldn't be Boris Caslov—reading through his file had made her blood run cold, particularly his history with women. She'd gotten lucky during her time in the modeling industry—while the advances from men hoping for more than a professional relationship were frequent, no one had ever gotten aggressive with her when she politely turned down their entreaties. She knew that not all girls—most girls, really, even those who weren't in the industry—had been so fortunate. She could only imagine the things Caslov had done that *didn't* make it into his official file.

Elizabeth decided she would like that drink, after all. She glanced around the terrace, hoping to catch the attention of a passing waiter, and instead found herself staring at a man who had just emerged from the restaurant. He paused in the shade of a large tree, his eyes passing from table to table, until he finally spotted her. He was tall, athletic, with lean and broad shoulders. As he came into the sunlight, she noticed his blond hair. It was Nikolai Mavich.

Elizabeth could scarcely believe her eyes; it had never occurred to her that Mavich would come himself to collect her. He paused to speak with the maître d', and she tried to get herself under control. The men back in Virginia had spoken about Mavich with a kind of begrudging reverence—he was an excellent spymaster, and not an enemy to be trifled with. She'd been more apprehensive about meeting him than anyone else. If she didn't get a hold of herself quickly, she'd ruin the whole operation.

She studied him carefully as he began to make his way over to her table. Although she knew he was thirty-five from his file, she wouldn't have thought he was a day over thirty if she didn't know better. He was dressed in a light-blue blazer with a scarf around his neck and dark blue slacks. The cut of his clothing was excellent. His skin was the color of light copper, an attractive contrast with his blond hair. As he made his way across the terrace, he moved with the smooth, lazy grace of a leopard. *And probably as dangerous as one, too*, Elizabeth thought to herself. He passed a table of women who were watching him admiringly, but he didn't seem to notice them. Maybe he was used to having women stare at him. In her old life, maybe he and Elizabeth could have discussed what that was like. But then, in her old life, why on Earth would she be talking to a man like Mavich?

He nodded to Elizabeth when he reached the table, and now she could see his eyes. They were an intense, startling blue: very clear, very compelling, and very cold. He sat down across from her, and then said, in excellent Spanish, "I see you recognize me." His voice was as cold as his eyes.

Elizabeth nodded, not trusting herself to speak yet. She was so nervous that she was sure her voice would shake. Nicola Neumann would hardly be nervous; she'd be relaxed, and flirtatious. Although, Elizabeth suspected that even Nicola might find it hard to flirt with this iceberg.

Mavich glanced down at the menu. "You haven't had lunch," he said. A statement, Elizabeth noticed, not a question. The moment he turned around, the maître d' himself came over to take his order. Mavich glanced back at Elizabeth.

"I think you would like the vichyssoise and the chicken curry. Both are excellent."

"Sounds wonderful, thank you," Elizabeth said, trying to sound cool, and immensely relieved that her voice hadn't quavered yet.

Mavich glanced up at the Mexican. "Make that two."

The maître d' asked Mavich if he wanted wine. Mavich nodded, and as the two men reviewed the wine list, Elizabeth watched him, glad for the chance to observe him unnoticed. His chiseled features were aloof and remote, with no sign of warmth or humor. And yet, he was an attractive man: high cheekbones, straight nose, a strong, clean-cut jaw, and those brilliant blue eyes. He had an air of cold authority about him, the air of one who has long been accustomed to immediate—and unquestioning—obedience.

As soon as the maître d' left, Mavich turned back to Elizabeth, his sharp, penetrating eyes studying her carefully. She met his gaze for a brief moment, but realized she wouldn't be able to fool this man for long. She glanced away, pretending to watch a couple throwing a frisbee in the swimming pool, hoping Mavich wouldn't notice her worry.

"You arrived in Mexico this morning?"

Elizabeth looked at him sharply, catching her breath. Was this a test? If he thought she'd arrived today, he must had been apprised of Nicola's arrangements for coming into the country. Wynter had been hoping he wouldn't know anything about them. She tried to keep her voice as cold as his when she replied.

"I didn't come in this morning," she said. She waited, and Mavich arched an eyebrow.

"Well?"

"I came in the night before last, and spent the better part of the night bouncing in a truck from Tampico to Valles," she said, letting a note of annoyance creep into her voice.

"Tampico?" Mavich questioned. He was staring at her with narrowed eyes.

Again Elizabeth felt a bead of sweat make its way slowly down her back. Obviously, Nicola had not planned to come in through Tampico. That was most unfortunate.

"We got word the Mexicans had set up roadblocks out of Vera Cruz, so I had to improvise."

"Roadblocks? Were they tipped off about you?"

"Hardly," Elizabeth said, doing her best to sound indignant. But secretly, she had never been more relieved—Wynter was right when he said that Nicola would come in through either Tampico or Vera Cruz. "Who would tip them off? No one knew when I was coming, even you. The Mexicans are always looking for contraband in Vera Cruz. An inconvenience, but nothing more. Tampico was unbelievably hot, even at night."

Mavich didn't look very sympathetic. But then, she hadn't expected he would. His sharp eyes were watching her intently.

"I gather you came in along the coast. Then what?"

Elizabeth allowed herself a quick breath; she'd gotten over the first hurdle, anyway.

"A truck was waiting for me, and drove me to Valles. I spent the night in Tamazunchale, and came on to Cuernavaca this morning."

PASSPORT TO DANGER

Mavich was silent, as though tracing her progress on a private map that he kept locked in his head. Finally, he shook his head.

"I'm a little surprised they didn't arrange a plane to pick you up in Tampico."

Elizabeth tried a scornful laugh.

"So am I. Would have been a damn lot more comfortable, and less of a hassle. But you know how these missions go."

"You must be tired after driving through those mountains," Mavich said. His voice could scarcely be called warm, but it was not quite as glacial as it had been at first.

"I'll feel better after I eat," Elizabeth said.

The waiter came towards them with a bottle of wine. He poured a small amount for Mavich to taste; when he nodded, the waiter filled their glasses. Elizabeth took a sip: cool, smooth, delicious. She leaned back in her chair and took a large gulp. Nicola, according to her file, was an excellent drinker. Elizabeth was glad for that detail now—she needed anything she could find to ease the nervous tension in her body.

Mavich was studying her openly now; Elizabeth half-expected him to ask her what she thought of the wine.

"You're not at all what I expected," he said suddenly.

Elizabeth nearly dropped her wine glass. She stared at him with wide eyes. Had he already made her out? If that was the case, what was she supposed to do now? She said nothing, trying to fight down her rising panic.

"I've often found that people's reputations have been exaggerated," Mavich continued. "In this case, I'm glad for it. I suspected you were going to be one of those bossy females who makes life miserable for everyone."

Elizabeth was astounded. He wasn't doubting her identity, just Nicola's reputation. She felt almost lightheaded with relief.

Mavich leaned forward on his elbows and spoke in barely a whisper—time, Elizabeth guessed, for business.

"When does the Leningrad arrive in Cuba?"

"In three days. It leaves again on the fourth, at night. Midas wants you to board it in the evening, right before it sails."

Mavich nodded.

"Makes sense. He wants our friend in Cuba for as short a time as possible."

He saw the waiter coming towards them with their soup and was silent until they had been served.

"Did Midas send any messages?" he asked.

Elizabeth, fortunately, had been prepared for this question.

"He wants to know why you broke radio contact."

Mavich's blue eyes became colder, if that was even possible. He spoke now in a low hiss, full of loathing.

"When I see Midas, I'll tell him why myself. His stupidity has gotten me into an incredible mess. I kept asking him for something, and he kept stalling. Because of him, the Mexicans had time to track down my radio."

Elizabeth did her best to look horrified.

"Do they have it?"

Mavich nodded grimly.

"Fortunately, my operator had time to destroy all the tapes and messages."

He was wrong about that, but Wynter would be delighted to learn that Mavich thought they did. Mavich didn't know that the operator had forgotten to destroy one message; either he had overlooked it, or he had been afraid to tell Mavich the truth, which was certainly understandable: You wouldn't want to report any sort of failure to this man.

"I don't suppose the Mexicans could have decoded your tapes, anyway," Elizabeth said.

"Maybe not, but the Americans could. If the Mexicans had discovered a tape they couldn't decode, they probably would have given it to the Americans, and that would have been...awkward. For all of us."

"Yes," Elizabeth said, nodding her head. She decided to try to change the subject. "By the way, how is...our friend?"

Mavich frowned.

"Not so good. When he discovered what Midas was really up to, he became quite angry, and uncooperative. I can't say I blame him. Midas has handled this whole operation poorly, which is standard procedure for him these days. I can only guarantee he'll be finished after this fiasco." Mavich laughed sardonically. "A plan like this, given the special importance of our friend, requires genius planning and scrupulous attention to detail. Midas is neither a genius nor particularly concerned with details. If we do get our friend to Moscow, it will be because the Americans gave him to us, and I'm afraid they aren't nearly fond enough of us to do that."

Elizabeth stared at him for a moment. Did this mean that Steve Brenner was right, and Sobokov really had been kidnapped? Or perhaps lured under a false premise? Either way, she couldn't believe what she was hearing: Why would a man as important as Nikolai Mavich go on a futile mission?

"If you thought things were this bad, then why are you here?"

Mavich once again arched an eyebrow at her.

"Because I'm getting paid a considerable amount of money."

Elizabeth looked shocked.

"Don't play the pious little party member with me," he said. "I know how much you enjoy the fringe benefits that come with this line of work."

Elizabeth sipped her soup, thinking quickly. This was a facet of Nicola's personality that Wynter hadn't known: Nicola was not a dedicated Communist. Maybe that was why she had been hoping to defect in the first place—maybe she had been sincere when she talked to Connor back in San Juan. Elizabeth made a mental note to incorporate this new information into how she acted going forward.

"If Midas wasn't paying me, I wouldn't have dreamed of getting involved in this mess. But, under these circumstances, I decided it was worth the gamble, and I like a challenge. I didn't realize that Midas would underestimate the Americans—as stupid as he is, I thought he would have more sense than that. Apparently, I was wrong."

"You aren't expecting trouble from the Americans, are you?" Elizabeth said. "They don't even know where our friend is."

Mavich regarded her mockingly.

"Don't be too sure of that."

The waiter arrived with two steaming plates of curry. Elizabeth sipped her wine, keeping silent until the waiter had moved on to the next table.

"What makes you think the Americans might have located you?"

"I'm not certain they have, but a few things make me wonder. I wouldn't be surprised—Midas may underestimate them, but I don't. The Mexicans finding my radio was innocent enough, given that Midas kept demanding updates and giving me nothing that I needed. But by now, the Mexicans have undoubtedly given all the equipment they seized to the Americans. I'm sure that's aroused their curiosity, and right after my radio was located, two men moved into the house to the left of ours. It's always empty this time of year; the owners live in France, and they're rich, so they don't even bother to rent it. Put that together with another few trifling incidents. Nothing particularly important, until you start adding it all up."

Mavich is adding it up all right, Elizabeth thought in dismay. *And coming up with all the right answers.*

"Why would the Mexicans give the equipment to the Americans?" she asked.

"The Mexicans would want to know who manufactured the equipment, and the Americans could tell them."

"But even if the Americans have your equipment, that doesn't mean they know where you are."

"True," Mavich said. His intent blue eyes were studying her. He seemed to be waiting for her to continue.

"Maybe the two men in the next house are relatives of the family," Elizabeth said. She nearly said "archeologist," and that would have ruined everything; Nicola had no way of knowing that information. She was surprised Mavich hadn't sent someone over to find out himself. "The timing of the radio seizure and the arrival of the men is probably a coincidence."

Mavich's lips curled into a wry smile.

"Most people in our profession don't believe in coincidences."

Elizabeth had no answer for that. She took a sip of wine to cover her silence. *You just made a terrible blunder,* she told herself angrily. What had Wynter told her? She had to think like a member of the KGB, and Mavich *was* right about these seeming coincidences. By trying to convince him that his instincts were wrong, she'd endangered her own position.

Elizabeth gave him a warm, charming smile.

"The world is full of coincidences," she said, "even if we refuse to acknowledge them for the sake of our own preservation. An occupational hazard, I suppose. Have you checked on the two men?"

Mavich shook his head, looking at her reflexively.

"You know, you're not at all like I thought you'd be."

Elizabeth's eyes turned cold as she glanced up at him—if he wanted the Nicola he thought he knew, this was the time to give her to him.

"What can you possibly tell about a person by reading a file? Maybe you've spent too long in the shadows, but when I'm on assignment, I'm acting a role. That's what you've seen, if you've seen any of my work: an act, and a damn good one. As for my file, suffice it to say that some of those reports are biased—sometimes for me, sometimes against me, depending on who wrote what and whether I could get to them first. You can't believe everything you read. I certainly didn't believe everything I read in yours."

Surprise showed in the intense blue eyes. Then Mavich laughed; a real laugh, not the bitter chuckles he'd offered her earlier. For a very brief moment, Elizabeth thought she could catch a glimpse of the man he might have been—attractive, warm, and personable—if he had chosen a different profession, but he hadn't. She must never forget, even for a single moment, that this man was a cold, hard machine, one who would dispose of her without a second thought if he ever doubted her identity.

Over dessert and coffee, Mavich questioned Elizabeth thoroughly about the details of her trip. Wynter had been right about his interest; this man was thorough. As she ate her pie, Elizabeth wondered if he was going to check out her story. Probably. It was just as well they had taken such elaborate precautions.

Mavich paid the bill and stood to leave. For a moment, Elizabeth remained seated, feeling relieved that the meal had gone well enough. Once more, Mavich arched an eyebrow.

"You're coming, yes?"

Elizabeth would have liked nothing more than to remain seated, order herself another glass of wine, and spend the rest of the day looking languidly at the tourists in the pool and thinking about absolutely nothing at all. But instead, she fixed Mavich with a small smile and stood.

"I hope your car is more comfortable than the back of a vegetable truck with a shot suspension."

"Will a Mercedes suffice?" Mavich said, obviously proud of his car.

Elizabeth brightened.

"I guess you were right—there *are* some perks that come with this line of work."

Again, Mavich allowed himself to laugh. As he lead her through the restaurant, Elizabeth could feel all the eyes of the diners following them out. She wondered what they must have thought of them; a young, attractive couple out to lunch together. *If you only knew*, she thought, as he led her to the waiting sedan that the valet had brought around to the front.

CHAPTER FIFTEEN

Nikolai Mavich was silent as he threaded the Mercedes through the narrow streets of Cuernavaca. Elizabeth looked out the window, trying to appear as if she had nothing more important on her mind than taking in the local scenery. Despite the way her heart was still thudding its berserk tempo against her ribcage, she couldn't help but notice that the city was beautiful: an extensive tropical garden, flowers of every variety and color imaginable, red tile roofs looming up among the ancient trees that shaded the houses from the warm sun. The walls of the houses bordering the streets were painted in bright colors—red, blue, yellow, green—and covered with bougainvillea, poinsettia, and large orange blossoms she had never seen before. Wynter had her read about the history of the city: It had been little more than a village before the Spaniards came, but after the conquest, Cortes had built himself a Governor's palace, now the state legislature. He had also introduced sugarcane from Cuba, and started the first sugar mill on the continent. Cuernavaca had begun to grow. When Maximillian was Emperor, he and his wife, Carlotta, had come here to relax. Ever since, it had been one of Mexico's resorts, popular for its balmy climate, old-world charm, and beautiful setting.

PASSPORT TO DANGER

Hardly the first place you'd think to look for a missing nuclear scientist, Elizabeth thought to herself. Suddenly, over the tops of the buildings and trees, Elizabeth saw the Baroque tower of the Franciscan church. Two stories of richly carved arches and pilasters crowned by a slender dome and lantern. The church dominated the city; everything else seemed small in contrast. It was easy to imagine the Spaniards in their armor, monks in their plain habits, and the royalty in their beautiful clothes gathering in the church for Mass while the subdued Mexicans huddled outside the church, awaiting their own Mass. It had been a brutal time, but Elizabeth sometimes thought it must have been less complicated then, absent of the looming threat of nuclear annihilation.

The car whispered through a tunnel of trees as it climbed a hill towards a residential area. *We must be getting close to the house,* Elizabeth thought, remembering the map laid out back at the house in Virginia. *But,* she reminded herself, *Nicola wouldn't have the faintest idea where we are. She'd be interested, though—wouldn't she?*

"Lovely," Elizabeth said, trying her best to sound droll. "Are we up here?"

"About a mile," Mavich said.

"Do you like the house?"

Mavich shot her a quick glance.

"It's comfortable," he said. "We have a tennis court, and a pool. No one could complain about that. The meals, though... the gardener, who lives on the property, has been acting as our chef. What he knows about cooking wouldn't make a sentence in a cookbook."

Elizabeth laughed lightly.

"Well, I'm glad I won't be around too long to enjoy his gourmet dinners."

Mavich glanced at her sharply.

"Back to Cuba?" he said.

Elizabeth shook her head.

"I've just come from that delightful island, and I don't ever intend to go back, if I can help it."

"So you aren't coming with us."

"I don't see why I would. Another person would just attract more attention."

Mavich frowned.

"I'd heard you might get recalled to Moscow, to be briefed for another mission."

Elizabeth studied the man behind the wheel for a moment—was this a test of some kind, or simply the back and forth between two agents, trying to show the other just how well they had mapped the territory? It was a shame, she thought, that Wynter wasn't here to enjoy these little surprises. If he had his way, soon she would set up the microphones that she had secreted in her luggage, allowing him to hear everything that went on in the house. But until then, she would have to rely on her memory, and her instincts.

"They've decided on someone else, thankfully. I'm being given a vacation."

Mavich looked vaguely surprised.

"You're fortunate. I can't remember my last vacation."

"They must not be keeping you busy, then," Elizabeth said.

Mavich gave a bark of laughter, and tightened his grip on the steering wheel. The car swung to the left, and just ahead, Elizabeth could see two intricately carved wooden gates swinging open to admit the Mercedes. Just before they went through, she thought she could see, in the window of the house they passed, a familiar face looking down on her from underneath a Panama hat. But that could just have been her imagination.

"Mavich went to pick her up himself," Alex Connor said from his posting by the window, not taking his eyes off the black sedan as it sped towards the Soviets' safehouse. Wynter and Brenner hurried next to him, the three men staring at the receding taillights as the gates swung closed behind the car.

"How could you tell?" Brenner said, craning his neck to see if he could get one last look at the car ferrying Elizabeth into danger.

"I got a decent view of the driver, for one thing," Connor said, "and for another, he doesn't let anyone else drive the Mercedes. He loves that car. I reckon he'll be sorry to leave it behind."

"Maybe we can offer him a trade," Wynter said. "He keeps the car. We get the scientist back. Everyone wins."

"Something tells me they don't drive Mercedes in the gulag," Connor said.

Wynter chuckled and said something about icy roads, but Steve Brenner was still looking out the window at the compound. He couldn't see anything, but he knew that even now, Elizabeth would be getting out of the car, preparing to convince the waiting men that she really was Nicola Neumann.

"You think Mavich bought it?" he said, trying to keep the anxiety out of his voice.

"Would he have brought her into the house if he didn't?" Connor said.

A long silence threatened to engulf the room after that comment, and Connor wished to hell he had kept his mouth closed. True, if Mavich had suspected something, he might well have left Elizabeth in the restaurant, not risking bringing a mole into his operation. But all three men at the window knew that, more likely than not, if he suspected her, he would have brought her back to the house with him to be disposed of quietly, and privately. The thought sent a chill down Brenner's spine.

"We'll have a team in place around the clock, from now until Elizabeth leaves the compound," Wynter said. "Any sign that things are going wrong, I'll send them in."

"How will we know?" Brenner said.

"Once she manages to get the microphones up and running, that should give us all the intel we need to properly assess the situation."

"*If* she manages to set up the microphones without anyone noticing," Connor said. He looked at the faces of the two men next to him and cursed quietly. "I'm sorry, boys. I don't know what the hell's gotten into me."

"Go get some sleep, Connor," Wynter said. "You've been glued to that window for the better part of the day now. We'll need someone on watch the whole time."

Connor mumbled something about coffee and headed back into the rented house, leaving Steve Brenner and Bill Wynter alone in the little study, looking out over the compound.

"I wish like hell it was me in there instead of her," Steve Brenner said after a time. Wynter tucked his tongue into his cheek.

"No offense, Steve," Wynter said, "but you'd have a hard time impersonating Nicola Neumann, even on a good day."

Brenner allowed himself a little chuckle and went back to watching out the window.

"She's going to be all right," Wynter said.

"Yeah," Steve said, leaving unsaid all the reasons he couldn't bring himself to fully believe the old spymaster. "Yeah, of course."

PASSPORT TO DANGER

The black Mercedes went up the circular drive and stopped in front of a handsome one-story house. Vines and flowers decorated the warm beige walls; the ornate black wrought iron grills that covered the windows were a stunning contrast with the lighter plaster. In the yard were fruit trees, oaks, and a magnolia with the largest blossoms Elizabeth had ever seen. She was admiring the garden—roses, jasmine, japonicas, azaleas, and gardenias—when Mavich opened her door.

"Not a bad place to lay low for a little while," she said lightly as she emerged from the car.

"I've stayed in worse," Mavich said with a small grin. He extended a hand and led her towards the house.

As they approached the front door, Elizabeth felt a stab of fear go through her. Things with Mavich appeared to have gone alright so far, or the man was a top-notch actor, but her real challenge would begin once she was inside. The only comfort she could find was by reminding herself that Steve and Bill were close by. Once she got the microphones up and running, they would know everything that was happening with her.

Mavich swung open the heavy wooden door and ushered Elizabeth into the living room.

"Wait here," he said, crossing over to a pair of glass doors that opened to the veranda and disappearing outside.

Elizabeth took a deep breath. *I'm finally here, and already desperate to leave.* She quickly cast such a fleeting and rueful thought aside—there was no time for regret now, and it was too late to back out. She tried to calm herself by studying the living room and thinking of herself within the miniature version of the house that had been so lovingly assembled back at the house in Virginia. Here was the long, wide room she remembered with its enormous marble fireplace. The furniture was clearly expensive, and on the walls were several fine paintings, including one that looked suspiciously like a Renoir. The Soviets had to be paying a fortune for a place like this. It was worth it to them, though, if it meant getting Sobokov back to Moscow in one piece.

She scanned the room again, this time looking for a place that might conceal one of the microphones that Wynter had sent her in with. Her eye found a bunch of artificial roses sitting in a silver urn. The room was too large for one microphone, but the flowers were quite a distance from the dining room table. If she placed one microphone in the urn, and another under the table, any word spoken in the area would be clearly audible to Wynter. Elizabeth was surprised to find that her pulse had slowed considerably in the few minutes since she had entered the house. Being able to focus on a concrete task, even one as dangerous as placing microphones around a Soviet safehouse without attracting attention, quieted the more anxious parts of her mind. It had the feeling of a puzzle, and Elizabeth had always enjoyed a crossword.

She was admiring a beautifully carved antique desk when she heard Mavich's footsteps on the tile floor. He looked preoccupied as he picked up her suitcase.

"I'll show you to your room. You can change into something…a little more comfortable. Then I'll introduce you to the others."

They crossed the living room, through another pair of glass doors, and entered the first bedroom on the arcade. To Elizabeth's pleasant surprise, it was large and comfortable, decorated in bright blues and greens, with the scent of roses in the air. Mavich left her suitcase on the luggage rack, and for a horrible moment, Elizabeth was sure that he was going to undo the zipper and examine the contents inside. The tools that Wynter had given her were well concealed, but would an experienced spy be able to find them anyway?

But Mavich appeared to have other things on his mind. He turned quickly to leave, telling her at the door that he would see her in a few minutes.

As soon as Mavich had closed the door behind himself, Elizabeth collapsed onto a chair. She leaned her head back against the soft leather and let her eyes fall closed. It hadn't been two hours since she'd met Nikolai Mavich, but she was already exhausted. She rubbed a hand across her forehead; she needed a minute. When she opened her eyes again, she looked around the quiet room. She could not remember ever feeling quite so lonely, or so worried. There was a lot depending on her, and she knew she wouldn't be able to deceive Mavich for much longer. Wynter had warned her, but there was no way to prepare herself for just how clever and perceptive the Soviet agent really was.

Suddenly, she bolted upright. She had forgotten something of vital importance: Wynter had told her to check the room immediately for a hidden camera, a two-way mirror, or microphones. Maybe someone was watching her now, wondering why an experienced agent like Nicola Neumann would seem so exhausted and scared. Her eyes scanned the walls quickly—no mirror. She rose easily from the chair, trying to adopt the sure, casual way that she had seen Nicola move through the world, now conscious of the possibility that she was being watched. She glanced up at the ceiling—plaster, no recessed lights, which meant no camera, either. But that didn't mean there wasn't one hidden somewhere in the room. For the next few minutes she conducted a frantic search of the room, but found nothing. She allowed herself a moment's relief before she unlocked her suitcase and found her new jewelry box.

Wynter had given her this jewelry box as a gift just before they'd left Virginia for the Mexican border. She had known, even before he showed her how it worked and what it held, that this was no ordinary jewelry box—Bill Wynter didn't seem the type for sentimental gifts. The false bottom was easy enough to work; Elizabeth wondered if there were other, more complicated mechanisms that they only entrusted to more experienced operatives. But what was inside, from what she could tell, constituted the best gadgets that Langley—or whoever else Wynter was sourcing his gear from—had to offer.

To begin with, there was the bug detector, a special device designed to indicate the presence of any hidden listening devices that might be in the room. Elizabeth took it now and turned it on, listening as the little machine beeped to life. Standing in the center of the room, the sound was faint, but the noise grew more and more intense the closer she got to the bed. But even after a thorough check, she couldn't find anything. She stood for a moment, frustrated with herself—she was running out of time, and even if Mavich allowed a lady like Nicola the proper time to freshen up, she could sense that there was a limit to his patience that she would do well not to test.

As she brushed a lock of hair off her forehead, her eyes came to rest on the telephone on the small bedside table. She shook her head: *Of course that's where it would be*, she thought, annoyed with herself. She took a nail file from her purse, sat on her knees beside the bedside table, and, very carefully, picked up the phone. She stared at it, taking a deep breath. Very slowly, she turned the phone upside down, holding it in place with her knees as she unscrewed the bottom plate. She remembered how surprised she had been when Wynter told her that she'd have to check Nicola's room for electronic listening equipment. He never explained why Mavich wouldn't trust his courier, who was also a Soviet operative and ostensibly on the same side as him. *If these people can't trust each other, then they really are in trouble*, Elizabeth thought as she lifted the plate.

Apparently, they couldn't: there was the microphone. She pursed her lips as she studied the little bug carefully. Clearly, they weren't taking any chances with Nicola. Not only would the microphone pick up any word she said in the room, but also, if she made a call, the number would be recorded, and Mavich would be able to find out who she was calling. Elizabeth replaced the plate and returned the phone to the table. That meant no radioing Wynter from her room; she would need to find someplace else.

She glanced at her watch again. Enough time had gone by that Mavich was probably starting to wonder what had happened to her. She rushed to her suitcase and took out a pale green Dior dress with two pockets and quickly got changed. Then she found her makeup kit and removed a heavy gold compact. Beneath the powder was another false bottom, this one holding a set of tiny microphones, each scarcely bigger than a dime. She emptied the microphones into her pocket. She checked the hairbrush with the hollow handle, a small set of universal keys hidden within. Next, she unzipped a small plastic bag and removed what looked to be a fountain pen...but was actually a special gun that, if need be, could fire two bullets.

Elizabeth had actually scoffed when Wynter had shown her the pen-gun back in Virginia.

"Your lab techs have spent too much time reading James Bond novels," she said, holding the unloaded pen gingerly and wishing that she could leave it behind. Wynter had chuckled.

"Where do you think Flemming got the idea from?"

"But I couldn't possibly shoot anyone!"

"If you ever find yourself in a desperate situation, you'll be surprised what you can do," Wynter said. "Desperation strips the civilized veneer off a man and shows him what he really is."

It sounded like a line that Wynter had said many times before to skeptical assets before he'd sent them into the field. Elizabeth had stared at him then, thinking that he really did live in a different world from any she'd known. *But I'm in his world now*, she thought, as she looked down at the fountain pen in her hand, *and I'd do well to remember that*.

Finally, she reached for the pack of cigarettes that Wynter had sent her off with. These scared her more than anything else in the luggage, since four of them were secretly explosives. It was enough to put someone off smoking for good, and Elizabeth had never adopted the habit herself, despite the urgings of the "coaches" at the Elizabeth Arden farm who had told her that nicotine made for a delightful meal replacement. Still, she'd rather have them on her person than sitting in a suitcase, waiting for whoever was nosy enough to go through her belongings.

She was almost ready to leave, but before she did, she dug down under the clothes in her suitcase and found the revolver—Mavich would expect her to be armed, so she put it near the top of the luggage, under her nightgown, so that it would be easily found. Then she picked up the thin nylon string that one of Wynter's men had attached to a hinge and looped it around a small screw; if anyone opened the case, she would know.

PASSPORT TO DANGER

Elizabeth locked the case and gave one last look around the room. Nothing was out of order; everything was just as it should be. She steeled herself for the ordeal ahead and opened the door.

A man was standing just down the hall, half-hidden in the shadows that the afternoon sun cast through the windows. It wasn't Mavich; Elizabeth could tell that much, even from here. There was a casual, almost slouching arrogance about this man, his whole body held loose like an athlete before entering the ring. The man had a small, terrible grin on his face.

A wave of cold panic ran through Elizabeth as she realized who this was. Boris Caslov, the man she least wanted to be alone with out of the entire house full of ruthless killers and professionals. She thought back to his dossier, trying to think of anything helpful, and found herself only capable of remembering all the horrors that had filled his file.

The man began walking towards her. Elizabeth thought about retreating into the room and locking the door. *Surely she'd have time*, she thought. Perhaps she could scream, and draw the attention of the other men. But instead, she stayed where she was, frozen, unable to talk, unable to move.

"Hello, Nicola," Boris said as he approached her.

"What do you think you're doing here?"

He grinned wolfishly.

"I think you know," he said. His eyes raked her slowly. "Your reputation has spread far and wide."

Elizabeth took one step backwards, and then another. Boris was coming at her quickly, closing the distance. All at once, Elizabeth lunged back towards the room and tried to close the door.

But the door held. Boris Caslov's foot was holding it open, and then he was in her room, closing the door behind him.

CHAPTER SIXTEEN

Elizabeth was, for a moment, frozen in place, her eyes wide with alarm as she watched Caslov standing between her and the only way out of the room. She vividly remembered everything she had read about him in his dossier. Mavich had surprised her with a certain gentility, and lured her briefly into believing that the men in this house might not be as bad as Wynter warned. Now, it seemed, she was sorely mistaken.

It felt as though all the moisture in her mouth had suddenly run dry; her tongue felt like sandpaper. Her voice, when she spoke, barely sounded like her own.

She attempted her previous question, trying to keep the fear from her voice—trying to sound as cold, or as much like Nicola Neumann, as she could. "What do you think you're doing here?"

Caslov brandished the same predatory grin.

"You're much prettier than your pictures, you know," he said.

Elizabeth looked around the room for any possible means of escape. If she screamed, he'd probably just cover her mouth to shut her up—or worse. Besides, the walls were so thick that she doubted anyone would even hear her. She glanced over to her suitcase and thought about the revolver lying just beneath the surface. If she could get to it, then she could threaten him. If he really knew Nicola, then he'd believe that she'd have no problem shooting him. She just had to hope that he wouldn't call her bluff.

"I thought women liked to hear how pretty they look," Caslov said.

"While we discuss my appearance," she said, "do you mind if I get a cigarette?"

"There's no need to waste time with discussion," Caslov said. His mouth looked hungry.

Elizabeth's throat tightened.

"I think you'd better leave," she said. The luggage rack was still a good seven feet away—too far to make it without Caslov getting to her first. Still, it was her only option.

Caslov came slowly towards her.

"I'll leave, but only after..."

Elizabeth leapt for the suitcase, and for a moment, Caslov stayed where he was, surprised by the sudden movement. Then all at once, he was on her. Caslov snatched her collar and jerked her backwards. Elizabeth heard the sound of silk ripping—her Dior dress was torn from the collar to the armhole. Elizabeth screamed as she fought to get away from him, but Caslov just took a firmer grip on her dress, causing it to rip to the waist. For a split second, Elizabeth stared incredulously—was this really happening to her? Caslov used the pause to grip her arm, twisting it viciously behind her. She screamed in pain as he shoved her towards the bed.

Was this really how this was going to end? She hadn't spent even an hour inside the house. She hadn't managed to set up any of the microphones yet—Wynter and Steve and all the others would have no idea what was happening to her. For a moment, she considered the possibility that Caslov might actually kill her. It seemed almost preferable to whatever else he had planned.

The door crashed open. Caslov dropped Elizabeth's arm like it was a hot coal and spun around, standing still as a statue as he stared at the doorway. Elizabeth whirled around nearly as quickly, clutching her shredded dress, and saw Nikolai Mavich watching them.

Mavich's cold eyes slowly took in everything that was happening in the room. Elizabeth held her breath—she knew that Caslov's behavior had been tolerated before, that it wasn't enough to keep him out of the field. The spymaster leaned against the door frame, studying Caslov with his icy blue eyes. When he spoke, his voice was barely louder than a whisper.

"Don't ever go near this woman again," he said. "Don't even consider it."

Elizabeth heard the sound of footsteps. Behind Mavich came another man—Yuri Betrin, she was fairly sure of it, his hazel eyes grim and mouth a tight line.

"You stupid idiot," he said between his teeth. "We've got enough problems without you attacking this girl."

"She was going for her suitcase," Caslov said, trying to sound disinterested. The other two men looked at her.

"For my gun," Elizabeth said. "I was ready to put a hole in his head if it was the only way to stop him."

"You see?" Betrin said. "We would've had the Mexican police down on us like a pack of wolves if the neighbors reported gunfire, never mind the problem of hiding your body. What in the hell do you suppose our American friend would have told him? That we were having a tea party in here?" He studied Caslov silently, then added in a quieter voice, "When your lust overcomes your sanity, you become expendable. If she hadn't shot you, I would have. If I were you, I wouldn't forget that. Now get out of here."

PASSPORT TO DANGER

He stepped aside so Caslov could pass him. The man left quickly, without glancing at anyone. Betrin turned to Mavich.

"He may be frightened now, but I'm afraid he might give Nicola some more trouble after we've gone to bed."

"I'll be ready for him next time," Elizabeth said. "I knew what kind of man he was, but I thought he might extend basic courtesy to a fellow operative. A stupid misjudgment on my part. It won't happen again."

Mavich considered this, and nodded grimly. "Even so, we'll put you in the room next to Sobokov." He turned to Betrin. "Find Avilova. Tell him to pack so that Nicola can change rooms with him. Boris won't bother her if she's in our wing. Then bring me some medicine and a bandage for her shoulder."

Betrin glanced sharply at Elizabeth's shoulder, eying the ugly gash. His face tightened as he hurried out to find Avilova. From somewhere deep inside, past her hurt and fear, Elizabeth registered the unusual name: *Avilova*. There had been no Avilova in the dossiers that Wynter had given her. Was it possible that she had forgotten someone? Or perhaps it was a nickname that the men used for one in their ranks? If not, that meant there was someone in the house who Wynter didn't know about, and that was a dangerous thing, indeed.

Mavich went over to Elizabeth. He examined her cut carefully. Elizabeth hadn't moved; she was still looking at the floor, holding her dress tightly around her.

"It's not pretty, but it doesn't look too deep," Mavich said. "We'll get that taken care of in just a minute."

He left her for a moment, and then returned with a towel from the bathroom, draping it over her shoulders.

"Does it hurt much?"

Elizabeth shook her head.

"How did he do it?"

"I don't know," Elizabeth said softly. She could feel herself shivering, and try as she could, she couldn't stop. Somewhere deep in the back of her mind, she wondered what Nicola would do in a situation like this. *Probably kill the man herself,* Elizabeth thought.

"We'll make certain that Boris doesn't have an opportunity to get near you again," Mavich said.

Elizabeth forced herself to meet his eyes.

"I'm fine now. Thank you for getting the towel." She shook her head. "If you hadn't gotten here when you did, one of us would have ended up dead, and I wouldn't have let it be me."

Mavich tucked a tongue into his cheek and nodded, thinking.

"We were all worried about him trying something. I just didn't think he'd be so stupid, so quickly. Fortunately, Yuri saw him going towards your room and came to find me. I'm glad I didn't waste any time."

Mavich crossed over to her suitcase, flung open the top, and felt among her clothes until he found the revolver. He checked to see if it was loaded and then regarded it thoughtfully.

"Would you have used it?" he said.

"Only if he was too stupid to leave," Elizabeth said. "I don't want gunfire here anymore than you do. But judging by the look in his eye, I'd say he was willing to risk a bullet rather than leave of his own accord."

At that moment, Elizabeth remembered the fountain pen in her pocket, the one loaded with two small-caliber bullets. Could she have gotten to it, if it had come to that? Possibly…but what would have come after, when she had to explain to the others in the house what had happened, and how she ended up with such sophisticated spy equipment? (Would the other agents have known it was American? Could she have convinced them that it was something she had picked up in her travels? Lies on lies on lies.... Elizabeth couldn't believe that this was her life now.)

"You couldn't have scared Boris," Mavich said. "He would have taken the revolver from you, easily."

"Then it's a good thing you got here when you did," Elizabeth said.

Yuri Betrin returned with medicine and the bandage. He handed them to Mavich.

"Boris is in his room. Avilova is having a long talk with him. I doubt we'll see Boris for a while."

Mavich raised his eyebrows.

"So old Ivan scared him."

"He told Boris that if he bothered Nicola again, he would personally see that Boris spent the rest of his life in Siberia." Betrin glanced at Elizabeth. "You must have impressed him when you were working for him. He seems to hold you in the highest regard."

Elizabeth felt a cold chill run down her spine. She had never heard of an Ivan Avilova before. *But apparently, Nicola Neumann had.*

Mavich dismissed Betrin and watched as he closed the door behind himself. Then he turned to Elizabeth.

"Let me put some medicine on that cut," he said.

Elizabeth's eyes widened.

"There's no need for you to do that. I can manage."

"Sit down," he said. The air of authority that she had noticed when they first met was back. She did as she was told. He took the cap off the bottle and poured some of the sharp-smelling liquid onto a ball of cotton.

"This might sting," he said, and then dabbed the cut quickly but thoroughly. "If you were to get infected, we'd need to find a doctor, and we don't need any more attention right now."

"I understand," Elizabeth said.

"Good." He put the bandage on her shoulder. Once he was satisfied with his first aid work, he went to leave the room.

"I'll wait outside while you dress," he said. "Then I'll take you to meet the others. If you're ready."

"Of course," Elizabeth said, trying to sound as steely as she imagined Nicola might be. But would Nicola have ever let Caslov get so close in the first place? How would she have dealt with the situation? Not even an hour in the house and already Elizabeth felt like she was completely out of her depth.

At the door, Mavich paused for a moment.

"I'm sorry about all this," he said.

"Let's forget it," Elizabeth said.

Mavich shook his head grimly.

"If I forgot it, then I'd be forgetting that Boris is an idiot, and entirely undependable. I made that mistake already. I don't plan to make it again."

He left her, and then Elizabeth was alone again. She drew a deep breath and let it out slowly. She reached back and touched the bandage on her shoulder. She had gotten lucky that Mavich had intervened when he did. But there was also one good thing about Boris's attack: Elizabeth was being moved next to Dr. Sobokov. It was an unbelievable stroke of luck, even if it came freighted with danger.

PASSPORT TO DANGER

She changed her dress quickly, freshened her makeup, and combed her tousled hair. She was careful to transfer everything from her pockets to the new dress—now seemed like a perfect time to try and plant the microphones, when any odd behavior could be explained away by what had just happened. But she didn't fully trust herself now. If she saw an opening, she would try and take it. The most important thing now, however, was to get herself back under control and convince everyone in the house that she really was who she said she was.

Especially Avilova, whoever he is. If he had really worked with Nicola Neumann before, then her mission might be doomed before it ever really got started. She'd have to hope for a little more luck.

Mavich led her back down the long hallway and out to an arcade. Two men were sitting at a card table, sipping coffees, while a third leaned negligently against a stone pillar, twirling a tennis racket and dressed all in white.

"Too scared of me to play today, Nikolai?" said the man with the tennis racket. He was dark, and handsome, with winged eyebrows. Elizabeth recognized him immediately: Carlos Mendoza, the Venezuelan.

"Do you and Carlos play often?" Elizabeth said to Mavich as they came out into the arcade.

"Every day," Mavich said.

"Every day he beats me, too," Carlos said, shaking his head. "A forfeit is my only real chance."

"I find that difficult to believe," Elizabeth said with a quiet smile. His handsome face was so benign, he didn't look like he would ever carry anything more deadly than a peashooter. But he did—Carlos was said to carry a stiletto blade on his person at all times, and be absolutely deadly with it.

Her eyes passed quickly to the two men sitting at the table. The first, smoking a cigarette, was Yuri Betrin, the man who had alerted Mavich to Caslov's assault and brought her the medicine. The two exchanged a cursory nod of recognition. The other man was older than everyone else in the house. He looked short, even seated, almost like a child sitting at the grown-ups table for the first time. But everything else about the man suggested the accumulation of many years. His face was round, with sagging jowls, bushy eyebrows, thick grey hair, and the brightest, shrewdest blue eyes that she had ever seen before. She was certain that she had never before seen this man in her life, in pictures, on video, or in any other way.

"Hello, Nicola," the man said in a deep voice. "It's been a long time."

Perspiration broke out on the palms of Elizabeth's hands. So Betrin was right: He really did know Nicola. Who was he? And what was he doing here?

The man rose from his seat with a grunt of exertion and came slowly towards her.

"Yes, it has been a long time," Elizabeth heard herself say in a remarkably steady voice. But how long, she wondered? Six months? A year? A decade? The man was rocking back and forth on his feet, studying her carefully.

"I must say, you look marvelous," he said. His eyes twinkled wickedly. "I believe you look younger every time I see you."

Elizabeth's heart nearly stopped. Did he know that she wasn't Nicola Neumann? She was afraid for a moment that she might faint. She took a deep, steadying breath to try and quell the buzzing in her ears, and then tried her best for a sweet smile.

"That's the best compliment you can give a woman," she said.

The older man was now looking at the water rippling in the pool, reflecting the deep blue sky and the tops of the trees. After a moment, he glanced back at her, and Elizabeth thought she detected a flash of malice in his eyes.

"You've changed, Nicola."

Elizabeth clenched her hands together so tightly that her nails scored her palms. The older man's amusement seemed to disappear—could he tell how nervous she was?

"You're different from the old days," he said—almost kindly. "The change becomes you."

Does he really believe Nicola's changed? Elizabeth wondered, teetering between hope and incredulity. She couldn't quite bring herself to believe it. But it was possible...

Mavich had settled himself at the table and was toying with a saucer.

"I didn't know you knew Nicola," he said coolly.

"There's a lot about me you don't know, Nikolai," he said. He sounded like a grandfather, amused by the antics of a young grandchild.

"That's the truth," Mavich agreed with a laugh. "Old Ivan Avilova, full of secrets."

"Nicola worked for a few months for a network that was under my supervision," he said. "We became friends during that time."

Elizabeth tried to swallow but found that she couldn't—it felt as though her throat had closed. What sort of game was this man playing? If he really knew Nicola that well, surely he could tell that she wasn't the agent who had worked for him.

"It must be nice to have a powerful man like Ivan as a friend," Betrin said. "It would make life at home less tense."

There was a glimmer of amusement in Avilova's bright eyes.

"Now, Yuri, you know it's the people in your line of work who make the rest of us tense. We could all breathe a little easier without an assassination squad looming over our shoulders."

Betrin laughed, and Elizabeth had the sense that this was some kind of long running joke between the two men. How strange to be in a world where assassination could be the subject of casual chiding between colleagues. Another reminder of how far she was from anything she had known before.

Avilova glanced at his watch, and for a moment, a flicker of worry crossed his face. But it was gone as soon as Elizabeth noticed it. She wondered if anyone else had picked up on the small cue.

"I'd better get back to Dr. Sobokov," he said. His eyes began to sparkle as they rested again on Elizabeth. "Until later, Nicola."

Much later, hoped Elizabeth. *Better yet, not at all.*

Mavich watched as Avilova made his way slowly from the table and entered the second door on the arcade. Then he turned to Elizabeth.

"You didn't recognize him," he said, a small note of accusation in his voice.

Elizabeth forced herself to stare back coldly.

"I did—but I was shocked to see him, even after Yuri's little warning. Midas neglected to tell me Avilova was going to be here."

And so did dear old Wynter, she thought, trying to keep anger from clouding her mind too much.

Mavich gave her a small, ironic smile.

"I'm sure Midas didn't know. He is obviously no longer in charge of the operation, or Avilova wouldn't be here. More important people are running it now, and they're sending in the top brass."

"So who's in charge now?" Elizabeth said, trying to imagine how disdainful Nicola would feel at being cut out of the loop. Mavich shook his head.

"I don't know, and if I did, I wouldn't tell you. Someone higher up the ladder than Avilova, that much is clear, and he's on the way up there himself. He's not about to explain the inner workings to pawns like us."

"Don't sell yourself short, Nikolai," Elizabeth said. "You're a bishop, at least. Maybe not a queen yet. But we can't all be."

Mavich laughed at this, a genuine laugh. This was enough encouragement for Elizabeth to try to learn a little more.

"What happened to Midas?" she said. If he was supposedly her Control, wouldn't it be natural for her to be interested in his fate?

"Nothing except for what that idiot had coming to him," Mavich said. "Apparently, our friends back home feel the operation is too vital to take a chance on letting Midas control it any longer. His performance has been poor—and they're not about to wait around for it to get any worse."

Mavich shook his head, looking rueful.

"He used to be a brilliant agent," Mavich said. "That's how I first knew him. But he became too important, too confident. He started getting sloppy. The only reason he hasn't been relieved of his duties is because he has some extremely influential relatives in the Politburo. But he could read the writing on the wall. That's why he started telling people that he could get Dr. Sobokov back to Russia—and get him to do it voluntarily, too. Naturally, they were interested. But Midas wanted to pick his own men and didn't want the hierarchy looking over his shoulder, second-guessing his decisions, giving him advice he didn't feel he needed. The KGB bosses, with more than a little nudging from his influential relatives, decided to let him try it. It would have been quite a coup, if he could've pulled it off." Mavich shrugged. "Unfortunately for him, he couldn't."

Elizabeth listened to this story with interest. Did this mean that Steve Brenner was wrong, and Sobokov hadn't been kidnapped, after all? What had gone wrong with Midas's plan? And, most importantly, what did all this mean in terms of where Nicola Neumann stood with regards to the operation?

"It makes it sound like I came all this way for nothing," Elizabeth said.

"On the contrary," Mavich said. "We need all the competent agents we can find. We have four days until the Leningrad departs. Who knows what will happen between now and then?"

He turned to Mendoza and cracked his neck.

"Shall we finish off our set?"

Mendoza nodded and pushed himself off the pillar. He nodded to Elizabeth and made his way out onto the tennis court. Yuri was sitting alone at the table now, smoking a cigarette fitfully. Elizabeth smiled and took a step towards him.

"I owe you my thanks, Yuri," she said. "I don't know what would have happened if you hadn't said something about Caslov to Mavich."

Yuri took a long drag on his cigarette and cocked his head to the side.

"The man is an animal," he said, "an occasionally useful animal, but an animal nevertheless. If it was up to me, he would never have been here. But then, I had very little to say about who is here and who is not."

Elizabeth tried to keep her smile from faltering.

"Well, thank you, all the same."

Yuri Betrin stubbed out his cigarette in the ashtray and sighed. "You know what it is I do, Nicola?" he said.

Elizabeth thought back to her drive with Steve, the two of them trading facts about the men in the house like they were back in high school, studying for a history exam. For all of Avilova's banter with Mendoza, it was Yuri Betrin who was the trained killer in the group, the ghost who the CIA had few, if any, hard facts to go on. She nodded.

"Then you know I'm just as dangerous as Caslov, maybe more so, because I won't be obvious about it. Just remember that I might not be there the next time you need saving."

Elizabeth frowned—the man said this completely calmly, as though he was discussing the care instructions for some clothing he was dropping off to be washed. Betrin lit another cigarette even though the last one was still smoldering in the ashtray. She nodded.

"I understand," she said.

"Good," Betrin said with a small smile. "Welcome to paradise."

"Excuse me," Elizabeth said. She suddenly wanted to be far, far away from this man—far away from all of them. But she also recognized that, with two of the men playing tennis, Avilova in with Dr. Sobokov, and Caslov apparently sequestered to his room, she might never have a better chance to plant the microphones that Wynter had given her. "I think I'll take a look around."

Betrin had nothing to say to this. He nodded and went back to casually observing the tennis game happening behind him. Mavich hit a big serve wide, and Mendoza swore in colorful Spanish as his return fluttered harmlessly into the net. Elizabeth pretended to watch for a moment, and then quickly walked back into the house, already thinking of where would be best to plant the little bugs.

CHAPTER SEVENTEEN

Elizabeth stepped back inside the house, the cool of the tiles badly needed against the heat of the day and the lingering feeling that the men outside left with her. She was safe from Boris Caslov, at least until one of the other men forgot to mind him or she was discovered. This Ivan Avilova seemed, against all odds, to believe that she was the same Nicola Neumann he had worked with sometime in the past. She had known she would need some lucky breaks for this plan to work, and so far, she had gotten them. But luck, as Elizabeth well knew, could run out at any moment, and it was foolish to expect it to continue unabated. She had to do what Wynter had sent her to this house to do, and fast, before she was discovered.

Through the glass doors and into the living room Elizabeth went. The room was sumptuously decorated: an ornate plate on one table, a piece of Steuben on another, a Serves vase on an end table, an elaborate gold bowl. Who, she wondered, had arranged all of this? When these men left, what would become of the house? She liked to imagine some functionary back in Moscow pouring over Western design catalogs and trying to decorate everything just so. More likely than not, the men had rented the house from some rich person who was friendly or smart enough not to ask questions. She shook this thought from her mind and tried to focus on the task at hand: This might be her best, and maybe her only, opportunity to plant the microphones that Wynter had given her.

She spotted an urn of roses on a sideboard that looked like the perfect hiding spot for one of the little bugs. Quickly, she removed the false bottom of the compact in her pocket and fumbled for one of the microphones. She parted the leaves and dropped it into the urn, and then looked around the room for somewhere else to place a bug. Glancing over her shoulder to make sure that no one was watching, she knelt and pressed a microphone underneath the tabletop. She waited for a moment to make sure the small metal device would hold to the wood, and then, satisfied that it was, pushed herself back out from beneath the table.

With everyone else busy, Elizabeth moved quickly through the house, trying to look as innocent and curious as possible as she went in case anyone was observing her movements. After all, wouldn't a good agent familiarize herself with new surroundings as quickly as she could? She affixed one microphone behind the coffee maker in the kitchen, another just beneath the framed map of the state hanging over a leather couch in the library, and a third near the French doors that led out to the atrium, where she hoped the device was powerful enough to pick up any chatter from the men who seemed to habitually assemble there. She made her way down the long hallway that led towards the bedrooms, including the room where Dr. Sobokov was staying—or being held, she reminded herself. She was kneeling beneath a side table, trying to get the microphone to hold to the bottom of the marble, when she heard a cough and froze.

"Lose an earring?" she heard from behind her. It was Avilova, done with his visit to see Dr. Sobokov much more quickly than she had expected.

PASSPORT TO DANGER

Elizabeth pawed at the carpet for a moment, and then brought a hand up to her ear, pretending to fix the earring back into place. She scooted back and brought herself up to full height, looking now at the Russian agent with the best fake smile that she could manage.

"The damned things just won't stay in," she said. "My own fault for picking beauty over practicality."

"I won't pretend I've never made the same choice myself," Avilova said, "but not where earrings are involved."

Elizabeth felt something cold run down her spine—after what had just happened with Caslov, was Avilova coming on to her, too? But as she looked at the man, his eyes twinkling slightly, she saw that her first instinct had been wrong. There was nothing leering or lecherous about the man. He reminded her instead of a kind uncle, the sort who might drink a bit too much at a holiday party and regale the family with old stories from a generation past. She reminded herself that this was probably no more than an act designed to put her off her guard. Of everyone in the house, Avilova now represented the biggest threat to her. It was only a matter of time before he realized that she wasn't the real Nicola Neumann and informed Mavich of his suspicions. It was incredible, really, that he hadn't mentioned it right away. Perhaps, he was bored and having some fun at her expense, the sort of casual cruelty that reminded her of children torturing ants. Either way, she had to get out of this house before he made his suspicions known.

"How is Dr. Sobokov?" she said, hoping to change the subject.

Avilova made a sort of shrugging motion and blew a little air out the corner of his mouth.

"As well as can be expected," he said.

When had Avilova arrived? Surely one of Wynter's men had seen him come in. Why hadn't he told her about it, or even cancelled the mission? Elizabeth realized that she had allowed herself, in all the time since she had left Virginia, to believe that everything was under control, and that the plan would work just as Wynter had promised her it would. Now, it was becoming clear that things in the field operated by their own berserk logic, and that there was nothing she could do about it now. *If I'd had any idea of what sort of surprises were waiting for me*, she thought to herself, *I would have caught the first flight to Athens.*

"You should be careful about exploring the house on your own too much," Avilova said. "Not everyone here is quite as trusting as I am."

Was he trying to threaten her? There was nothing malicious about the way he said it, but how else was Elizabeth supposed to receive this kind of advice? Had he, in fact, seen what she was up to, and was merely stringing her along now? Elizabeth could feel her panic rising as she tried to think of something, anything, to distract the man from the truth.

But before she could, footsteps began to sound from down the hall. For a horrible moment, she was certain that it was Boris Caslov, returning to finish what he had started earlier. But to her tremendous relief, it was Carlos Mendoza. The man had changed into black slacks and a red knit shirt with a white V at the neck, and he was carrying the luggage from her room.

"Nikolai thought you might need some help with your bags," he said, carrying the heavy suitcase as though it weighed nothing at all.

"What a gentleman," Avilova said, and Elizabeth thought she could hear an edge of sarcasm in the older man's voice now. But apparently Mendoza didn't, because he grinned at Avilova and kept on walking. Avilova gestured for her to follow the other man, and retreated back out towards the atrium. Elizabeth couldn't shake the idea that he had seen something, though—maybe he was on his way, even now, to reveal his suspicions to Mavich. If that were the case, there was nothing to do about it now, so she pushed that from her mind and followed Mendoza down the hallway.

"How did the tennis match come out?" Elizabeth asked with a smile. Mendoza grinned.

"Nikolai always beats me. The only reason I play is for a little exercise, and because I get so damn bored here otherwise. I'm not in the same league as Nikolai as a player."

"Don't you ever win?" Elizabeth asked.

"He was well on his way again today, before Boris's little interruption. I finally won a set off him afterwards; he seemed distracted. He almost never shows emotion on the court, and today he was swearing like a sailor every time he hit an error. Boris's antics must have really thrown him off."

"Antics," Elizabeth said, shaking her head slightly. Mendoza looked back and grimaced.

"A poor choice of words, perhaps," he said, "but I'm surprised you don't know about Nikolai's skill on the court. He plays real tournament tennis. Surely, you've read about him?"

Elizabeth swallowed, then glanced up at him and smiled.

"I'm seldom in the Soviet Union anymore," she said. That was just a small lie; she'd never been there before in her life.

Mendoza looked surprised, then pleased.

"So you avoid it, too?"

"As much as possible."

"It's so damned dreary and cold," Mendoza said. "I get better accommodations in our so-called 'backwards' Latin American countries than I do in Russia."

He sounded bitter to her, and Elizabeth tried to make herself sound as sympathetic as possible.

"I know. They treat me the same way. They're deplorable hosts, even though we risk our lives for them."

Mendoza looked at her warmly. Clearly, he was glad to have found someone who shared his feelings on the Soviets' lack of hospitality. Elizabeth was grateful. She needed all the allies she could muster in this house, for however long she had to stay there.

As they reached the other wing of the house, Elizabeth eyed the four doors leading off the main hallway speculatively. Dr. Sobokov was behind one of these doors, but which one?

"You'll be safe over here," Mendoza said, mistaking her curiosity for fear. "Boris wouldn't think of bothering you here...not while Nikolai is so close."

Elizabeth glanced up innocently at him, hoping that he would understand her unspoken question.

"Nikolai has the end room," Mendoza said, trying to reassure her. "Yuri the next one, and our friend is staying in the room next to yours. You'll be sharing a bathroom with him for the time being, until we can get Yuri to switch rooms. It would have taken him some time to pack, and Nikolai wanted you over on this side of the house as quickly as possible."

Elizabeth could scarcely believe her luck. Her new room would give her more or less immediate access to Dr. Sobokov! Was there anyone in with him now? She knew Avilova had just paid him a visit, but what about the others in the house?

"Is there...anyone with Boris right now?" she said.

PASSPORT TO DANGER

Mendoza smiled reassuringly.

"Yuri is keeping an eye on him. There's no need for you to worry."

Elizabeth gave Mendoza one of her warmest smiles.

"Thank you, Carlos. For everything. I think I better rest before dinner."

"Of course," the man said. "I'm sure it's been a long day."

If he only knew, Elizabeth said. He opened the door to her new room and put her suitcase on a chair.

"Don't worry about a thing, Nicola," he said as he was leaving.

The minute the door closed, Elizabeth hurried to her suitcase, opened it, and got out her makeup bag. She took out the hairbrush, unscrewed the handle, and tilted the brush until a little set of keys dropped in her hand. She looked at them thoughtfully, hoping they were as good as Wynter said—he'd claimed they would open any lock, and said it was their best option, since there was no time to teach Elizabeth how to pick a lock herself.

She let herself into the bathroom, closed it behind her, and locked it from the inside. On the far wall was another door. She tested the handle first—locked, as she had expected. She looked back at the keys. Everything depended on them now. If they didn't work...well, no use thinking about that now.

"We have ears on the house," Connor said from the room where the radio equipment was kept. Steve Brenner was standing by the window, smoking yet another cigarette and looking out onto the same streetscape he'd been staring at for the past three hours. He stubbed the cigarette out in the ashtray and hurried over to the other room.

Alex Connor had a big pair of headphones over his ear and was fiddling with the dials before him. Wynter came bounding up the stairs more quickly than Steve would have guessed the older man could move, his jacket abandoned to the Mexican heat and his shirt sleeves rolled up. There was a very fine sheen of sweat on his forehead.

"How many?" Wynter said. Connor raised a hand as he made some more adjustments.

"Two...no, three...no, four!" he said, looking incredulously down at his equipment as he confirmed the radio sources. "At least four...maybe five...how many did you give her?"

"Eight," Wynter said, rocking back onto his heels with a slight smile on his face. "She must be waiting for something to plant the others."

"I can't believe it," Steve Brenner said, steadying himself with a hand against the rustic wooden chair by the desk. Ever since Elizabeth had gone off with Mavich, he'd been halfway holding his breath, waiting for something to go wrong. The whole plan still seemed absurd to him, some desperate Hail Mary by an old spymaster backed into a corner and out of options. He realized now that it had never occurred to him that this might actually work—that he'd never allowed himself to contemplate the possibility that Elizabeth might actually be able to pull off the series of unlikely events that Wynter had put into motion. Now that she had, he didn't quite know what to do with himself.

Connor let the headphones slip from his ears as he shook his head, apparently feeling the same way that Steve did.

"She's doing a damned good job," he said. There was admiration and surprise in his voice.

"Maybe you underestimated her," Wynter said.

"I did," Connor admitted soberly.

"What are you picking up?" Wynter asked. Connor put the headphones back on and quickly scanned through the different broadcasts from the little bugs down the road.

"Nothing...nothing...sounds like someone cleaning up, or maybe moving around...wait a minute, here we go," he said, fine-tuning the dial until the signal came in clearly. He fiddled with a few things and then pulled the headphones out of the jack, the sound from the radio now filling the little study with the sound of Spanish conversation.

Steve strained to make out what the men were saying—he spoke a bit of the language from a childhood spent on a cattle ranch in Texas, but it had been a long time since he'd listened to fluent speakers talking among themselves instead of trying to make himself intelligible to a patient waiter at a restaurant.

"What are they saying?" he said finally, unable to follow and desperate to know what they were saying. Most likely, it had nothing to do with the mission at all—there were a lot of dead hours to kill, even on a mission with stakes as high as this one, and agents became adept at finding ways to pass the time and deal with the suffocating boredom. For all he knew, they were listening in on a card game, or a discussion of when the heat was likely to break, in which case he would tell the men to go on waiting forever. Connor and Wynter both held up a finger for him to be quiet, and Steve couldn't help but notice the growing look of worry beginning to cloud both of the men's faces.

"Well?" he said quietly after a time.

"They're talking about Nicola," Connor said. Steve felt a bead of sweat drip down the back of his shirt.

"What are they saying about her?"

"It's Mavich, right?" Connor said to Wynter. Wynter pursed his lips.

"We don't have audio of him from before so there's no way of knowing for sure, but that's my read, too. I can't tell who he's talking to, though."

"Any chance we missed someone?" Connor said. Wynter shook his head, and then paused.

"I wouldn't have thought so, but I wouldn't put it past Mavich.... We'll have to double check all the comings and goings from the house, even the ones that the agents dismissed as routine...."

All the men went silent again as the conversation started up in earnest, Steve straining for comprehension. After another few minutes, Connor and Wynter looked at one another with something akin to horror on their faces.

"For God's sake, what it is?" Steve said. Wynter shot him a quick look, his grey eyes full of worry.

"Mavich is beginning to wonder if that girl is really Nicola Neumann."

CHAPTER EIGHTEEN

The three Americans huddled around the little receiver in the study of the house in Cuernavaca, straining to listen to the conversation happening just a stone's throw from where they stood. Connor began taking notes in a furious shorthand. Wynter stood back with his arms folded across his chest, wondering if this was it, the beginning of the end. He'd had plans implode on him in the past, an unavoidable part of a job that required improvisation and long-shot bets, but it never got easier; especially not when he was standing alongside the man who loved the woman he had put directly in harm's way.

"She's not what I expected," Mavich said in his lightly accented Spanish.

"Well, go ahead," the other man replied curtly. Who was this? Wynter was kicking himself for allowing an unfamiliar man into the house without his knowing. He'd known Mavich was an accomplished spymaster, but apparently he'd still managed to underestimate the Soviet's abilities; and if this man knew the real Nicola Neumann...it was a stroke of impossibly bad luck, at a time when they could scarcely afford any.

"For one thing, I wouldn't have expected Nicola to panic when Boris started making advances."

Wynter heard Steve Brenner inhale sharply next to him and wondered how much of this the scientist was getting, his Spanish unpracticed before a few days earlier. He was grateful he would have a chance to try and explain it to him. If Steve had been hearing this unfiltered, he might already be charging over to the house, guns blazing and hell-bent on rescuing Elizabeth. Then they would all be sunk.

"You can never tell what a woman will do in a case like that," the other man said, "even a woman like Nicola."

"Avilova, you're not hearing me," Mavich said. Connor scribbled the name down on a sheet of paper and passed it to Wynter with an arched eyebrow. Wynter shook his head—he had never seen the name, and didn't know the man. Somehow, this made him even more concerned than he had been already. "She told me that if she'd been able to get to her pistol, she would've shot Boris if she hadn't been able to frighten him off. I just can't believe a woman with Nicola Neumann's experience would jeopardize our entire operation. Can you imagine how quickly the police would have been on us if the neighbors reported gunshots?"

"She's read Boris's dossier," Avilova said. "Did you really expect her to just submit for the good of the mission? If there's anyone you should be angry with, it's Caslov."

"Believe me, I am," Mavich said. "If it was up to me, he would be halfway around the world, working on his suntan somewhere out in Siberia. But you can't say her behavior hasn't surprised you, can you? How long has it been since you've seen her?"

"It's been several years," Avilova said, and Wynter felt his blood run cold. This man *knew* Nicola Neumann—the real Nicola Neumann, not the pale, beautiful imitation they'd tried to pass off.

He heard Connor inhale sharply as he took in this information. Steve Brenner frowned.

"What are they saying?" he whispered. Connor held up a hand to shush him as the men continued to talk.

"I admit she's changed," Avilova said, "but for the better. She's…mellowed. Not as tough as she used to be."

There was a pause then—Wynter could imagine Mavich thinking this over, weighing the report against his own instincts. He was surprised that this man, Avilova, was willing to give Nicola the benefit of the doubt. He had to hope that Mavich might be convinced, too.

"That's unusual," Mavich said. "I've found that most of the women in Nicola's profession get harder over time, not softer. It really hasn't occurred to you that this girl isn't Nicola?"

"I only saw her briefly today," Avilova said. "She was rattled. I think it's a sign of her experience that she understood the danger Caslov presented to her."

Another long pause then.

"I want to look at the films of her again," Mavich said, "compare what's there against the woman in this house."

"I'm afraid that's not possible," Avilova said.

"What the hell do you mean?"

"The projector is broken."

"Broken? What happened?"

"We don't know for sure, but—"

"Maybe the girl did it," Mavich said. "She knows I've got the films and she doesn't want me to have an opportunity to look at them again."

Wynter looked down and saw that he was clutching the back of Connor's wooden chair so hard that his knuckles had turned white. Could Elizabeth have really thought that far ahead? It seemed unlikely to him—the risk of being caught destroying the device was high, and it would only matter if the agents in the house already suspected her.

"No, Nikolai," Avilova said. "She didn't do it. Yuri thinks the gardener did it by mistake when he was cleaning the room—it was fine before he went in there, and broken afterwards."

Wynter heard Mavich curse quietly in Russian.

"So much for the films," he said.

"Tell me again why you're so worried about whether or not the girl is really Nicola," Avilova said.

Wynter couldn't believe what he was hearing, and neither, apparently, could Mavich, judging by the protracted silence that followed Avilova's question.

"That's the most absurd question I've ever heard."

"You're the one who's acting absurd. Think about it: That girl is either Nicola or someone who looks like her, and who, besides you and Midas, knew that his courier was going to be Nicola Neumann?"

"I told the others here," Mavich said.

"Only after you arrived in Cuernavaca. You're the only one who's had any connection to the outside world, through the radio. Once that was gone, there was no way for Midas to contact you, other than through Nicola."

"What are you trying to say?"

"You and I both know Midas. Imagine him back in Moscow, under house arrest, everything riding on this mission. He's already told you that Nicola will come to tell you how to get our friend back to Russia. Then he isn't able to find her. What do you think he would do in that case? Cancel the mission? Send someone else who he knows you would reject, because he had no way to update you? No! He would tear the Soviet Union apart trying to find someone who looked like Nicola, hoping that she'd deceive you. Because the radio was down, he had no way of warning you."

"Do you really believe what you're saying?" Mavich said. "Because it sounds very unlikely to me."

"You've always got to go by the book, Nikolai. Sometimes that's good. Sometimes it isn't. In this case, your Control was afraid to play the game by a different set of rules because he was worried you'd take your ball and go home."

"So you've known from the beginning that she wasn't Nicola?"

"I didn't say that. I'm still not sure she isn't, frankly. But I have my doubts."

"Why didn't you tell me?" Mavich said. Wynter could hear the anger rising in the spymaster's voice and understood it: If one of his men suspected something like that, and kept it from him, he would be apoplectic.

"She had the information on the Leningrad," Avilova said. "*Someone* obviously sent her. If she really is a substitute, she's probably had a hell of a time. I feel sorry for her."

"You feel *sorry* for her?"

"If she isn't Nicola, then I doubt she's even an agent at all," Avilova said. "I wonder what pressure Midas used on her."

"I intend to find out when I talk to her."

"Go easy on her. She's young, and if she isn't Nicola, she's frightened. Midas shouldn't have sent her. It's tantamount to sending a lamb into the lion's den."

"Yeah. Sure," Mavich said. There was the sound of footsteps, and then they stopped, like the man had one more thing to say before leaving. "You know Midas well enough to know that he does what's expedient for Midas. He's never given a damn about what happens to anyone but himself, so don't worry. I'll be nice to her."

Over the radio, Wynter heard the sound of a door opening, then the feed was silent. The conversation was over, and Mavich was on his way to go interrogate Elizabeth.

For a few moments, the room was quiet, Connor frantically scanning across the other radio channels with his big headphones on and Wynter standing back, lips pursed and expression thoughtful. Had this been a regular mission, he would have aborted it by now: sent in the men, extracted his agent, and chalked the whole thing up to bad luck. But how long had it been since he'd had a "normal" mission? This one was especially abnormal, with the heightened dangers to match, and if Elizabeth hadn't managed to get the passcode from Sobokov yet, then years of advanced missile research would be lost at a minimum. The house was full of trained killers, ready to fight their way out if necessary, and if Mavich already half-suspected Elizabeth, what were the odds he would just let her leave? It was an impossible situation.

"Is someone going to tell me what the hell is going on?" Steve Brenner said, breaking the tense silence.

Wynter and Connor looked at one another. Connor winced and went back to the radio. Wynter cleared his throat.

"How much of that did you catch?" Wynter said.

"Enough to know that something's off," Brenner said. He lit a cigarette and exhaled. "They know, don't they?"

"We don't know that for sure," Wynter said.

"But they suspect her."

"Mavich is a suspicious man," Wynter said.

"Oh come on, Bill," Brenner said. "Don't give me that bull crap. Elizabeth is in danger and you know it."

"She was in danger from the moment she set foot in Mexico. You knew that. She knew that."

"Jesus Christ," Brenner said, starting to pace back and forth in the little office.

"This other man, Avilova...he doesn't seem as convinced as Mavich," Wynter said.

"That's the other thing: How the hell did someone get into the house that you didn't know about?" Brenner said, stopping just long enough to point a finger at Wynter's chest. Wynter looked down at the extended digit for a moment, then back up at Brenner, a new cool reserve on his face.

"I don't know," he said, "but I'd be careful where you point your finger, Steve."

Brenner sighed and went back to pacing.

"We need to get her out of there, ASAP," Brenner said.

"You know we can't do that," Wynter said.

"What's the good of having half a battalion of former Marines in a little nowhere town in Mexico if you can't storm a damn compound?"

"If we moved on them now, we'd be jeopardizing not only Elizabeth's life, but Dr. Sobokov's as well, to say nothing of my men. I won't do it, Steve."

"So you're just going to let Mavich do whatever he wants with her?" Steve said. There was a strain of desperation that was edging into his voice now, and for the first time, Wynter started to wonder if it had been a mistake to bring him along and let him work his way so intimately into the operation.

"We're going to wait and listen," Wynter said. "I don't know what you thought you were getting yourself into, but that's most of what this job is. It isn't glamorous. It isn't adventurous. But it gets results."

Steve Brenner let out a bitter chuckle and stubbed his cigarette out on the ashtray next to the radio.

"My father used to take me and my brother hunting," Steve said. "My brother hated it. He complained about how boring it was, sitting in a blind all day, waiting for some buck to wander by. My father used to say to him, 'That's why they call it hunting, not shooting.' I don't mind being patient, Bill. What I mind is sitting around with my thumb up you know where, doing nothing, while Elizabeth is in danger!"

"What would you do, in my shoes?" Wynter said. Seeing the look on Brenner's face, he continued, "I'm serious. Maybe I'm missing something. What would you do?"

Brenner thought for a long moment, staring out the window in the vague direction of the house that was partially obstructed by the trees that lined the street.

"I'd put my men in position to take the house," he said. "Keep Connor glued to this radio. And the minute I hear that something's going down, I'd take it."

Wynter and Connor looked at each other again. In the universe of requests that Brenner could have made, it was far from the most damaging. Wynter nodded.

"I'll get the boys set up," Wynter said. "Quietly. But no one moves until we hear something that means we have no choice. Agreed?"

Brenner thought about it for a moment, then nodded. Wynter reciprocated the gesture, slapped Connor on the shoulder, and then headed downstairs to get the tactical team ready to move if necessary.

The first key did nothing at all—just rattled aimlessly around the lock like a tourist on layover in some remote, impenetrable city. The second didn't even fit into the opening. Elizabeth was beginning to wonder if any of the toys that Wynter had given her were good for much of anything at all.

There were signs of promise with the third key—it seemed to catch on something inside the mechanism. But when Elizabeth went to turn the key, the door wouldn't budge. Was it possible it was deadbolted from the inside, too? She had been so sure they'd be focused on keeping Dr. Sobokov in that she hadn't figured they might be trying to keep others out. If that was the case, she couldn't see how she was going to be able to get to him alone. The whole mission would be ruined.

She held the fourth and final key aloft. It reminded her of the key to a diary she'd been given by some of her parents' friends in the days after the accident—a hazy time in her memory, more blank than terrible really, the enormity of what had happened settling in slowly rather than all at once. She had brought the diary up with her to Canada, and then onto the boarding school, where one of the prefects had taken it, claiming that secrets weren't allowed at St. Catherine's. Elizabeth had been too meek and too scared to protest, too numb to tell the gangly girl everything that had happened. She hadn't thought about that diary in a long time.

She fitted the key into the lock and turned. The thick wooden door opened with a groan, and Elizabeth stepped into the dark room.

The shutters in the room were closed up tight, allowing only scant sunlight in through the gaps in the slats. The air inside the room was hot and thick with the slightly sweet, rancid smell of sick and sweat. Trying to make as little sound as possible, Elizabeth made her way over to the bed, where a figure lay beneath a bundle of blankets. As far as she could tell, Dr. Sobokov hadn't heard her come in.

She tiptoed over to the bed and stood over him, looking down at his gaunt, grey face. For a moment, she worried that she was looking down at a corpse. But no—he was breathing, if just barely, the faintest trace of respiration present in the gradual rise and fall of the blankets piled atop his body. He looked awful.

"Dr. Sobokov?" she said quietly. Nothing. She reached down and gently shook his shoulder. "Dr. Sobokov, wake up."

There was no response. He seemed dead to the world. Had he been drugged? She couldn't see why the Soviets would risk drugging him—with the men in this house, it would be easy enough to keep him from escaping. But clearly, there was something wrong with the man.

She took the last microphone that Bill Wynter had given her and knelt beside the bed, pressing it firmly against the wood beneath the side table. Even if Dr. Sobokov was drugged, this way the Americans would be able to hear anything that transpired between him and the Soviets.

Suddenly, she stiffened, listening intently. There were footsteps coming down the hall. Was someone coming to check on Dr. Sobokov? The footsteps stopped, and she heard a knock against her door in the next room. She bit her lip, wondering what to do. If she didn't answer, would whoever had come for her think that she was asleep, and leave her be? Or would they come into her room and find her here, with Dr. Sobokov? There would be no explaining herself then. The horrible thought sent her tiptoeing back through the shared bathroom, closing the door to Dr. Sobokov's room behind her, just as she heard a key scraping in the lock for her door.

"Just a minute!" she called out. She wondered who would be waiting for her, and realized that there was no good answer to that question—just a series of bad to worse men who all would wish her harm if they found out who she truly was and what she was doing in that house in Cuernavaca.

CHAPTER NINETEEN

Nikolai Mavich was waiting on the other side of the door, a slight frown on his face and something churning behind his eyes. Something was wrong, Elizabeth knew it.

"What is it?" she asked.

"Pack your suitcase," he said. "We leave in ten minutes."

"Leave?" Elizabeth said. "But why?"

It was too late. Mavich was gone, heading to tell the others, maybe, or to make whatever preparations were necessary for this last-minute flight.

As she stuffed her clothes back into her suitcase, Elizabeth tried to imagine what had gone wrong. Had Avilova finally revealed to Mavich that she wasn't Nicola Neumann? If so, why would he still bring her with him? It must have been something else, she thought, though for the life of her she couldn't say what. That was the problem: When everything looks like danger, and anything might be going wrong, it can be hard to pinpoint where exactly the risk is coming from.

The rest of the house was thrumming with activity as she dragged her suitcase out of her room, the men rushing all about, stripping the borrowed house of its essentials and anything they didn't want to be discovered. Elizabeth paused for a moment and looked down the long drive towards the gate, currently unmanned. She considered her options. In all this chaos, it might just be possible for her to slip from the house unnoticed. Would Wynter and the other men watching the house would be able to track her once they left? What was waiting for her, when they arrived? She didn't like the answers to any of these questions. If there was a time to make a break for it, it was now.

But then she thought about the sad figure of Dr. Sobokov lying under the sheet in his bed, pale and barely breathing, looking as though he were on death's door. If she left now, then the mission would be a failure. The research would be lost. And Dr. Sobokov would end up either back in the Soviet Union or dead. If she stayed with Mavich, then there was still a chance of finding out his passcode and maybe even getting the man to safety. The rules of the game seemed to be changing, but Elizabeth felt that she needed to keep playing.

Which meant she *had* to find out where they were going. She couldn't rely on the Americans to effectively follow the cars—Mavich was too good for that, too cautious not to notice a tail, especially after something had clearly already spooked him. But how?

Avilova came out of his room holding a small case, a wide-brimmed hat set on his head. He did not rush or move with any noticeable alarm, but Elizabeth could tell that there was purpose in the efficiency of his movements. How many times, she wondered, had the old spy slipped from one place or another, leaving at a moment's notice? She could imagine the way a thing like that could get into one's bones, a hair trigger on the animal part of oneself that knows to leave, combined with the training and history of knowing just how to get away. She saw him glance her way, shaking his head slightly. She was about to go to him when she saw Yuri Betrin step out of the afternoon shadows and join him.

"Paranoia?" Betrin said. Although he spoke in a low voice, Elizabeth could still hear him.

"Is it still paranoia if he's right?" Avilova said.

"So you think…"

"I don't know. But I trust Mavich. I would think you do too, after all this time."

Betrin groaned and cracked his neck.

"'Go to Mexico,' they said. 'An easy mission,' they said. 'Nice and relaxing.'"

"And you believed them?"

Betrin let out a low bark of a laugh, seasoned with more than a little bitterness, and shook his head.

"Where to, then?"

"Acapulco," Avilova said. "A friend has a house there."

"And will that one be any safer than this one?"

Avilova shrugged. The two men carried their cases into the living room. Elizabeth followed them, dragging her own suitcase behind her. But as soon as she got into the living room, she gasped. The two men looked at her, concern on their face.

"What is it?" Avilova said.

"I've forgotten my makeup case," she said, shaking her head. "I couldn't stand to let you all see me like that."

"Hurry up," Avilova said. "I have the sense Mavich does not want to be left waiting."

Elizabeth hurried back to her room and closed the door behind her. There wasn't any time. She sat down at the dressing table and took out her lipstick, then wrote across a little scrap of paper: *ACAPULCO*. When she had finished, she rolled the paper as tightly as she could, removed the cartridge from her lipstick, and slipped the paper into the empty case. She left the tube sitting on the top of her dressing table, where it would look, she hoped, like something left behind or discarded in their haste to flee. She just had to hope that Mavich wouldn't perform a final sweep of the house before leaving—if he did, there would be no explaining this to him.

Two cars were waiting out in the driveway, one in front of the other, engines already running. The headlights of the first car were battling against the weak light of the late afternoon sun, already beginning its stately descent in the west. Mendoza was at the wheel, Betrin beside him, with Caslov and Avilova in the backseat.

Mavich was standing in the driveway, tapping his foot impatiently, then came forward to grab Elizabeth's bag from her.

"Get in," he said. He hurriedly opened the door of the Mercedes, and Elizabeth saw Dr. Sobokov stretched out in the backseat. If possible, he looked even worse than when she had seen him just a few minutes earlier, his breathing irregular and jagged.

"What's wrong with him?" Elizabeth said. Mavich frowned.

"He needs to rest," Mavich said as he stashed her suitcase in the trunk. "Come on."

He signaled to the gardener, who was standing at the huge wooden gates. The Mexican man swung the gates open, and the first car charged out of the driveway, turning left. Within thirty seconds, another car followed, driven by two men wearing suits and sunglasses. As soon as the tail car had passed, Mavich nosed the Mercedes out of the gate and took a right. He headed fast down the street, tires screaming as the car whipped around the corner.

It wasn't until they were on the highway that Mavich finally spoke.

"It looks like we have the road to ourselves," he said.

"I feel like I've been on a roller coaster," Elizabeth said, hoping to sound irritable enough to cover her worry. She had been hoping that someone might be following her—some sign that Wynter and the other Americans would know where she was going. But it seemed as though, for now, she was all alone with the Soviet spymaster.

"Why are we tearing away from Cuernavaca like this?" she said. "In broad daylight, no less."

Mavich shot her a quick glance.

"The house was being watched. Didn't you see the car follow after Mendoza when he left?"

"I saw *a* car behind Mendoza," Elizabeth said, "but I don't know who it was. For all I know, it was a neighbor running out to the market for limes before it closed." She heard Mavich snort with incredulity. "But my instincts might not be as finely tuned as yours. How did you know someone was watching?"

"I saw them," he said. "There's been a car parked on the street beside the house with two men in it. They've been sitting there for two hours now, not doing anything. Just waiting, and watching. Across the street, in a supposedly empty house, a man was smoking a cigarette in a second story window. Does that answer your question?"

Elizabeth shook her head. One cigarette and Wynter's plans for rescuing Dr. Sobokov were ruined. "How do you think the Mexicans found you?"

Mavich said nothing. Elizabeth wondered if he had heard her, or if he was lost in thought, playing through their narrow escape and planning for what was to come. She was about to repeat her question when Mavich cleared his throat.

"Before we talk any more about this," he said, "there's another conversation that you and I need to have."

"Oh?" Elizabeth said. She could feel her palms beginning to sweat.

"As you know, I've never met Nicola Neumann," Mavich said. His eyes stayed on the road, his voice calm, but Elizabeth could barely breathe for all the tension that now suffused the Mercedes. He was waiting for her to respond.

The way she saw it, Elizabeth had two choices. She could keep pretending to be Nicola Neumann—though if he doubted her already, she didn't think it would be possible to change his mind. Likely, he had already discussed his suspicions with Avilova, who surely must be thinking the same thing if he had met the actual woman. But she couldn't tell him the whole truth—he would shoot her instantly, and leave her body in a ditch along the Mexican highway for some unfortunate trucker to discover. Elizabeth sighed and leaned her head back against the cool leather of the seat.

"I wondered how long it would take you," she said. "Did Avilova say something to you?"

Mavich glanced over at her, surprised to hear this.

"He was actually willing to give you the benefit of the doubt," Mavich said. "He said it had been years since he'd seen you."

"I didn't know he was going to be here," Elizabeth said. "I don't know if they would have sent me if they knew someone in the house had met the actual Nicola Neumann."

"That must have been a nasty shock for you."

"Very nasty," Elizabeth said, forcing a light laugh that came out sounding more like a choked sob.

"This will all be much easier if you just answer my questions and tell me the truth," Mavich said. "Who sent you?"

"Midas, of course."

"Midas?"

"Well, I didn't know him by that name. To me, he was just Uncle Grigory, an old friend of my father's. If I had known..."

"You know him?"

"Grigory Valenkov?" Elizabeth said. This was her trump card—Mavich was the only member of the operation who knew the true identity of Midas. If she was going to convince him, everything had to start from this. "I wish to God that I didn't. But yes, I know him. I know him well."

Elizabeth looked over and watched as Mavich took in this new information. She searched her mind now for everything that Wynter had said about the man in charge of the operation back when they were at the house in Virginia, but it was difficult to recall anything right now. The past few days all blended in her mind, too many names, faces, facts, and factions to keep straight.

"What's your name?" Mavich said.

"You can keep calling me Nicola, if you like," Elizabeth said.

Mavich sighed.

"Come now. No more games. Who are you?"

Elizabeth let her head hang down for a moment, then let loose a sigh of her own.

"My name is Elizabeth. Elizabeth Villemont."

"Villemont," Mavich said, rolling the syllables around his mouth like it was a fine wine. "French?"

"Yes," Elizabeth said.

"Elizabeth is not so common a French name."

"My grandmother was English," Elizabeth said. "I was named for her."

"And what is it that you do, Ms. Villemont?"

"You mean when I'm not impersonating international spies?"

Mavich chuckled drily at this.

"Yes, the rest of the time."

"I'm an interpreter."

Mavich looked over at her in mild surprise. Elizabeth allowed herself a brief moment to consider again how different her life would be if the UN really had hired her as an interpreter a few years earlier—no modeling, no chance meeting with Steve Brenner, and certainly not this car ride to Acapulco with a Soviet spy intent on discovering who she really was.

"I can't speak as many languages as you," Elizabeth said, "but I'm fluent in English, French, Spanish, and German."

Mavich looked openly shocked.

"So you're not Russian."

"Nicola isn't, either," Elizabeth said. "German, from what they told me."

Mavich nodded.

"So," he said, "how did a French interpreter end up in a house in Cuernavaca with a kidnapped American nuclear scientist?"

It was the first time that Elizabeth had heard anyone call what had happened to Dr. Sobokov a "kidnapping." *Steve was right*, she thought, glancing back briefly into the back seat until she had seen the scientist's chest rise and fall.

"I'm afraid it's a long story," Elizabeth said. "I suppose you'd like to hear it?"

"We have a long drive ahead of us," Mavich said. "Start from the beginning. Tell me everything, and, Ms. Villemont?"

"Elizabeth, please," Elizabeth said.

"Elizabeth," Mavich said, the corners of his mouth curling up into a subtle cruel grin. "Just remember: I'll know if you're lying. You've fooled me once already. I don't plan to make a habit of it."

"I understand," Elizabeth said, before proceeding to tell the biggest lie of her life.

Once they had secured the garden and cleared the rest of the house, the Americans began to tear the house in Cuernavaca upside down. Bill Wynter was in the living room, trying to find Elizabeth's microphone in the vase of roses. It didn't matter now, of course, but it helped to focus his mind on something; he liked putting himself into Elizabeth's shoes, trying to guess where she had slipped the little listening bugs.

Steve Brenner was on the sofa, chain smoking again and looking around irritably.

"They just left?" he said for probably the tenth time since they'd watched the cars peel out from the driveway and head off to God knows where.

"They just left," Wynter said, not sparing a single slance towards the anxious scientist.

"But, my God, Bill, why?" Brenner said. "Do you think it's because they found out about Elizabeth?"

"Possibly," Wynter said. "But the men we placed on heightened alert down the road seem to think that Mavich noticed them and caught onto their presence."

"Don't try to put this on me!" Brenner said, rising from the couch to point a finger across the room. "Elizabeth was in danger!"

PASSPORT TO DANGER

"And now she's in much greater danger," Wynter said, looking up wearily from the vase. "For the record, Steve, I don't blame you. This was my call. I have to wear it, whatever happens here."

This seemed to briefly mollify Steve Brenner—he stopped pointing, sighed heavily, and then plopped back down. He looked exhausted, Wynter thought. They all did. But he could understand why the man would be so defensive. His instincts had been to protect the woman he loved. He just didn't know how, hadn't spent enough time in the field to understand what a delicate game they were playing, and how the slightest of moves—even ones made in the name of caution and preparation—could suddenly throw everything off.

Connor came charging into the room, holding up something small and golden in his hand.

"Bill!" he said. "We found something."

"Are you sure it's your color, Alex?" Wynter said. "I'd think you'd do better with a more neutral tone, what with your complexion."

"Har har," Connor said. He undid the cap and handed it over to Wynter. Inside, scrawled on a torn sheet of paper in smudged red lipstick, was a single word: *ACAPULCO*.

For what felt like the first time in weeks, Wynter smiled.

"Smart girl," he said.

"What is it?" Brenner said.

"Where we're heading," he said. "That girl of yours is full of surprises."

"You don't think he'll tie in her arrival with everything else?" Steve said. Wynter sighed and shrugged.

"He'd suspect her even if she was innocent. But she's not, which means that time is not on our side." He looked at one of the men across the room, currently inspecting the safe behind one of the large ornate paintings. "Call if you find anything."

"Where are we going?" Steve said, rising from the sofa to follow Connor and Wynter out the door.

"Acapulco," Wynter said. "This isn't over yet."

Not by a long shot, Wynter thought, as the three men hurried out of the house and towards the waiting car.

CHAPTER TWENTY

Elizabeth Villemont, the French interpreter, had led a more or less normal life.

She had known, vaguely, that her father had been involved with Communist politics after the war—but then again, so had De Gaulle, and nobody thought less of him for it. She had lived in Paris her whole life, taken to languages as a young woman, and found herself delighted by the ways she could hear echoes of one language in another—the more she learned, it seemed, the easier it became to pick up another. Becoming an interpreter was the most logical thing in the world. She had led a nice, quiet life. She was happy.

But all of that had changed at a party in Paris a few years earlier. That's where she had met Midas—under a different name, of course. She could still remember how surprised he was the first time he saw her. At the time, she didn't think much of it. Elizabeth Villemont was not vain, nor was she naive enough to ignore the way that men looked at her. It had been that way her whole life. She did her best not to let it affect her too much.

It was only later that she learned the real reason that Midas had stared at her, dumbfounded, from across a crowded room in the 6th Arrondissement. Grigory Valenkov had made his way over to her that night and introduced himself as one of her father's old friends. She had been pleasantly surprised that he wasn't one of the lecherous old men intent on telling her how beautiful she was, their barely disguised lust hidden ineptly behind tired jokes and the veil of old age. Now, she wished to God that he had only been interested in her for her beauty. How much simpler her life would have been.

"My father had worked for Midas over the years," Elizabeth said. "I knew nothing about it. He is a jeweler; his trips were always for business: Antwerp, London, and occasionally New York. But as soon as he met me at that party, Midas had told my father that the time might come when he found me particularly useful. I guess he was thinking, even then, that Nicola might not be around forever."

"The woman had a reputation, that's for sure," Mavich said, shaking his head. "But I'm surprised anyone, even a committed Communist, would get you into a mess like this."

"My father refused, at first," Elizabeth said. She felt strangely, almost preternaturally calm, as though she were in a trance. "After Nicola disappeared, Midas told my father he wanted me to go to Cuernavaca in her place. I knew something was strange between them—Midas showed up at strange hours, and I could hear them yelling at one another. Actually, that wasn't so strange—they were always yelling at one another, usually in good fun, I thought, the way old men do. But after he left, I found my father crying. That was new.

"After my father refused, I learned that Midas was trying to exert a considerable amount of pressure on him. He threatened his business, his family, revealing his secret life to the world. My father would have been run out of Paris with nowhere to go. He would have been ruined...absolutely ruined. So I decided to seek out Midas myself. I wanted to hear what was involved, at least, and if there was any way I could help fix what had been broken between them. I thought he was our friend. I thought he would want what was best for me."

"And your parents?" Mavich said, his steely eyes still on the empty road before them.

"I haven't seen them since," Elizabeth said. "They are Midas's hostages. He told me that once I'd done the job, he would let them go."

"This all must have come together quickly," Mavich said.

"I had forty-eight hours of training," Elizabeth said. "Just enough to be briefed on Nicola and everyone else with you in this house here. Everyone, that is, with the exception of Ivan Avilova."

"Ah, yes," Mavich said.

"Who is he?" she asked.

Mavich hesitated, as though deciding whether or not it was worth telling her anything. She couldn't tell which was more dangerous: If he didn't say anything, it meant he didn't trust her. If he told her everything, maybe it meant he didn't think she was a threat—either because he believed her, or because he planned on disposing of her, anyway.

"There are...many rumors about Ivan," he said finally. "He's a powerful man in the Politburo. Some say he's one of the top men in the KGB. He's important—that's all I know, and all that matters."

"Sounds like you don't really know who he is," Elizabeth said. As soon as the words were out of her mouth, she was shocked by the boldness of them. What did she think that would help? But Mavich seemed to take it in stride.

"It's the business. You're never quite sure who anyone is. You must know that by now."

"I'm beginning to sense that, yes," Elizabeth said.

"So you've really never met Nicola?"

"No. I've seen her photos, studied the films of her. But we've never met."

Mavich was silent for a time, thinking over what Elizabeth had said. In the passenger's seat, Elizabeth gripped the leather of the seat as hard as she could, feeling her fingers digging into the luxurious material. Mavich had discovered that she was not Nicola Neumann—it had taken barely any time at all. Wynter's plan had been foiled almost immediately. And yet...she was still alive. She hadn't really allowed herself to think about—all those hours in Virginia and then on the long drive to Cuernavaca with Steve—what would happen if she was discovered. But now, she knew that some part of her had simply assumed that if she was found out, she would be killed. These were ruthless men she was dealing with, playing a very dangerous game. What was one more body to them? And she was hardly an innocent in these matters: She was an agent for the United States, sent to subvert their mission.

But she was still here. Blood pumped yet through her body. She could hear her heart beating above the low growl of the engine as the Mercedes sped along the Mexican highway.

Telling Mavich the story of Elizabeth Villemont had come so naturally to her that it unnerved her a bit. How had she managed it? The details might be different—no Communist father, no English grandmother. But the core truth of what she felt was real. She was a random woman who had the misfortune to look like a Soviet spy, who had been pressed into service in her stead. All that fear, all that uncertainty, and the sense of unreality that had pervaded her life since that chance meeting with Steve Brenner—

all of that was real to her, the truth of what she had felt for days now. Would that be enough for Mavich to believe her? Or was that a bridge too far?

She closed her eyes briefly and thought of Steve. Would they have found the note she left behind in Cuernavaca? Even if they did, would they be able to find her in Acapulco? She thought of his face, knitted with concern, and wondered if she would ever see him again.

"Are you a Communist?" Mavich said finally. Elizabeth took in a sharp breath, wondering what to do.

"No," she said after a moment. It had the virtue of being true. Besides, she knew nothing about Communism, really—no depth that Mavich couldn't expose with a few choice questions. "Just my father."

"You realize that this puts me in an awkward position."

Elizabeth nodded but found that her voice was gone. She could imagine how a man like Mavich typically resolved his awkward positions.

"You know too much," he said.

"Midas said you'd be suspicious of me," Elizabeth said. "I don't blame you. I would be, as well."

"And I expect you think it's just a coincidence that our American friends made themselves known as soon as you showed up?"

Elizabeth said nothing.

"Let me review a few facts for you," Mavich said. "Three days before you arrived, my radio was discovered by the Mexicans. I'd be incredibly naive to think there wasn't a possibility the Americans were involved. A day later, two men moved into the house on the right, a house that's always vacant this time of year.

And on the day you arrived, the area was suddenly teeming with intelligence agents."

"I thought you only saw three men?"

"When you can see as many as three, you know you're surrounded," he said. "Like cockroaches. Or spiders."

"That sounds like them getting nervous, and sloppy," Elizabeth said. "If they thought I was Nicola, then they must have thought you were getting close to leaving. If they were smart, they would have stayed quiet."

Mavich laughed at this, a harsh and mirthless sound.

"An answer for everything, this girl."

"Please," Elizabeth said, letting a little bit of the desperation she was feeling edge into her voice. "I have as much at stake as you do. Maybe more. This is my family. I don't know what they'll do if you don't get that scientist back to Moscow."

Almost on cue, a low moan issued from the back seat. Mavich and Elizabeth both looked back at Dr. Sobokov, writhing a bit under his blanket now like a feverish infant. He did not look well. Elizabeth wondered if he would make it all the way back to Russia in this state.

"What's wrong with him?" she asked.

"That is no longer your concern," Mavich said, staring back out at the road. Then, "How much do you know about him?"

"Nothing."

"I find that hard to believe," Mavich said.

"I know he's a scientist," Elizabeth said. "I know Midas cares very much about getting him back. Beyond that, why would he tell me anything? He knew what a risk he was taking, sending in someone with no training. No need to take any more risks than necessary."

"Hmm," Mavich said. Elizabeth could see the muscles in his jaw working as he thought something over.

"You're going to kill me now, aren't you?" Elizabeth said. Mavich looked over at her, surprise plastered across his face. She supposed it wasn't a way he allowed himself to look very often.

"What makes you say that?"

"You don't know if you can trust me," she said. "It would be easy enough to tie up this loose end, dump me by the side of a Mexican highway. You'd be in Cuba before anyone connected you to me."

"Is that what you would do?" Mavich said. Elizabeth couldn't tell if he was mocking her or not.

"Me?" Elizabeth said. "I'd drive me to a luxury hotel by the water in Acapulco, put me up in a suite, and tell me not to come out for a week. Order up room service, read a book. By the time I felt the sand beneath my toes, you'd be long gone."

Mavich laughed again.

"I think we're a bit beyond that, sadly," he said.

"I know," Elizabeth said, sighing and staring out the window. "But it's a nice thought, isn't it?"

"Let's focus on getting to Acapulco first," Mavich said. "We can continue our little conversation there."

Then quiet returned to the car. Elizabeth watched the flat expanse of scrubland rise before them. She was still alive. That, for now, was enough. But her mind was already whirring: What would happen once they got to Acapulco? Was there any way that she still might do what she had been sent to do? A few minutes earlier, this had seemed impossible. But now, she could sense that Mavich was content, for the time at least, to believe that she really was Elizabeth Villemont. How much longer that would last...was another question entirely.

In a car speeding towards a private airfield, Steve Brenner lit another cigarette. Next to him, Bill Wynter rolled the window down, the early evening air whipping against them as Alex Connor raced through the empty streets of the sleepy town.

"You're going to smoke us all out here, Steve," Wynter said. Brenner sighed and stubbed the cigarette out in the car's ashtray.

"God damn it all!" he said. When no one answered him, he slapped a hand against the side panel and slouched back into his seat.

"You think being angry is going to fix things?" Wynter said. "I thought you were a man of science. Rational. Cool headed. That's what I thought, anyway."

"There's a world of difference between this and lab work," Steve said. "People's lives are at stake here!"

"You really think I don't know that?" Wynter said. "And not just Elizabeth's, by the way. Do you know what happens if they get Sobokov back to Moscow? Even if he doesn't give them anything, that's five years gone in our missile program. Puts the Soviets at par with our systems, if not ahead, which means we're playing from a disadvantage; which means people start to take risks; which means people make mistakes. Don't talk to me about lives at stake. That's the job, Steve."

No one talked for a few minutes. Connor pressed the pedal against the floor. The car tore around a corner, barely missing a curb. Brenner grabbed for the hanging strap by the door to keep himself from hurtling to the other side of the car, then noticed that the other two men were wearing their seatbelts.

"You trying to get us killed?" he said.

Connor shot him a look in the rearview.

"Our pilot doesn't like it when people are late."

"Has it occurred to you that he might like it even less if we don't show up at all?"

Connor chuckled, and the tension broke in the car. Steve groaned and leaned his head back against the seat.

"I'm sorry, Bill. I know you've got a lot on your plate without me barking at you."

Wynter shrugged in the front seat.

"It means you care, Steve. That isn't a bad thing."

"At least we know where they're going," he said. "But how the hell are we going to find them in Acapulco? They could be anywhere."

"I've got a team on the way there now, canvassing any known Soviet safehouses," Wynter said. "If they're moving this quickly, Mavich has somewhere in mind. Somewhere he thinks will be safe."

"And if we don't find them?"

"There's a chance Elizabeth still gets herself out of there. Mavich has enough on his plate to be too worried about someone who's clearly not an agent."

"But how would she even know where to go?"

Alex Connor took another hard turn, and then cleared his throat.

"You know the old chestnut about how to find someone in New York?" he said.

"New York?" Brenner said.

"Two people are in New York," Connor said. "They know they have to meet up, but they haven't set a time or a place for the meet. How do they do it?"

Steve Brenner thought about this for a moment.

"You mean they just wander the city, looking for each other?"

Connor caught his eye in the rearview mirror again.

"I'm asking, what would you do?"

Brenner thought about it for a moment.

"I guess you'd go somewhere obvious. Somewhere everyone knows. Probably at some nice, round number of a time, figuring the other guy will guess it as well."

"What does that look like?" Wynter said, craning around in his chair to look back at Steve. He took a deep breath.

"I guess...maybe the clock at Grand Central? Noon? Something like that?"

Connor and Wynter grinned at one another.

"We'll make a field agent of you yet, Brenner," Wynter said.

"But what does that mean for Acapulco?" Brenner said.

"I could think of a few places," Wynter said. "My first guess? Condesa Beach. I'll put agents at every other tourist attraction, with instructions to be on the lookout, but that's where we'll start."

"If she can make it out," Steve said.

"You would have lost money betting against that girl so far," Wynter said as the air strip came into view. "No reason to start now."

"No," Brenner said as Connor brought the car to an abrupt halt and threw open the door, the plane's propellor engine already whirring to life. "I guess not."

CHAPTER TWENTY-ONE

Sunrise found Steve Brenner on the patio at the Presidente Hotel with a cup of strong coffee and a cigarette. The beach down below was slowly coming to life, vendors setting up for the day in preparation of the throngs of tourists who would soon populate the white sand beaches, hoping to spot an American celebrity down for a getaway. His eyes scanned the early crowd: Could Elizabeth somehow be here already? He already knew that she wasn't. He would have noticed her immediately. For an unguarded moment, he had the thought that he might never see her again. He cursed and stubbed out his cigarette. It did no good to think like that, no good at all.

Bill Wynter came and sat next to him. The spymaster looked old and tired this morning, with heavy bags beneath his eyes. He ordered a pot of coffee from the passing waiter in fluent Spanish and then sighed before turning to Steve.

"You should bring Elizabeth back here when this is all over," he said. "Give her a proper vacation. She's earned it."

"I'm guessing she'll never want to step foot in Mexico again," Steve said.

"You'd be surprised. Beer never tasted as good as it did on a beach in Haifa in '67. Something about making it through to the other side...there's nothing like it."

"How did this all go so sideways, Bill?"

The waiter arrived with the coffee and poured a cup for Wynter. He took a long sip and then turned back to Steve Brenner.

"All the usual ways: carelessness, bad luck, and a lack of better options. Tell me, knowing what you know now, is there anything you would have done differently?"

"I never would have let that poor girl into my cab in the first place. I would have let her stick it out in the rain on her own and keep her out of this whole mess."

"You're too much of a gentleman to ever let a woman face the elements alone," Wynter said. "Especially if that woman looks like Elizabeth."

Steve said nothing to that and looked back out on the beach.

"Any leads on the safe house?" Steve said.

"We're looking. The local authorities are being exactly as helpful as you'd expect."

"Did you tell them what you're looking for?"

"Of course not. They think we're scouting possible vacation homes for Elizabeth Taylor's next trip."

"Christ, Bill."

"We're in Acapulco. Trust me, that'll get them moving more quickly than if we told them there's a Soviet sleeper cell with an American nuclear scientist somewhere in the city, especially since we don't know who to trust."

"So in the meantime, what? We sit here drinking coffee?"

"Until cocktail hour, at least."

Steve stared across the table at Wynter, barely keeping his contempt in check.

"How can you possibly be so glib at a time like this?"

Wynter sighed and took off his sunglasses.

"Do you have any idea how much of this job involves sitting around and waiting? I suspect that's what drives most of the men out of this line of work, more than the danger, the long hours, and everything else that comes with it. Waiting around for an informant to come in for their daily coffee, or for the man you met at the bazaar to finally finish up a deal with his cousin, or for the general who swore he'd make time for you to leave his mistress's apartment. It takes patience and an iron stomach. If you have to pick one, I'd prefer a man with a weak stomach and a limitless reserve of patience."

"Yeah, well, my stomach's heading that way, at least," Steve said.

"Just give it another twenty years," Wynter said.

For a time, the two men looked out over the beach, watching the waves gently lap against the white sandy shores. It was beautiful here, even more so than Cuernavaca, with an energy and a verve that the sleepy little hamlet didn't have. If he and Elizabeth managed to get out of this mess in one piece, maybe he would bring her somewhere, someplace far away. She had been planning to go to Greece before he came crashing into her life. He could take her there. That might be nice.

He looked over at Bill Wynter, ready to say something else about the safe house. But the CIA man was looking intently at the beach, like a bird of prey circling above a clearing. Steve turned back to the beach, straining to make out anything from their perch. There was a young mother playing with her children on the sand; an old man walking slowly down the beach, slightly stooped over as he made his shambling way; a few men from the hotels and resorts tending to their fiefdoms of chaise loungers and towels. Nothing out of the ordinary, as far as he could see. But then there came a man, well dressed in a pair of linen pants and a clean white guayabera, a Panama hat on his head and big sunglasses over his eyes. He was tanned and healthy-looking, with the posture of a man who could use his body well if necessary.

"Is that..." Steve said.

But Bill Wynter was already up out of his seat, ignoring the query that the waiter called out after him. Steve threw a few pesos down on the table and followed the old spy. Who knew what had brought Nikolai Mavich out to the beach at this hour of the morning? But it was the first stroke of luck they'd gotten since they'd left Virginia, and they weren't about to let it go to waste.

• • •

Elizabeth Lamont came out of her deep sleep as quickly as she had entered it. She sat up, brushing her dark hair out of her eyes, and glanced around the bedroom. Faded peach wallpaper; pale pink bedspread; high ceiling; antique furniture; crème damask drapes. An almost pretty, if somewhat tired, room. It might be purgatory—too comfortable to be hell, not quite enough to be heaven. But Elizabeth was fairly sure that she was still alive, and that was no small feat, especially after her conversation with Mavich.

By the time they had arrived in Acapulco, it had been the middle of the night, and Elizabeth was exhausted. She and Mavich appeared to have settled into an unsteady sort of truce, though Elizabeth couldn't tell if the man genuinely believed her story or was only allowing her to think as much before he decided what to do with her. She'd managed to fall asleep in the car—she'd been faking it at first, to avoid any more questions from Mavich, but soon found herself giving in to the bone-deep exhaustion. She had always slept well in cars. Anything that moved seemed to soothe her. Then they'd reached the house, and she'd woken up long enough to stumble upstairs, to this room, where she'd promptly fallen into bed and gone right back to sleep.

She glanced at her watch, then again with surprise. Nine o'clock already? She wouldn't have guessed she'd managed to sleep that long. *I was more exhausted than I realized*, she thought. She crossed the room to the nearest window and pulled back the heavy drapes, then opened the French doors that led onto a small balcony. Across from her was a small island, lush with tropical foliage. Down below her was a lawn as smooth as green velvet, punctuated with date palms and fruit trees that ran down to the edge of a cliff, seventy-five feet above the gleaming Pacific Ocean. The emerald grass contrasted vividly with the turquoise sea and the blue sky, the deepest blue she'd ever seen.

At the far left of the yard was a swimming pool surrounded by a hedge of rhododendrons and a garden of azaleas, gardenias, roses, and lavender bougainvillea. Two men were sitting at a table by the side of the pool, shielded from the sun by a coral and white umbrella. Both dark haired; neither was Nikolai Mavich. Another man was walking down a path towards the pool. She watched as Ivan Avilova stooped to test the water with his fingers.

That left two of the men unaccounted for: Mavich and someone else. Where were they? With Sobokov? She hoped not. After seeing him in the car, she didn't know how much time he had left. And as soon as she had tried to speak with him, she was going to get out of Acapulco as quickly as she could. She took a final deep breath of the fresh, sweet air, filled with the tangy scent of the fruit trees, and went back inside.

She changed into an aqua bathing suit with a matching dress and slipped her fountain pen, lock-picking keys, and the packages of cigarettes—an unusual pack, since four of the cigarettes were explosives—into her pocket. She allowed herself another moment to collect herself before leaving the room. Somehow, she had managed all of this okay. She was still alive. She was safe, for now, and soon, all this would be behind her.

Someone had left a pot of coffee and a sweet roll on a tray by the door. A fly had come to land on the sweet roll and was looking up at Elizabeth, as though trying to stake its claim. That was enough to put Elizabeth off the coffee too. She didn't like the thought of men being in her room without her noticing.

She crossed the room over to the bedroom door and listened intently. When she didn't hear anything, she put her hand gently against the doorknob and pulled.

Nothing happened. The door was locked fast.

Elizabeth frowned down at the doorknob. Locked from the outside. For a moment, she considered the universal key that Wynter had given her—it had worked well enough in Cuernavaca. But she could see no mechanism by which she might be able to unlock the door from this side.

So Mavich hadn't believed her, after all. She was a prisoner now.

She went back over by the window and studied the movement of the men below her. None of them were paying her any mind at all, a small figure above them hidden in the shadows. Cautiously, she went back out onto the balcony and assessed the situation. It was too far from the balcony down to the lawn below to risk any sort of jump or fall—besides, that would be sure to attract the men's attention. If she called to them, maybe she could pretend that she merely believed that her door had gotten stuck, play ignorant and hope that they might judge her so harmless that they would come and let her out. But if Mavich had ordered her to be locked away, there was little chance of them falling for any rouse like that. The longer she could remain undetected by them, the better. She bit her lip and looked to the side, thinking.

And then she saw it: A little way beyond her own balcony was a second balcony, jutting out from another room, the curtains closed tight against the French doors. If she could make her way over to that, could she escape through that other room? It was risky—even if she didn't fall and break her neck, there was no guarantee of getting into the room. She couldn't imagine trying to explain how she ended up on the balcony of the wrong room to Mavich. If he didn't trust her before, he certainly wouldn't trust her after something like that.

Elizabeth slipped out of her shoes and tiptoed out onto the balcony, taking care to keep herself as hidden from view as possible. She stood on the edge of the balcony, as close as she could come to the railing, trying hard not to look down at the lawn below her. If she leaned over the edge, could she reach the other balcony? No, it was well out of her reach. Down below, one of the men started to laugh, a harsh and bitter sound. She did not want to be trapped here with these men. Mavich had been her savior once before, but now, he represented perhaps the gravest danger to her. She wondered if he had told the other men about her new identity as the French Elizabeth Villemont. Or worse—now that he was in Acapulco, did he have some way of contacting Moscow to confirm her identity? Staying put was no longer an option. She had to move.

She put a foot hesitantly up on the wrought iron of the railing, testing to see if it would take her weight. It groaned a bit under the pressure but seemed to hold firm. Would the fall kill her if she misjudged the distance? And, if it didn't, what would the men do with her then? She took a deep breath and pushed that thought from her mind.

She brought her other foot up onto the railing now, her fingertips lightly grazing the stucco wall of the villa. A gust of wind blew off the water. She could smell the salted air and felt her legs begin to tremble beneath her. Elizabeth looked down one more time to make sure that she hadn't been spotted.

And then she jumped.

For a terrifying moment she was suspended in mid-air, legs beneath her in a passable jete, arms outstretched for the coming railing. Her front foot cleared the railing, and her hands came crashing down against the pavement of the opposite balcony. She felt a sharp, hot pain in her back foot as it caught against the wrought iron and brought a hand up over her mouth to stifle her scream of pain. She pushed herself so that her back was up against the building, looking down at her injured foot. There was a long, nasty gash across the top, blood already starting to flow. She held her leg with both hands and willed her ankle to move. To her relief, it did. She could walk on it if she needed to, and it was clear that she couldn't stay on this balcony forever.

After a few moments, she crawled to the edge of the balcony and peeked back down at the men on the lawn. Remarkably, no one seemed to have noticed her death-defying leap. She closed her eyes and gave thanks for small miracles, then went back towards the French doors and tried the handle. Locked, again. She pulled from her pocket the key that Wynter had given her. If she couldn't pick the lock, what would happen to her? She couldn't imagine what Mavich would do if he found her out here. Maybe just push her off the side and let gravity do the rest.

PASSPORT TO DANGER

She pushed the key into the lock. It caught on something. She fiddled with it carefully, trying to replicate the easy way the technician had used in back in Virginia. How simple it had looked then, with no pressure and nothing at stake. Now, everything depended on it working. It had to work. It just *had* to.

Elizabeth heard a click. The handle turned. She heaved a sigh of relief and pushed into the room, shutting the door quietly behind her.

Inside, the room was dark, the air thick and sweetly sick in a way that felt eerily familiar. From amidst the gloom, she heard a noise. Someone was groaning in pain. She held her breath and strained to see through the darkness.

"Dr. Sobokov?"

CHAPTER TWENTY-TWO

There were many times when Bill Wynter found himself doubting his chosen profession: when he lost a man in the field; when he had to apply leverage to a source who thought he could trust him completely; when, despite all of his best efforts and intentions, his mission still failed, and he knew the repercussions would echo through the free world. At times like that, he sometimes found himself wondering what his life would be like if he had followed in his father's footsteps and become a dentist, settling down with a little practice outside Minneapolis, a cabin on the lake for the long summer days and a boat he could take fishing. Leave any thoughts of spycraft to the paperback books and the inside pages of the Star-Tribune.

But deep down, he knew how quickly he would grow bored of a life like that. The Army had been informative, in that way—Korea had been the first place he'd felt a real sense of purpose, rather than feeling as though he were merely following the steps of a life that had been prescribed for him by convention and family and expectations. For all the sleepless nights, agonizing days, and gut punches that came with this job, he wouldn't trade it for anything.

Never was that more clear than when he was in pursuit.

PASSPORT TO DANGER

He was careful as he followed Nikolai Mavich. A man like him would be attuned to anything out of the ordinary; his casual demeanor and resort wear disguised a mind as watchful and attentive as Wynter's. It was rare these days to have the chance to be out tracking someone like this; one of the downsides of his own success is that he had graduated from the work that had made him fall in love with espionage in the first place. But how quickly it all came back to him—the innate sense of how far back to remain to avoid detection; the ways in which details filtered past him now; the singular focus and purpose. He could sense Steve Brenner behind him, straining to keep up. But that didn't matter now. All that mattered was the man in the smart Panama hat coming off the beach now and heading to a table with a beautiful view of the water, where an attractive woman in her late thirties was waiting for him.

"Who is that?" Brenner hissed behind him.

Wynter shook his head slightly, not taking his eyes off the pair as Mavich planted a pair of kisses on either cheek and sat down next to her. She was clearly wealthy—he noted the bikini with the Belgium lace jacket, the kind that you might find in the best couture shops of Paris; the expensive cosmetics; the frosted hair, which had to have constant protein treatments and expensive rinses to look that shiny and silky; and, most tellingly, the enormous diamond, nearly the size of a grape, on the woman's left hand.

Wynter came off the beach now, fairly sure that they had avoided detection so far. Other than a cursory glance around when he first sat at the table, Mavich had given no indication that he knew he was being watched. He imagined all the things on the Soviet spy's mind. *How noisy it must be in there*, he thought. He led

Steve to a table behind where Mavich was seated, close enough to hear the pair over the crashing of the surf and the laughter coming from the beach as the tourists began to enjoy the sand. He let Steve order a pair of coffees from the waiter who approached them and focused instead on the other table.

"Where is Tony today?" Mavich said.

"Mexico City," the woman said breezily. "He'll be flying in tonight. Why don't you have dinner with me? We can wait for him together. I know he'll be anxious to see you."

"I'm sure he will," Mavich said drily. "Though I had the sense the last time I saw him that he'd happily murder me if given the chance."

"Oh, stop that," the woman said, papering over her anxiety with a laugh. "Tony knows nothing about us, and even if he did, what of it? I know he has girls in every town he visits. Why shouldn't I be allowed to have a little fun, too?"

"Is he really meeting with his mistress at a time like this?" Brenner whispered under his breath. Wynter shook his head but said nothing. If Mavich thought it was worth risking detection to speak with this woman, then he was after something more than a romantic tryst.

"I can't make it tonight," Mavich said. "Things are...beginning to get more interesting. I'll need Tony's helicopter."

"The helicopter?" the woman said. "Whatever for?"

"I have a friend who needs a ride," he said, "and a nice big boat waiting for him. It's not far. I'd have the helicopter back before Tony ever gets home."

"Nikolai," the woman said, a new tone of a concern in her voice, "what's happened?"

"We were being watched in Cuernavaca," he said.

"Oh, you boys and your paranoia," the woman said, waving a hand at the idea. "Always someone watching, or listening, or following you. You've grown afraid of your own shadows."

"I do not have time for your banter, Marie," Mavich said. "I need that helicopter. When can I expect it?"

The woman tutted her tongue and leaned back in her seat, considering. The moment seemed to stretch on interminably.

"Do you remember Copenhagen?" she said finally. Mavich let out an exasperated sigh.

"Not this again."

"I thought to myself, 'Finally, here is a man I can really talk with. A man who understands me.' I thought that again in Athens, when you called me to get you out of that jam. And even after you got sent to, where was it? Hanoi or somewhere? I felt that there was a real connection there. A soul connection. The sort of thing that Tony and I have never managed. Oh, don't misunderstand. I don't mind being a Countess. There are worse ways to live. But now, I'm wondering if I had it all wrong. Tony asks so little from me. But every time I see you, there seem to be new demands."

"Marie," Mavich said, "I am a desperate man. I have nowhere else to turn, and no one else I can trust in this Godforsaken town. I would like nothing more than to be able to leave this all behind and just be with you. But right now, I can't. Do you understand that?"

"You say that as if any of this will ever change."

"If you help me, it just might."

"How do you mean?"

"If I manage to actually get our friend out of here, back to where he belongs, I expect I'll have earned a nice, long vacation," he said. "The sort of vacation where I might bring someone along, if they still had feelings for me after all this time. No more games. No more asks or demands. Just the two of us. Is that something you might like?"

"Oh, Nikolai," the woman said, practically swooning at the table. Wynter stifled the impulse to groan. Was the woman really so naive as to believe that a man like Mavich would ever really change? He would say whatever he needed to get what he had to from her, and then disappoint her all over again. Was she really so blinded by love that she couldn't see that?

"Remember: I need that helicopter as soon as you can," he said. "I'll send you a message once we're safely in Cuba. Oh, and Marie? Try to make sure that Tony doesn't intercept it this time."

"Oh, you're so bad, Nikolai," the woman said. Then, after a quick glance around, she came across the table and planted a long, slow kiss on his lips. Mavich rose from the table, gave her an affectionate pat on the shoulder, and then turned to leave. Though he couldn't see him, Wynter knew that the smile melted from Mavich's face the moment he turned away from the Countess, now that he'd gotten what he'd come for.

The Countess was still fawning when Wynter passed her table, Steve Brenner hurrying behind him. Mavich was out in front of the hotel now, waiting on a taxi. Wynter led them into the lobby and positioned them behind a potted plant, where they would be obscured if Mavich looked back inside or decided he had a sudden need to use the telephone.

"Who was that out there?" Brenner asked.

"A very rich, very silly woman who's about to find out she's playing a game she has no business involving herself in," Wynter said. "She'll wish their little affair ended in Athens, or Copenhagen, or wherever else she and Mavich have had their little rendezvouses. I've seen this before. It never ends well."

PASSPORT TO DANGER

Mavich stepped into a waiting taxi. Wynter came striding out of the lobby and held up his hand for the next one, keeping an eye on the cab in front as it waited at the exit for traffic to clear. The next cab pulled up and Wynter piled inside, nearly closing the door before Steve Brenner had a chance to get in behind him. Wynter reached for his wallet, took out all the cash he had inside, and held it aloft. He saw the driver's eyes go wide in the rear-view mirror. Wynter pointed at the cab ahead of them, now nosing its way into traffic.

"Follow that car," he said. "Keep your distance if you can. But whatever you do, don't lose it. If you do all that, this cash is yours. Understand?"

The cab driver nodded vigorously, and then stepped on the gas, the cobblestones of the hotel drive bumping beneath the wheels of the car. Wynter sighed and leaned back against the scuffed leather of the back seat. They were back in the game. They had a chance. Now, they just had to pray that their luck held out a little longer.

• • •

A gaunt man was sitting up in bed, regarding Elizabeth with hostile brown eyes. Elizabeth studied the haggard man in front of her; it was hard to believe that this was the same man whose photographs Bill Wynter had shown her back in Virginia. Still, she knew that it was him: the dark hair peppered with grey; the straight, thin nose; black eyebrows arched like a satyr's; the fine, deep-set brown eyes; the high cheekbones. As a young man, he would have been handsome; as an older man, distinguished. Now, he looked exhausted and ill, his face grey and drawn, his eyes sunken into his skull with dark circles underneath.

"To what do I owe this unwelcome intrusion?" he said in English. His voice was as hostile as his eyes. He was watching Elizabeth closely, tracking the look on her face. "Are you here to kill me?"

"What?" Elizabeth said. "No, of course not!"

Dr. Sobokov let out a chuckle that abruptly warped into a long coughing fit. He reached for a handkerchief on his nightstand and spit out a glob of phlegm, then took a small sip from a glass of water. He sighed and leaned back in the bed.

"It might be a mercy, at this point," he said. "I'm shocked I'm still alive."

"Please, Dr. Sobokov, I don't think we have much time," Elizabeth said, carefully crossing the room to approach the sickly scientist. She lowered her voice even further. "I'm a friend of Steve Brenner's."

"Steve?" Dr. Sobokov said. For a moment, his eyes flashed with recognition. But then, the steely reserve returned. "Another one of Mavich's tricks, maybe. How do I know I can trust you?"

"Please lower your voice," Elizabeth said in a faint whisper. "If one of Mavich's men find me in here..."

"Yes, yes," Dr. Sobokov said, as though he had heard all this before. Elizabeth suddenly felt as though all the warmth had suddenly gone from the room; she shivered slightly against the cold. She watched as the scientist studied her face closely, and as he did, something seemed to shift again in him. "You're frightened, aren't you?"

"No," Elizabeth said, almost automatically, but they were past lying now. She let her shoulders slump to the side. "Of course I am. I'm terrified. I have no idea what I'm doing."

"Who are you?" he said, his voice quieter now, if not exactly friendly.

"I really am a friend of Steve's," she said. "The whole story is rather complicated, I'm afraid. Apparently, I look just like the courier who was supposed to bring Mavich a message. A man Steve knows in the CIA decided to use me as a substitute, in the hopes of finding you."

"And she never arrived?"

Elizabeth shook her head.

"Dead, I suppose," Dr. Sobokov said. "And you managed to fool Mavich?"

Elizabeth hesitated for a moment, and then explained the story she'd told Mavich on their drive from Cuernavaca, about being a French translator with the Communist father who was being held hostage by Midas. By the time she had finished her story, Sobokov was frowning.

"He didn't believe you, of course."

"I'm still alive," she said, "but I did wake up in the room next to yours, and its locked from the outside."

Dr. Sobokov let out another small laugh that ended in a cough. He closed his eyes and leaned his head back against a pillow.

"And how is my old friend Steve?"

"Wonderful," Elizabeth said. "When we get out of here, I'm hoping that we might get married."

Dr. Sobokov opened one eye and appraised the girl.

"I don't know which part of that sentence is crazier," he said. "But it's too crazy for you to be lying, which means you must be telling the truth. How about that?"

"Please, Dr. Sobokov," she said. "We don't have much time before Mavich is back. We need to be out of here by then."

"Out of here?" Dr. Sobokov said. He flung his arms feebly out to the side. "Look at me. I'm not going anywhere I'm not carried at the moment. And I can't imagine a little thing like you making it very far with me draped over your back, even if I have practically wasted away."

"So you really are a defector," Elizabeth said, stepping back from the bed. Dr. Sobokov frowned.

"Who said that? Just because I can't move under my own power doesn't mean I'm happy about any of this."

"So what happened?"

Dr. Sobokov groaned.

"I fell for one of the Communist's oldest tricks. I'd like to think that any other time, I would have seen it for what it was. But they happened to catch me just a few hours after I'd received some earth-shattering news, and, well, let's just say they either got very lucky, or I had the worst luck imaginable. And now, here I am."

"What was it?" she said. But Dr. Sobokov stayed quiet. Elizabeth went over to the window, hoping that the space would convince him to get his thoughts in order. She was careful to stay to the side of the drapes so the men down below couldn't see her.

"Are they still down there?" Sobokov asked tensely. Elizabeth nodded.

"I wonder where Mavich is, though?"

"Arranging transport, I'd imagine," Sobokov said. "Coming here wasn't part of the plan. Now, he needs to improvise if he hopes to get me to Cuba undetected."

"How did you know..."

"I'm an invalid, not an idiot."

Elizabeth looked back down at the pool.

PASSPORT TO DANGER

"Everything is too relaxed," she said. "I don't like it."

"I can tell you why no one is worrying about you."

Elizabeth looked at him sharply.

"Why?"

"They expect you to be sleeping. Soundly."

"Then they must think I'm awfully tired. Just how long do they expect me to sleep?"

"It depends on the drug they put in your breakfast."

Elizabeth stared at him. Sobokov grinned.

"I'm guessing you didn't eat from the tray in your room. Good girl. If you did, you probably wouldn't have even made it back to your bed. These characters don't fool around with the light stuff. They have quite a heavy hand, in my experience."

"They've been drugging you."

"Aggressively. It's a miracle they haven't made a mistake with the dosage and put me under for good. Though to tell you the truth, I wouldn't altogether mind it."

"Oh, enough of that!" Elizabeth said. "You're in a mess, I'm in a mess. No use moping about it. Now, are you going to help get us out of here or not?"

"You're feisty," Sobokov said. "I can see why Steve would like you. He never did well with wallflowers."

Before Elizabeth could say anything else, Dr. Sobokov held up a finger.

"Before we continue," he said. "Do you see that switch on the far wall?" Elizabeth nodded. "Flip it on."

Elizabeth hid her surprise and did as she was told. The overhead fan creaked to life. *Is he warm*, she wondered, *or does he want to drown out the sound of our voices?*

"Check on the men," he said. Elizabeth went over to the window.

"They're still there," she said.

"Tell me what you already know about me," he said.

Elizabeth sighed. Did they really have time for this? But if she was going to get the code for his work, and possibly convince him to escape with her, she was going to need him to trust her. They had, at least, until Mavich got back. So she told Sobokov everything she knew: that he had defected to the United States thirty-four years earlier; that he was in London with a group of physicists and managed to get away from the NKVD; that he had asked for refuge at the American Embassy and was flown to the United States that evening; that he had gone on to become one of the leading scientists in America.

"I'm telling you what I was told by our Intelligence," Elizabeth said. "I could imagine they missed a fact or so."

"Yes."

"And they are?" she said, trying to keep her voice more relaxed than she felt.

Sobokov let loose a long sigh.

"Once, I was in love," he said, "and now, it will be the end of me."

CHAPTER TWENTY-THREE

"The girl I was in love with was a young scientist," Dr. Sobokov said. He was sitting up in bed, and Elizabeth could see the sweat beading on his forehead from exertion. "We were deeply in love. My wife had died of pneumonia the previous winter. I was going to marry Lydia."

"But then the trip to London came up," Elizabeth said. Dr. Sobokov nodded.

"I didn't want to go," Sobokov said. "But she pleaded with me. She wanted me to escape if I had the chance. Can you imagine?"

"I can," Elizabeth said. She thought of Steve again, and the things she already knew she would do for him, if she had the chance. That was part of being in love, being strong enough to want the best for the other person. "But what does Lydia have to do with any of this?"

"Her father was an important member of the underground. Anything that was known about him, or his family members, was recorded. That is how my little affair made its way into the official files, and then, shortly after I left Russia, I heard that Lydia's father had been caught and executed. My brother decided to marry Lydia, hoping the Secret Police would think she was just a harmless housewife and mother, and wouldn't prosecute her as they had the rest of the family."

"Mother..." Elizabeth repeated quietly. She noticed the look of deep sorrow in Sobokov's eyes.

"That's right. She was pregnant. I didn't know or I wouldn't have left." He began to cough, violently, and motioned for Elizabeth to bring him the glass of water sitting on the far side table. She brought the glass to his lips and he took a few feeble sips before leaning back against the pillow. "Several months later, I heard that my brother and Lydia had been taken to Siberia. The purges were beginning again, and anyone thought to be connected to the resistance was rounded up and either killed or shipped off to the labor camps. The Secret Police picked up Lydia and my brother when they were standing in a bread line. What could be more Soviet than that?"

"And your son?"

Dr. Sobokov squinted his eyes and stared at Elizabeth.

"How did you know he was a boy?"

"Lucky guess," Elizabeth said. A timid smile hid the fact that some part of her had known—intuition, maybe, or something in the tone of Dr. Sobokov's voice.

"He was with neighbors that day. They didn't get him."

"I'm glad," Elizabeth said softly.

"So was I. I couldn't bear the thought of him dying in a labor camp. I hoped it made that time easier for Lydia. You see, she could hope that he would live. We can tolerate almost anything if we have hope, and very little in its absence. Life in those labor camps is very hard. You have to be as strong as an ox to survive in one. Neither Lydia nor my brother were that strong. They died four months later."

Sobokov was silent for a moment. Elizabeth fought the urge to check outside the window again: She had the sense that this was a story that gave Dr. Sobokov great pain, and he would tell it only once.

"Around that time, the United States government approached me. They asked if I would work for them. They had checked on me, I suppose. They knew all my relatives were dead. There was no one left in Russia the Communists could threaten. But the Americans knew nothing about Lydia. Or my son."

Dr. Sobokov shook his head.

"I wanted to work for the United States, to find a way to contribute to the country that had taken me in, and hopefully strike a blow against the regime that had cost me so much. I didn't think they could ever use my son to blackmail me: As far as I knew, there was nothing to link us together. To the rest of the world, he was merely a nephew I had never met. He had been only twelve days old when his mother had been hauled off to Siberia. Even if I had wanted to, I had no way of finding out where he was, or if he had survived."

"But why has this come back around after all this time?" Elizabeth said.

Sobokov studied her with worried, unhappy eyes.

"A most unfortunate coincidence. You know the man Midas, the one supposedly in charge of this whole operation?"

"Grigory Valenkov," Elizabeth said. Sobokov nodded.

"Yes, him. We have a connection, the two of us. His father was the man who vouched for me in 1938—the one who promised the Party that I wouldn't defect if they allowed me to go to London. He was wrong, and he lived the rest of his life in disgrace because of that mistake. His son always hated me for it. I can't say I blame him. He grew up to become a successful agent, until the KGB kicked him down to the Department of Records because he couldn't handle his assignments any longer. While going through some old NKVD records, he found my files. That's the Secret Police for you. They're like pack rats, never throwing anything away."

"And your files had notes on the affair."

"Yes."

"So Valenkov found out about Lydia."

"And must have guessed that her son was mine instead of my brother's. The baby was born six months after my brother married Lydia. Not unheard of. But maybe he found the birth records, and guessed that a child born three months prematurely wouldn't weigh eight pounds. Or maybe it was just a lucky guess. But with that information, Valenkov saw an opportunity to recoup all his lost prestige, avenge his father, and make his big come back."

A noise came from outside the window. Elizabeth peeled back the curtain and looked down. One of the men was laughing at something, the others shaking their heads in disbelief. None of them were paying any attention to the house.

"He checked with the labor camp and discovered that Lydia had been transferred. The woman who had died at the time of my brother's death was merely someone fitting Lydia's general description. Unbelievable? No, not necessarily. There have been mistakes of this sort made before. Valenkov went to the camp where Lydia had been sent and found her, alive. He brought her back to Moscow and then spent the next six months searching for our son, eventually finding him teaching school in a small village outside Kiev."

Elizabeth looked at the sick man propped up in the bed, dumbstruck by his story. Then she felt something cold harden within her, and frowned.

"It isn't true, is it?"

Sobokov sighed and looked up at the ceiling. He seemed even more tired than before.

"No. But it could have been. He found a woman who looked like Lydia, and a clever young actor who could make himself up to look like a composite of me and Lydia. He took films of them together and used these as proof to some KGB officials that he'd found Lydia and our son. It was enough to get an official blessing for this operation.

"Valenkov sent three men to see me in Chicago. Two of them posed as CIA agents. The third told me he was a Soviet defector, and that he knew a man being held by the CIA at a farm outside the city. He said this man knew quite a lot about Lydia and my son, that he had even seen them. They were alive and had been smuggled by the Underground through Yugoslavia to Greece. The stranger told me things about Lydia and her family that I knew to be true and managed to convince me that he was for real. At another time, would I have believed him so easily? Who can say. But I had learned a week earlier that I had terminal cancer and had six months to live."

Elizabeth couldn't help herself; she gasped. Sobokov chuckled, the phlegm in his chest rattling at the sound.

"I know, I know. Hard to believe, considering how good I look," he said.

"Dr. Sobokov, I'm so sorry."

"That makes two of us. But, what is that saying Americans are so fond of saying, the one that means nothing at all? 'It is what it is.' An elegant tautology, no?"

"So it isn't just their drugs that are making you like this?"

"Well, they certainly aren't helping. But no, it's not just that. Maybe it was the diagnosis, the sense that, finally, my time was drawing to a close, but I found myself full of this foolish desire to believe that Lydia and my son were alive, and to hear something about them. I was even foolish enough to think I might go to Greece and see them before I died. So I went with them, willingly, to go meet with the defector. It wasn't until we left the city limits that I began to have second thoughts. I realized I should have asked for proof, contacted friends in Washington to find out if the men actually worked for Langley. But when I asked to use the telephone, I got a shot in the arm instead. If I came to in the next twenty-four hours, I don't remember it, because I have no recollection of anything before waking up in my bedroom in Cuernavaca."

"I don't understand," Elizabeth said. "If they were going to kidnap you anyway, what did it matter if they lied to you about Lydia and your son?"

"They tried to keep the ruse going, remarkably," Sobokov said. "Mavich told me that Lydia and my son really were alive in Russia, and that I hadn't been told this in the States because they felt I wouldn't have believed them. Apparently, Valenkov had offered to give Lydia and my son free passage to Switzerland if I would help the Soviet scientists in a certain area of their missile weapons program. If I didn't, they would be killed in front of my eyes."

"And you didn't believe him?"

"Mavich tried his best to sell me on the story. I think he truly wanted to believe that Valenkov had given him something solid to work with, not some half-cocked bluff. But I told him that he had been duped by Valenkov, and that to prove it, he need only ask Valenkov to find out my old nickname for Lydia—she was the only one who knew it. He radioed Valenkov dozens of times for the nickname. But each time, Valenkov came up with some new excuse. Eventually, he just ignored him. Finally, Mavich realized that Valenkov had deceived all of them when he'd claimed he'd found Lydia and my son, and that he was a desperate man making a last effort to recover some lost prestige.

"I told him not to take it too hard. I was never going to help the Soviets, even if Valenkov's story had checked out. If Lydia had been alive, she would have much rather died than see me help the same men who had killed her father and so much of the rest of her family. I also told him that if he was hoping to torture me into submission, he had to work delicately, and quickly, because I wouldn't live through much. When he confirmed my diagnosis with the doctors in Chicago, it was a real blow for him. Poor bastard."

Elizabeth pursed her lips and leaned back against the wall. This was so much information, and so different from the story she'd been expecting to hear.

"Why doesn't Mavich let you go, if he knows you won't help?"

"Because his job is to get the American scientist onto a boat heading for Moscow. If I'm not cooperative when I arrive, well, that's hardly his fault, is it? Valenkov will take the blame if it comes to that, and I don't have the sense that there's any love lost between those two."

Elizabeth felt a small sense of anger flare unexpectedly through her. After all this time, and all this work, and all that she'd risked, it was startling to find a man so apparently resigned to his own fate.

"So you're just going to let them take you?"

"If you'd rather smother me with a pillow now, I'd at least consider it."

"Oh, stop it, none of that now!"

"Do you have any weapons on you?"

Elizabeth frowned, and then nodded.

"A fountain pen that I can fire like a gun. And a package of cigarettes, four of which are explosives, like little grenades."

Sobokov started to laugh again, holding his sides as tears rolled down his cheek.

"A pen gun and cigarette grenades? What, was the cane hiding a sword too conspicuous?"

"They didn't exactly give me a tour of the armory or free rein to choose whatever I wanted."

Sobokov muttered something in Russian, still laughing.

"Americans," he said, with no further elaboration.

From somewhere within the house, Elizabeth heard the sound of a door slamming shut. When she peeked back out the window, there was one less man now than there had been before. Someone was coming to check on Dr. Sobokov. *Or to find me*, Elizabeth thought. Either way, time was running out.

"Are you planning to use those funny little cigarettes?" Dr. Sobokov said finally.

"I'm very much hoping not to."

"Then give them here," Sobokov said. "I might find a use for them."

Elizabeth took the pack from her pocket, and then hesitated.

"You're not going to try to get out of here with me, are you?"

"No," Sobokov said. "I've made my mistake. No need to compound it by slowing you down."

"We could figure something out," she said. "I could distract the men. Get you into the car. I'm sure Steve, Bill, and all the rest of them are hot on Mavich's trail. If you can just hold out a bit longer…"

"Look at me," Sobokov said. "I'm already gone. It makes it easier, in a way. I made a foolish mistake at the end of my life, yes. But that doesn't matter, not against the rest of it."

The footsteps were getting closer. Elizabeth had to get out of that room, and fast.

"Then tell me the password," she said.

"Password?" Sobokov said.

"They told me that the research you were working on was protected, somehow," she said. "That without you, five years' worth of work would go to waste."

Sobokov cursed under his breath, and then laughed again, looking at the ceiling.

"The things you forget about when you find out you have cancer, and then get kidnapped by the Soviets," he said. "Yes, of course. *Antonin.* My son's name."

"That's a beautiful name," Elizabeth said.

"Thank you."

She glanced back towards the door. "I can't stay here any longer. Are you sure you won't consider coming with me?"

"What, out onto that balcony?" he said. "Even if you could get me up and out of this bed, which I doubt, the only thing I'm doing off that balcony is a swan dive." He looked up thoughtfully for a moment. "I *was* quite the diver in my youth, you know. It could be quite elegant."

Elizabeth took a deep breath. From her pocket, she produced the pack of cigarettes and placed it on the scientist's bedside table. He looked down at them, and then back up at her.

"My doctors told me no more smoking," he said with a slight smirk on his face. "Though I don't really see the difference it would make at this point."

"Just in case," Elizabeth said. Sobokov peeked inside the packet and peered down into it.

"You said there are four of them?"

"Yes."

"And you're sure you don't need them?"

"I'm fairly certain I'd blow my arm off if I tried. We didn't have the chance to do much in the way of training before they sent me down here."

"And yet, even so, you came," he said. "I'm sorry this won't be quite the rescue you were dreaming of."

"I'm sorry, too," Elizabeth said. "About everything."

There came a scraping sound at the door, like a key being fitted into the lock, and Elizabeth stole one last glance back at the dying Russian scientist before slipping back out onto the balcony and closing the door behind her.

Elizabeth looked back down at the lawn.

The men were gone, the pool chairs empty.

Something was up.

She glanced across to her own balcony. Soon, she supposed, someone would be coming to find her too, and she didn't like to think about what they would do when they found her. The grounds were seemingly abandoned now. Was this her chance for escape?

She was two stories up, too far to risk the jump without breaking an ankle and dashing any hopes she had of running away without being spotted. Her leg was still hurting from where she had sliced it against the iron railing. Down below her, she could see where the roof of the garage jutted out a few feet. It would be risky, but staying put was even more of a risk now. If she could get herself down to that roof, there were trees beside the garage, and hedges below them. It wouldn't be easy, but it was possible.

From behind her, she could hear the sound of voices speaking in hushed tones. How much longer until one of them noticed that something was off, and thought to look out onto the balcony? Or, worse, went to her room and found her missing? It was now or never.

Once again, Elizabeth hooked a leg over the wrought iron railing, holding on tight with both hands. She looped the other leg over and stood like that for a moment, looking like the figurehead on the prow of some impossible ship. She took one final deep breath, counted backwards from three, and jumped.

She landed hard on the garage roof, feeling a surge of pain in her leg. But nothing felt broken. The adrenaline was enough to keep her going. There would be time to tend to her scrapes and wounds later, if she was lucky.

She couldn't stay there on the roof. She had to keep moving. After she had caught her breath, she scrambled to the edge of the roof and climbed down the tree. The voices coming from Sobokov's room were getting louder, and angrier.

She headed quickly for the hedge and crouched there for a moment, surveying the grounds. She saw no one. Beyond the pool was the long driveway; if she could make it to the road, she had a chance. She began to run, moving fast now. She was doing it. She was going to make it out. She tried to imagine the look on Steve's face when she was in his arms again, and she could tell him everything that had happened.

Elizabeth didn't even have time to turn around before she felt someone's hands around her ankles. Then she was falling, heading towards the concrete around the pool. She felt a sharp pain on her head. And then, nothing.

CHAPTER TWENTY-FOUR

Bill Wynter was frantically trying to make the miniature radio work as the cab careened down the roads of Acapulco, Mavich's car just barely in sight ahead of them.

"Connor, you're not hearing me. I need a tactical team yesterday. Do we know anyone with surface to air missiles?"

"Oh sure, Bill," came back the staticky sound of Alex Connor's voice, the furious honking of traffic nearly drowning him out. "I packed a couple of Stingers in my carry-on."

"Well, you better find some, or I'm going to hurl *you* at the damn helicopter to bring it down."

"Not with that trick back of yours, you aren't."

"For the love of God, Connor..."

"I'm on it, Bill. The boys will be thrilled to hear they might actually get to see a bit of action. If they try anything with that bird, we'll bring it down."

"Good. I'll send you the final location when we get there."

"I've got the map out. Only so many places he could be heading to. I'll start mobilizing ASAP."

Wynter pushed down the aerial on the miniature radio and sat forward in the backseat of the cab. He could see the veins in Steve Brenner's forehead pulsing as he stared out the windshield. This was how it went—so many days of preparation, so much time spent waiting around, all on the off chance of actually getting to do something that might change the course of the free world.

"You play any ball growing up, Steve?"

"I was a halfway decent fullback."

"Well, then consider this my little halftime speech. I don't know what we're going to find at that house. They don't know we're onto them yet, but that won't last long. I'm going to do everything I can to get Elizabeth out of there safely. But Dr. Sobokov is our top priority. You understand me?"

Brenner gritted his teeth and nodded.

"Yeah. I read you."

"Good. Then strap in."

Elizabeth emerged slowly from the dark nothingness, the pain radiating through her forehead somehow less foreboding than the cold shiver of fear wracking her body. She took care to lay still—as long as they didn't know that she was awake, she felt she might be safer.

"Move over," said a cold voice above her. She recognized it as Avilova. "What happened?"

"I was only trying to stop her," Caslov said. "She was making a break for it. I didn't mean…"

"She seems badly hurt. Do you know what Mavich will do to you for this?"

She heard a few choice curse words in Russian.

"We've got to find a place to hide her," Caslov said. "Before Mavich gets back."

"There's nowhere here where he won't find her."

"Then where?"

"The car," Avilova said. "Put her in the car. We'll take her out of here."

PASSPORT TO DANGER

It was all Elizabeth could do to keep her body from trembling. It was one thing to be held captive by Mavich—the man was cold and brutal, but not, as far as she could tell, unreasonable. She mattered to him only insofar as she represented a threat. There was a chance that, when all of this was over, he might let her go. But these men did not think in the same way, Caslov in particular. She did not want to get in that car.

"But what if the Americans are onto us?" Caslov said. "Won't they follow the car?"

"They want Sobokov," Avilova said. "They don't care about you. They'll think you're abandoning a sinking ship."

"But what about the helicopter?"

"If the Americans find out, do you really think they'll let him take off? They'll blow this whole place sky high to keep Mavich from taking Sobokov to Cuba." Avilova's voice eased a little. "As soon as we get rid of the girl, we'll hire a boat to take us out to the yacht."

Elizabeth peeked one eye carefully open, just a fraction, to see if there was any space for her to make another dash. But the waves of pain were coming more quickly now—she was in no condition to move, let alone outrun a pair of Soviet agents. She heard the two men talking low among themselves now.

"All right, let's go," Caslov said finally.

"Good. Lie the girl on the floor I'll get on the backseat."

Elizabeth kept her eyes shut tight and her body limp as she felt the unwelcome hands of the Russian grab her roughly and hoist her over his shoulder. She did not like how insubstantial she felt in his grasp, and how easily he maneuvered her body around. There was such a casual cruelty to the way he used his body. She hoped that, whatever happened to her, he wouldn't make it out of Mexico alive. The woman of the world would all be better off without Boris Caslov still in it.

She heard the sound of a car door open, and then her body was being dumped below the back seat. It took all her strength not to yell out in pain as her head connected with the carpeted floor of the car. She heard Avilova grunt as he got into the back seat and closed the door behind him, and then the sound of a motor running. It felt like being in a nightmare, unable to move or do anything to change her fate, forced to see as it progressed to the terrible conclusion she already knew was coming.

Elizabeth heard the sound of the tires on grass and felt her body thrown around as Caslov turned the car sharply around. He charged down the driveway, heading for the gates.

"Hang on," she heard Caslov tell Avilova. The car didn't even slow down for the gates, knocking them open. Then it was through, rocking on its springs, before it swung to the left and shot down the street.

The black Mercedes emerged from the gates and screamed past the cab, Brenner and Wynter both craning their necks to watch it as it passed.

"What was that?" Brenner said.

"Did you see who was driving?" Wynter asked.

"Looked like Caslov to me."

"Me, too. Mavich will be mad someone else is driving it."

"Where the hell does he think he's going?"

"Got spooked, maybe," Wynter said. "Realized the only way out of this mess was either in handcuffs or a body bag. Perhaps neither option appealed to him."

Wynter got on his radio.

PASSPORT TO DANGER

"Connor? Yeah, tell Hank we've got a black Mercedes sedan heading his way. Get a helicopter on it if you can. I'm guessing he'll head for the coastal road. The pilots are to let him get out of town before they try to stop him. Tell them to keep me informed. And let me know when you get the roadblocks up."

The car driving Mavich pulled into the house, the gates now obliterated. Wynter shoved a handful of cash at the driver and told Brenner to stay low. The two men scurried out of the cab and behind the fence of the house facing where Mavich had gone in, looking for any signs of motion in the upper windows. The shades were all drawn tight.

A few minutes later, the calvary began to arrive. A cream-colored van pulled up quick on the sidewalk and Alex Connor jumped out, running to where Wynter was crouched and mopping his face with a handkerchief. Wynter looked at him in mild surprise.

"You're out of shape."

"The hell I am," Connor said. "Jessie Owens would be exhausted running around in that humidity. Damn it's hot out there!"

"Caslov took off," Brenner said to him.

"Well, good riddance is what I say," Connor said. "One fewer guy shooting at us. I remember his dossier saying that he knew his way around a rifle."

"He does," Wynter said. "If only we could convince Mendoza to take off, too, we'd be in pretty good shape."

"He's even better than Caslov?"

"Unfortunately."

Connor shrugged and then began his report.

"I've got agents going up and down the block telling folks to stay put for the next couple of hours. I think we spooked them pretty good."

"Any of them ask to leave?"

"No one yet. You know how this goes. They'll probably be hiding under their beds for the next few hours, which I wouldn't mind doing myself, to tell you the truth."

Wynter grinned and picked up his radio.

"Get the boats in position," he said. "Seal off the street in both directions. No one is to leave or enter. No one."

More vans were arriving now, agents pouring out of them carrying automatic rifles and moving with purpose to take positions around the house. Steve Brenner couldn't believe how quickly they had all arrived: He imagined them poised and waiting since they got the call yesterday of trouble in Acapulco, just itching to be deployed. Connor took off his sports coat and rolled up the sleeves of his white shirt, checking his revolver for ammunition. He noticed Brenner looking at him and grinned.

"Get rid of that jacket, Steve. It's too hot to wear it and makes it harder to maneuver your weapon."

Brenner smiled.

"I was afraid you wouldn't trust a nuclear physicist with a gun."

Connor laughed.

"I might not, but I'd trust the son of a Texas rancher any day."

Connor took a long gun from the back of the van and handed it over to Brenner, who checked the magazine and then briefly sighted it. He watched the other men around him with a mixture of amazement and anxiety. They all sounded relaxed as they talked, but he could tell they were each making preparations of their own, getting ready for the confrontation ahead. This wasn't their first rodeo, that much was clear.

Brenner looked across the road at the house and thought about Elizabeth. God, he hoped she was alright. Had Mavich already figured out who she really was, and who she was working for? Mavich was certainly the type to get rid of anyone he didn't need, Brenner thought, and felt his stomach muscles tighten painfully. *Don't think about it*, he told himself. *Or else you won't be of any use to anyone, least of all Elizabeth.*

A blast of static came from the radio in the back of the van, and Wynter hurried to answer it.

"Go for Wynter," he said.

"We've got eyes on the Mercedes," said the voice of a pilot, the huge sound of the helicopter propeller going behind him. "Looking like it might be more than one man inside."

Wynter and Connor exchanged looks—maybe they were going to get lucky, after all.

"Keep on them," Wynter said. "And don't engage until I give the order."

"Roger that," the pilot said. "Over and out."

Connor shook his head.

"Mavich isn't going to like that his soldiers are fleeing like rats off a sinking ship," he said.

"No, he's not," Wynter said. "Unless there's something happening that we don't know yet."

The men thought about that for a moment, then turned their attention back to the house across the street. From somewhere in the distance, Steve Brenner thought he could hear the sound of helicopter propellers.

The Mercedes was traveling rapidly along a curving mountain road, the sea a hundred feet below on the left and dense jungle on the right. The water pounded the rocks at the base of the cliff so hard that Caslov and Avilova had to raise their voices to be heard over the roar.

Elizabeth lay huddled on the backseat floor, her head resting against the door and throbbing something awful. The men hadn't yet noticed that she had regained consciousness, but she figured it was better that way.

"If Nikolai makes it back to Moscow…" Caslov was saying. Above her in the backseat, Avilova clicked his tongue impatiently.

"There's no way Mavich is getting away from the Americans. Sobokov is too important to them. He could do too much damage to the Americans. They won't be taking any chances."

"He's a dying man," Caslov said. "He won't work with our scientists, and there's no way we can make him."

"Think, Boris, think," Avilova said. "There's still the information he has about the American's latest missile systems: the Poseidon submarines, the Minuteman forces. He's an expert on MIRVs, well acquainted with both systems. How many MIRVs are on each missile? How do their decoys work? Our ABM systems in the Moscow-Leningrad corridor might be useless. Sobokov could tell us for sure what needs to change. He could be of a vast help to us, even if we can't force him to work for us."

"And there's no chance Mavich trades him to the Americans, once he realizes he's trapped?"

"No chance," Avilova said. "What do you think the Center would do to him?"

"And what will they do to us, for running out on him?"

Avilova chuckled. *Such a bitter and frightening sound*, Elizabeth thought.

"They trust me," he said. "I'll tell them that our operation was compromised by an American agent posing as Nicola Neumann, that we got rid of her and escaped. They wouldn't want to see me captured, with what I know, and I'll tell them I needed your help."

PASSPORT TO DANGER

Elizabeth didn't hear what Caslov said next, for Avilova's last words had confirmed what she had been fearing since they'd placed her limp body in the backseat. *They're going to kill me*, she thought with rising panic. *That's why I'm in this car; they're going to kill me.*

The entire left side of her face throbbed painfully, and the skin over her forehead felt very tight over a large lump. Had anyone noticed them leaving? Did Bill and Steve even know about the house yet? But what did any of that matter now? They were going to kill her, and there was nothing she could do about it now.

Or was there? Moving slowly so as not to attract attention, she felt in the pocket of her dress. There it was, the fountain pen Wynter had given her, lying so innocently in the fabric under her right hand. If she could get it without Avilova seeing it, somehow, she would have a lethal weapon. It might not be enough against these two trained killers, but it was better than just accepting her fate.

The car took a sharp turn, and the pen jolted from her pocket and started to roll around on the running board of the car. Elizabeth groped desperately for it as Avilova clucked his tongue.

"For God's sake, Boris, be careful. That's a long drop down to the sea...and I'd hate to find out just how long."

Without opening her eyes, Elizabeth slowly felt around on the ground, searching for the pen. She had to find it—without it, she was a sitting duck.

"Where do you want to dump the girl?" Caslov said from the front seat.

Elizabeth felt her throat go dry. He sounded so matter of fact, as though dumping a person over a cliff was no more spectacular than taking out the garbage.

"Anywhere is fine," Avilova said. "The undertow is strong. She'll be out to sea in a couple of hours."

Elizabeth's fingers hit upon something metallic and cold. For a moment, she felt a flood of relief. But when she tried to pick it up, she found that she couldn't. It wasn't the pen—it was a bit of metal at the base of the driver's seat. She kept searching as she felt the car begin to slow.

She squinted open her right eye, hoping to get a glimpse of the terrain. They didn't know she was awake: Did she have any chance if she made a run for it? The jungle was a thick undergrowth of bushes and trees—plenty of space for someone to get lost in. *Or to hide a body, if they decided on that instead.*

The car continued to slow. Elizabeth felt her muscles tightening. Her heart was pounding so fast that it actually hurt. *This is it*, she realized as the car rolled to a stop. Both eyes open now, she scanned the ground once more for the pen. She saw a glint of gold in the corner, and risked a glance up at Avilova. His eyes were focused on where Boris sat in the front seat. Elizabeth reached down—the fountain pen was just beyond her fingertips. She pushed further, feeling the strain in her shoulder. She felt a bit of the metal as the pen spun uselessly away from her grasp.

Then, finally, Elizabeth got hold of the pen. Slowly, she brought it along her side, feeling for the mechanism that Wynter had showed her back up in Virginia. *This is it*, she thought again. *I'll have to be quick...and lucky.*

She heard a car door open, and then heard Caslov's feet crunching gravel as he came around to the back of the car. Every muscle in her body was held taut now, waiting. She would only have one chance at this. If it failed, then she was as good as dead.

CHAPTER TWENTY-FIVE

Elizabeth held the pen firmly in her palm, her thumb hovering over the mechanism that would fire the little bullet contained within. Caslov was her target: He would be the one to try and kill her, she figured. She might even make it to the undergrowth before Avilova had a chance to shoot her. But even if she didn't, it would be satisfying to know that no one would ever need to fear Boris Caslov ever again.

Caslov was nearly to her door now. But in the seat above her, she heard Avilova say, "Boris, come here a minute. I have a suggestion for you."

Caslov stopped, the gravel no longer crunching beneath his feet. Then it resumed as he made his way to the other side of the car, to Avilova's window.

"What is it?" he said. He sounded irritable—in a hurry now, anxious to get this job over with and make it to the boat docked offshore.

Avilova said, "I think it would be much better if you—"

He never finished the sentence. A loud *bang* rang out. Then Elizabeth heard the sound of something hitting the side of the car, and a thud against the gravel. Still she clenched her pen tightly. It was only once Avilova told her to open her eyes that she realized she'd shut them tight.

"You can put that silly fountain pen away now," he said, his voice soft and almost kind, "before you hurt someone with it."

Elizabeth stared at the man with wide, incredulous eyes. He was unscrewing the silencer on his pistol; he dropped it into his pocket and slipped the gun back into his shoulder holster. He glanced down at her. Elizabeth wondered what he saw—her face pale and terrified, eyes enormous. It had been a very long week.

"It's all right," he said. "I'm not going to hurt you."

"But why?" Elizabeth said.

Avilova chuckled softly.

"You forced my hand a little, with that runner you did back at the villa. But, in the end, it wasn't such a bad idea to get you away from the house. Of course, Boris had to come along, which was no fun for you, I'm sure. But I have to tell you that I've been nervous ever since I saw you take that damn pen out of your pocket. Let me see that."

Elizabeth looked down at the pen still in her hand. Was this some kind of trick that Avilova was playing? Maybe he was tying up loose ends before he made his escape from Mexico, and didn't need Boris telling Moscow all the ways in which the Cuernavaca affair had been a fiasco. But there was something trustworthy about the man. If he was a liar, he was a very good one indeed. But wasn't that the way of spies?

"Is Boris dead?" Elizabeth asked. Avilova opened the car door, stuck out a foot, and kicked at something on the ground. No sound came.

"Very much so, yes," he said.

"Who are you?" Elizabeth said.

Avilova sighed and leaned back against the plush leather of the Mercedes. He looked old, Elizabeth thought, and tired.

PASSPORT TO DANGER

"That is a very long story," he said, "one I will tell you when we have a bit more time. But right now, we need to say hello to your friends."

"My friends?" Elizabeth said. Avilova nodded a head out the window. Elizabeth could hear a sound, faint but growing, an almost mechanical kind of buzzing.

"Come on," Avilova said, standing with a sigh and getting out of the car.

By the time Elizabeth was out of the car, it was twilight. She could hear the enormous sound of the chopper as it circled in search of a good place to land. Avilova fiddled with Boris Caslov's body for a moment, performing a cursory search of the pockets. Finally, the helicopter began to descend, touching down lightly on the widest bit of the road roughly fifty yards away from them.

Two young men scrambled out of the chopper: dark-haired, clean-cut, and capable looking. Both of them carried automatic pistols, the bright metal gleaming in the dying light of the day as they kept them trained on Avilova.

"Stop right there," said the man in front, holding up his opposite hand. Avilova calmly raised his arms, a bemused smile on his face. The man turned to Elizabeth. "Are you alright?"

"I'm fine," she said, fingering the bruise on her forehead. "Thanks to him."

The two Americans studied Avilova carefully, their young faces taut, guns still trained on him. *Probably nothing in the handbook for what to do in this situation*, Elizabeth thought. After a moment, Avilova said, in a brisk, authoritative manner, "Radio your Control and tell him I want to talk to him before he goes in after Mavich. I may have some helpful information for him."

It was clear that he had caught them completely off guard. Elizabeth watched as his grin drew wider in response to their surprise. One of the men ran back to the helicopter and got on the radio.

Avilova said, "If we drive back now, we'll be there in fifteen minutes."

"Why not take the helicopter?" Elizabeth said. Avilova turned to her, smiling more broadly now.

"As much as I'm sure our new friends would love to give us a lift, it'll be faster if we drive. That neighborhood is terrible for helicopter parking."

"Wait!" said one of the men as Avilova turned to move back to the car. Avilova sighed, his hands still raised. "I didn't say you could go!

"Look, I imagine your friend is a little busy at the moment," Avilova said, "and you've got, what, half a battalion outside that house, waiting to go in? Not to mention a dead KGB assassin lying in the middle of the road. I understand that this is all quite a lot to take in, but I need you to get up to speed, and fast. We don't have much time."

The man, his gun still trained on Avilova, glanced back in the direction of the helicopter. His partner stepped down and gave him a thumbs up. Avilova smiled and offered a gracious bow.

"Do you mind cleaning this up for us?" he said. "I usually hate to leave a mess, but pressing matters."

"I'm...sure we can figure something out," he said, holstering his gun as he glanced down at the body lying in a pool of blood by the side of the car.

"Good man," Avilova said, stepping around towards the driver's side of the car.

PASSPORT TO DANGER

"Thank you for coming when you did," Elizabeth said to the young man.

"I don't think we were much help," he said. Then he shook his head. "Who *is* that guy?"

"I'll tell you when I find out," Elizabeth said, giving the man a wave before stepping over Caslov's body and into the passenger seat of the Mercedes. Avilova put the car into gear, and Elizabeth watched as the two young, capable men stood over the dead body of Boris Caslov, trying to decide between themselves what to do about him.

Ivan Avilova drove the car quickly but skillfully over the winding mountain roads, barely decreasing his speed as he took the curves easily. Elizabeth allowed herself a moment to relax against the seat. Now that the adrenaline was wearing off, her head was aching painfully. She looked out towards the mountains before them, a broken line of green shouldering up into the brilliant blue sky. A hawk was circling above the avalanche of trees sliding down the hill beside the road. They passed a dark-eyed boy driving two goats and a donkey laden with straw. For a moment, the world seemed almost normal again. But it would be a long time before Elizabeth forgot what she had just been through, if it truly was over.

She looked at the man beside her, wondering who he was and why he had helped her. Had he decided to defect to the Americans, rather than die in a futile attempt to get Sobokov to Cuba? Or was there something more complicated at play? Elizabeth wasn't sure she would ever get the full answer—these people didn't deal in full answers, information being too powerful to dole out without receiving something just as valuable in return. He seemed to feel her eyes on him, for he shot her a quick glance and smiled.

"You look a hundred percent better," he said. "Except for that lump on your head. The bruise should look better in a day or so. Settle into a nice shade of emerald."

"I've always bruised like a peach," Elizabeth said. It was true—the slightest bump, even something she scarcely remembered, would bloom into the most spectacular shades of purple and yellow. She shook her head. "Why did you help me back there?"

Ivan Avilova looked immensely amused.

"Back there? I've been trying to help you ever since you joined us!"

"What do you mean?"

Avilova let out a theatrical sigh.

"Remember when we first met? I told Nikolai that you had worked for me. I'd never met Nicola, but I thought that if *I* didn't doubt you, Mavich wouldn't, either. I was quite wrong about that, and my attempts to convince him that you had changed didn't delay him much either. I had to break the projector just to make sure he didn't go back and review the films."

"That was you?" Elizabeth said. Avilova nodded.

"After Boris attacked you, I told Nikolai that you and Boris couldn't stay in the same house together, that one of you had to go. I figured he'd let you leave, but he didn't want to. The only thing left to do was convince him that you were a substitute for the real Nicola, and I think that bought us, oh, maybe a few extra hours."

Elizabeth looked at him cautiously. "How did you know I wasn't a substitute?"

"Because the only man authorized to make a substitution was Midas. He was placed on house arrest, at my suggestion, before he had a chance to send another courier."

"But you knew I wasn't Nicola."

"I knew she had disappeared."

"How did you know that?"

A small smile played around Avilova's lips.

"Because my American contact told me."

"Your American contact," Elizabeth repeated, staring at him, her muscles taut as violin strings. "Who is he?"

Avilova laughed.

"I didn't know his real name, just as he doesn't know mine, though I have a guess now. His code name is Thunderbird."

"And yours?" Elizabeth asked.

"Cobalt."

Her eyes widened in amazement.

"Bill is certainly going to be surprised. He thought you'd been arrested when he lost contact with you."

"No, no. It was Midas who was arrested. I finally found out who he was and let some important people know he wasn't handling the operation properly. He was taken into custody, and I was sent to Cuernavaca."

"So you knew from the beginning that I was working for the Americans?"

Avilova nodded. Elizabeth was silent. When she thought back on it, she could see how much he had tried to help her, all while being careful not to attract any attention to himself, or do anything that might make the other men, Mavich, most of all, doubt him.

"So what now?"

"Now, we go and try to save your scientist friend," Avilova said. "Though I don't think things are looking very good for him."

"I meant, what now for you?"

"Ah," Avilova said, "now there is a question."

"Will it be safe for you to return to the Soviet Union? Or will you come with us?"

Avilova shook his head.

"I can be of more help to the Americans where I am, and I suspect I could never completely disappear, even with all the help I'm sure I would get from the Americans. So I will go back, and keep doing what I'm doing."

"Trying to undermine the USSR?"

Avilova raised one hand and shifted it back and forth, in something of a half-and-half gesture.

"Your country and mine, we have been on a collision course for some time now. Even before the trouble with Cuba and those missiles, I could see it. I thought that I could help, in some small way, to minimize the danger of that collision. One day, perhaps, if we can keep the status quo between our two superpowers, my people will get a leader with some vision; someone more interested in his people than his own personal power; someone who will allow our people to voice their views without being sent off to Siberia. Perhaps, this is a crazy dream—who knows? But I will keep trying."

Elizabeth watched him thoughtfully, wondering what kind of life a man like this—a double agent—must lead, how lonely it must be for him.

"Not long now," he said as he drove around the curve. "I expect your friends will be delighted to see you."

For the first time since leaving the house, the enormity of everything that had happened seemed to wash over Elizabeth all at once: how much danger she had been in; the low odds of making it out alive; and the fact that, even now, she was speeding towards the man she loved, who she thought she might never see again. She felt a sob suddenly rise in her chest and fought to keep it down—there would be time for tears later.

"Yes," she said. "I should think so."

Steve Brenner stood just outside the air-conditioned van, the setting Acapulco sun beating down on his shoulders while he squinted through the dusky haze at the house across the way. There were figures in the upstairs windows now, braced behind overturned wooden tables and other makeshift barricades. The rifle in his hands felt reassuringly heavy. It had been a while since he'd seen any action like this, and, truthfully, he didn't mind. But Elizabeth was still somewhere inside that house, and he'd be damned if he didn't try anything he could to get her out of there alive.

Inside the van, Connor and Wynter were coordinating with the assault teams, getting men in position and considering possible entry points. They had the advantage in terms of manpower and firepower, but Mavich was a canny operator, and he had the thing that they wanted most: Dr. Sobokov. He'd be sure to use that to his advantage, which meant proceeding more cautiously than they might have otherwise. Connor was advocating for the use of something called LMX, some kind of simulated fire. Apparently, Mavich had been deathly afraid of fire ever since he'd been caught in a house fire as a child, a neat bit of background research that Connor was justifiably proud of having found. If they could smoke them out, maybe they'd have a better chance.

His thoughts were interrupted by the sound of a car roaring down the empty street. Wynter stepped out of the van with a frown on his face as the black Mercedes got closer. Brenner shouldered his rifle. Had the Russians called in backup? But Wynter put a hand gently on his shoulder.

"No need for an itchy trigger finger, Steve," he said as the Mercedes came to a stop. When Brenner looked back at the older spy, the man was smiling broadly.

The passenger door of the Mercedes opened, and out stepped Elizabeth Lamont. She looked like she'd been through hell: her hair a mess, a massive bruise across her forehead, clothing dirty and ripped in places. Still, Steve was absolutely certain he'd never seen anyone more beautiful. He let his rifle fall beside him and ran to where she was standing. Elizabeth fixed him with a smile so wide and bright that it felt like the sun was finally shining again after a season of darkness. She flung her arms open wide and Steve grabbed her up, spinning her around, unable to contain his glee. They were both laughing deliriously now, like they'd just heard the funniest joke that anyone had ever told, tears streaming down Elizabeth's cheeks. When he finally set her back down on the ground, Steve just shook his head.

"How?" is all he managed to say.

"I'll tell you later," she said, "when all this is over."

All this...right, Steve thought. Dr. Sobokov was still inside that building. A helicopter was incoming. There would be time to celebrate later, time to indulge in the joy of building their lives together. But first, there was work to do.

The man who had been driving the car got out now. He was an older man, with a deeply lined, intelligent face and a small, disbelieving grin on his face. He made his way over to where Bill Wynter was standing and extended his hand.

"Allow me to introduce myself," he said. "I'm Cobalt."

Connor stuck his head out of the van, about to tell Wynter something, just in time to catch this exchange. Steve Brenner heard his whoop with laughter. Wynter looked stunned—a posture that Steve couldn't remember ever having seen before—but recovered himself and shook hands with the man who called himself Cobalt.

"I was worried about you," Wynter said, "though I suppose I didn't need to be."

"In this line of work, it's always nice to be worried about," Cobalt said with a grin.

Wynter nodded, his face growing more serious now.

"I'm glad you were there to help Elizabeth. We've been more worried than I can tell you."

"With good reason," Elizabeth said quietly. "My cover was blown. Avilova saved my life."

Steve came forward to shake the man's hand and introduced himself.

"It sounds like we owe you everything," he said.

"Well, this isn't over quite yet," Avilova said. "I want to hear about Mavich's position. Is there someplace we can talk?" He wiped his brow against the still sweltering heat. "Someplace cooler, perhaps?"

Wynter nodded towards one of the vans. He turned crisply to Connor.

"Join the men. Have them hold their positions for now, but be ready to go on my signal. Radio me if there's any activity in the house, any at all."

Connor nodded, then patted Elizabeth on the shoulder.

"Glad to have you back," he said with a warm smile.

"You have no idea how good it is to be back," she said with a laugh.

Avilova and Wynter stepped into the waiting van, leaving Elizabeth and Steve standing together on the street, both smiling uncontrollably at the other. It felt like a dream to Steve, after so much worry, to finally have her back and safe.

"You were right, by the way," Elizabeth said. Steve frowned slightly.

"About what?"

"Dr. Sobokov didn't defect."

"You talked with him," Steve said.

"I did," Elizabeth said. "I even managed to get the password for his research."

Steve's eyes went wide. In all his worrying, he had forgotten entirely about Elizabeth's mission. How many lives would be saved, how many years and manhours of work preserved, because of her bravery?

"Elizabeth Lamont," he said. "I'm beginning to suspect I may have underestimated you."

"Well, don't make a habit of it, mister," Elizabeth said with a smile. "Now, where can a girl get a very large, very cold glass of water around here?"

CHAPTER TWENTY-SIX

"What's Mavich's position now?" Avilova asked. He wiped his forehead with a handkerchief, glad to be in the air conditioned cool of the CIA van.

"The helicopter arrived five minutes before you did," Wynter said, "with an unwelcome surprise: three more men, all of them armed. It seems like every Soviet in Mexico showed up for the party."

Avilova pursed his lips, frowning.

"They'll try to keep your men busy while Mavich gets Sobokov to the helicopter," he said. He eyed Wynter curiously. "You didn't try to stop the helicopter from coming in?"

Wynter shook his head.

"I couldn't. It came in over the city."

"That would have been Nikolai's order," Avilova said, a light twitch drawing his lips upward. "He's quite good, you know."

"So I've learned," Wynter said.

"I realize that if Mavich and Sobokov manage to get in the chopper, you'll have to bring it down. But what if you didn't?"

"I'm listening."

"He's going to go for the yacht. That's my bet, at least, unless he thinks I've left without him. You can exchange the crew on the yacht waiting for Mavich with your own men. I know the exact location."

Wynter mulled it over for a moment.

"I'd like to keep Sobokov alive, if I can, but if Mavich thinks something's wrong with the boat, and he heads inland..."

"I know," Avilova said. "You'll have no choice."

"Let's hope he feels like taking to the waves," Wynter said, picking up his radio to give the orders for his men to remove the crew of the yacht. He handed the radio over to the man he'd only known as Cobalt for years to give them the location of the boat.

The door to the van opened, and Alex Connor stuck his head in.

"It's starting," Connor said. "They just opened fire on that helicopter you've had circling the yard. The pilot is moving out."

"They're getting ready for Mavich to make his move."

Connor looked at the old Soviet double agent.

"Do you need a weapon, Mr. Avilova?" he said.

Avilova laughed and waved a hand.

"I'm getting too old for this cowboy stuff, and I'd rather not have any of the men on the other side of that gate see my face, just in case. Besides, the air conditioning feels so nice!"

Wynter chuckled and set the radio to the frequency of the operation.

"Cowboy stuff, huh...? I can trust you to behave yourself back here?"

"You can," Avilova said. "But if you're really the Thunderbird I know, you won't trust me or anyone else."

"Good answer," Wynter said, peeling off his jacket and leaving it draped over one of the chairs. "Come on, Alex."

PASSPORT TO DANGER

• • •

Elizabeth saw Bill and Alex getting out of the van. The commotion around her had intensified in recent minutes, and from somewhere on the other side of the wall, she could hear the distant sharp popping sounds of gunfire. Steve was looking over there now, his face a mask of concern, one of her hands still clasped in his.

"I don't suppose there's any way I can convince you to stay here with me?" she said.

"It's an all hands on deck sort of situation," Brenner said. "I have to help them."

"I know," Elizabeth said quietly. It was remarkable, really, how in such a very short time he'd become the most important person in her life. The whole time she'd been in that house with Mavich, Caslov, and all those other brutes, it was the thought of being back with Steve that had kept her going. To lose that now, after such an unlikely escape, was too cruel a fate even to contemplate. She'd already lost one man before. She couldn't go through it again.

"Be careful, Steve," Elizabeth said softly.

"I will," he said. He tried to smile, but couldn't. Instead, he held her close to him, his cheek against her hair. Connor and Wynter were waiting for him now, their weapons drawn and sleeves rolled up. Steve kissed her, and then picked up his rifle. He nodded to Wynter, and the three men made their way to where the others had the house surrounded.

Alex Connor handed his binoculars to Wynter, the two of them crouched together behind a large rhododendron bush.

"That's Mendoza in the downstairs window," Connor said. "He's got a heavy table turned over to use for cover. The two men in the upstairs windows have done the same thing."

Connor watched Wynter's taut, worried face. *He's thinking the same thing I am*, Connor thought. *We're going to be sitting ducks, and we won't be able to see them at all in those dark rooms with decent cover.*

"We'll just have to aim at the windows and hope we hit something," Wynter said, handing the binoculars back to Connor. "Lay down enough suppressing fire to keep them pinned and let our men move towards the helicopter."

Wynter took note of the positions of his men. There were six on this side of the driveway, and six on the other, all of them hidden behind a bush, a hedge, or a tree. Not the best cover in the world, but better than nothing. His radio sounded, confirming that the team had swapped out the staff on the yacht for some of his men. Everything was in position.

He signaled to his men to move forward.

He watched as they went, moving carefully, finding their cover and getting to it quickly. They weren't shooting yet. They were waiting.

But as soon as the men began to head for the house, the sound of gunfire rang out in the courtyard, the windows of the house exploding outwards as thin lines of gun smoke eddied up towards the Acapulco sky. The Americans responded with a blast of their own gunfire, dashing from cover to cover. Those without adequate cover inched forward on their bellies. The acrid smell of gunpowder filled the air, overwhelming the sweet fragrance of the gardenias. Gone were the gay sounds of birdsong; the birds had all departed as soon as the first gunshot had rang out. Now, the only sound was the repeated firing of the rifles.

PASSPORT TO DANGER

Wynter paused behind a palm tree, assessing the field. His men weren't making as much progress as he had hoped; they were still nowhere near the house. A man half-hidden by a shrub yelped in pain as a bullet struck his leg. His radio crackled.

"Mavich is headed for the back!" came the staticky sound of the helicopter pilot. "He's firing at us; I'm going to have to pull back."

Wynter cursed and put the radio back in his pocket. He turned to Connor just as the agent let off three shots in rapid succession, the rifle butt held tight against his shoulder.

"Some of our guys are going to have to get around to the back of the house," Wynter said.

"They'll need something to draw their fire!" Connor shouted back.

A decoy, Wynter thought to himself. *Well, you're elected.*

His lips and jaw tightened. He drew a deep breath. And then he began to run, zigzagging down the driveway, moving from tree to tree.

"What the hell is he doing?" Brenner shouted, watching as Wynter made a mad dash for the house. All the men in the house seemed to be concentrating their fire on him now.

"Being a goddamned hero is what," Connor said, grinning and shaking his head. "Come on! We need to get around to the other side!"

One of the Americans ran forward, holding something in his hand. He drew back his arm to throw it, but before he could, a bullet caught him in the side. The grenade rolled from his hand, and a moment later, the driveway exploded in a shower of dirt, the ground sheared away.

"Now!" Connor said, practically dragging Brenner along as the two men fired and then started to run. Wynter was still running in his zigzags towards the house. Brenner saw a quick flash of red mist as a bullet entered his shoulder.

"Bill!" he shouted.

"Come on!" Connor said.

"We have to go back!'

"Why the hell do you think he was running at the house in the first place?" Connor said. "So we could do this! Come on!"

Brenner cursed softly and followed the agent, peeking back over his shoulder to see one of the other Americans dragging Bill Wynter to the relative safety of cover.

When Brenner and Connor reached the back of the house, they saw Yuri Betrin and another man, presumably the pilot, crouched low behind the helicopter and taking occasional pot shots at the agents coming around the other side of the house. Suddenly, Nikolai Mavich moved out of the house, holding Dr. Sobokov in front of him. The old scientist looked barely strong enough to walk on his own; Mavich was supporting most of his weight, but he made for an effective shield nonetheless.

"Hold your fire!" Connor shouted. Slowly, Mavich dragged the scientist towards the helicopter.

"You're just going to let him get in?" Brenner said.

"If you can hit him without hitting Dr. Sobokov, be my guest," Connor said. "It takes more than growing up on a Texas ranch to hit a shot like that."

Brenner sighted his rifle, watching down the barrel as Mavich made his slow, halting progress towards the helicopter. Yuri Betrin saw him and fired off a quick round, forcing Connor and Brenner to duck back behind the house.

PASSPORT TO DANGER

"Any other ideas?" Brenner said.

Connor peeked back around the house, came back, and then turned, firing suddenly. From around the corner, Brenner could hear the sound of a man screaming. Connor came back to cover, his forehead shiny with sweat.

"It'll be hard to take off without a pilot!" he said.

By this point, the other Americans had made it around the house now. Yuri Betrin leaped up from behind the helicopter, firing his gun furiously, but was quickly mowed down in a barrage of bullets, his rifle swinging in a crazy arc as he died, spraying small branches and leaves into the air.

"We've got them!" Brenner said. But no sooner were the words out of his mouth than he heard the sound of helicopter rotors. From around the corner, he watched as the helicopter rose gracefully into the air.

"Hold your fire!" Connor shouted again, the men on the ground all training their weapons on the rising helicopter. Everyone was watching intently. Connor thought he could see Mavich in the pilot's seat. If it headed inland, there was a mortar waiting to bring it down.

But no—it was heading out over the water! They would have one more chance to get Sobokov back, alive.

Connor and Brenner raced back around the house to where Bill Wynter was sitting, propped up against the palm tree, a medic already tending to the bullet wound in his shoulder.

"They're heading towards the yacht," Wynter said. "We've got a chance."

"How badly are you hurt?" Brenner said.

"Oh, you know," Wynter said. "It hurts like hell, but I'll live."

Elizabeth was running across the courtyard now, tears in her eyes. Steve motioned for her to stay back—he couldn't possibly know if it was safe yet—but the woman would not be stopped.

"Are you okay?" she said.

"I'm fine," Steve said. His arms went around her, holding her close, and then he bent his head down to hers, kissing her long and hard. "It's all over. It's finally over."

"I'm so glad you're all right," Elizabeth said, her eyes sparkling.

"No get-well kiss for me?" Wynter said from the ground. Elizabeth looked down, as though surprised to find him there, and then both hands went to her mouth when she saw the bullet wound.

"You're hurt!"

"I'm okay," Wynter said, gritting his teeth slightly. "If I don't get one of these every couple years, the brass back at Langley starts to wonder what the hell I'm still doing in the field."

"I thought the point was to not get shot," Connor said. "You always told me that."

"Yeah, well, you can't miss 'em all," Wynter said.

The men all turned to watch the helicopter now, making its way out to sea. Wynter shook his head.

"Mavich is good. Damn good. I'll give him that. But I'd like to see his face when he gets to the boat and finds—"

Before he could finish his sentence, a red flash lit the sky. A streak of coral and gold followed, turning the sky into a spectrum of red, platinum, green, and violet. And then came the sound of a terrific explosion. Pieces of fiber glass fell slowly into the cool glittering sea waiting below, powerboats on the water already speeding towards the wreckage.

For what seemed like an eternity, no one on the lawn spoke. Then everyone seemed to move at once: men helping the wounded into the house; the bodies of the dead Soviets being picked up and moved; Wynter jabbering into his radio to have the yacht brought in—they wouldn't be needing it anymore.

Avilova had made his way out of the van and onto the lawn by now, shaking his head as the bodies of his dead would-be comrades were paraded before him. Wynter glanced up at him and got unsteadily to his feet. Alex Connor looped Wynter's good arm around his neck.

"I'm going to get patched up and see to my men. Then you and I have a lot to discuss."

"Take your time," Avilova said quietly. "I'll be here."

Wynter grinned.

"I was afraid you might be in a hurry to get out of Acapulco."

"Not that big of a hurry."

Wynter nodded, obviously relieved, and then headed for the house. Brenner told Elizabeth he was going to do what he could to help, but that he'd be back out as soon as he could. He gave her shoulder a quick squeeze, and then followed Connor and Wynter.

Elizabeth stood on the edge of the cliff, her hair blowing in the breeze, and watched the sea rising and falling, almost purple in the light of the setting sun. It was very quiet except for the wind in the trees, the water lapping the rocks below, and the song of the cicadas.

The powerboats were still circling the wreckage of the helicopter. She wondered what the tourists on the beach must think. Would they tell them it had been an accident, something wrong with the fuel line? Or play it off as Hollywood producers shooting footage for an upcoming action movie? One thing was certain: None of them would never know the truth.

Ivan Avilova came over to stand alongside Elizabeth. For a time, neither said anything, content to stare out into the water and the setting sun.

"It's my fault he's dead, you know," she said. "I gave him the explosives."

Avilova took her hand and held it.

"Dr. Sobokov, he didn't have much time left, and it wouldn't have been pleasant," he said quietly. "A quick and painless ending, doing what he felt was right, and making sure the Russians knew they could never take him alive."

Avilova sighed.

"And, for me, it's a bit of good luck that Mavich is dead. I don't have to worry about him guessing the truth about me, and that news somehow making it back to Moscow. For that, I have you to thank."

He fell silent again as he looked out at the deep indigo sea, rippling like a sheet of silk in the breeze. He turned back to Elizabeth with a small smile.

"My advice? Don't think too much about it. I know it sounds impossible, but tomorrow, it will be easier. The next day, even easier than that. Until one day, you will go to bed and realize the whole day has passed without you thinking about any of this at all. That is the only grace there is."

"I hope you're right," Elizabeth said.

"Of course I'm right!" Avilova said with a chuckle. "You wouldn't believe how much I've forgotten."

Elizabeth allowed herself a light laugh too. Avilova gently squeezed her shoulder.

PASSPORT TO DANGER

"Your young man will be here soon. I think you two have much to talk about."

Elizabeth glanced quickly over her shoulder and saw Steve Brenner coming towards them. When she looked at Avilova again, he was watching her with amusement.

"Eyes in the back of my head," he said with a teasing grin. He kissed her hand, and then left her. When he passed Steve Brenner, the young American man barely noticed Avilova, for he had eyes only for the auburn-haired girl in front of him.

"How is Bill?" Elizabeth said.

"Oh, he'll be alright. He's a tough old thing. It looks like everyone's going to make it."

"Even the guy with the…"

"Yup. Even the guy with the grenade. He's got a nice little collection of shrapnel in his leg, but he's already joking about how he'll never hear the end of it from his old Army buddies. Apparently, they always told him that he threw like a girl."

Elizabeth laughed a little and rested her head on Steve Brenner's strong shoulder.

"Steve?" she said.

"Hmm."

"There's something I've been thinking," she said.

"Yeah? What's that?"

"I'm thinking, now that this is over, I want to go on a trip somewhere."

Steve looked down at her and grinned.

"Another tour of the motel rooms of rural Mexico?"

Elizabeth crinkled her nose and shook her head.

"I was thinking Greece."

"Ah," Steve said. "With your friend Susan, right?"

"I actually had someone else in mind," Elizabeth said.
"Won't Susan be heartbroken?"
"Oh, I think she'll understand," Elizabeth said.

Somewhere in the distance, a band began to play softly. She turned and found Steve Brenner's lips, thinking that nothing in the world had ever tasted quite so sweet.